# THE SMILE
## ON THE
## FACE OF
## THE TIGER

# THE SMILE
# ON THE
# FACE OF
# THE TIGER

香港

Douglas Hurd and Andrew Osmond

THE MACMILLAN COMPANY

Library of Congress Catalog Card
Number: 77-90223
First American Edition 1970
Originally published in Great Britain in 1969
by William Collins Sons & Co., Ltd., London
The Macmillan Company
866 Third Avenue, New York, N.Y. 10022
Printed in the United States of America

# Contents

*Part One*

# MALAYA
## 1957

It was only a tiny sound, but they all heard it and froze. Pershing heard it; still, he kept on walking, watching his feet, until he collided with the brengunner.

1

Then it came again, a soft jangle like a far-off cowbell, somewhere below and to the left.

The Gurkhas shifted their heads, trying to get a bearing on the noise. A family of gibbons whooped and jabbered along the ridge, crashing from branch to branch, and the chorus of crickets never stopped—insistent rising scales, like a lot of people running their fingers along a lot of fine-tooth combs. But the Gurkhas listened only for a repetition of that false note. In all the racket of the Malayan forest a sound which does not belong is the ring of metal touching metal. Metal means man, and in that particular place man could only mean terrorist.

The brengunner eased the sling on his shoulder to bring the barrel down and flicked the change-lever to automatic. Pershing glanced at his carbine, as if surprised to find it in his hands, and pushed the safety button to the left.

They stood listening for another minute. Pershing eyed his men, poised with perfect balance on the steep hillside, and knew they had forgotten him. Some of them had been on this job for nine years. He was their commander, but now that the moment had come, nothing he could do would make any difference. If there was time they would ask him for orders, as a matter of form; he would ask for their suggestions; and whatever they suggested, he would order them to do.

Then they heard it again, and now even Pershing knew what it was. Someone was washing tins in the stream. Two of the Gurkhas pointed decisively downward along a line about eight o'clock from their original line of march. The Corporal edged forward to where Pershing stood and whispered in his ear. Pershing nodded.

At a sign from the Corporal the section sank gently to the ground, each man clearing a patch in the dead leaves, which would crack like giant potato crisps at the touch of a knee or foot, then kneeling with his rifle at the port.

Pershing thought it out. They were climbing a steep valley, trying to hold to a line halfway up the right bank, with the stream below them on their left and the ridge of the spur above and to the right. They knew the camp was on this stream, and the old courier route, ambushed by the Special Air Service a month ago, ran up the other bank— that was all. By now the Sergeant would be scattering the rest of the platoon across the bottom of the valley, covering the stream, the courier route and the left bank. Pershing had taken one section up the right bank, dropping four men and leaving himself with an assault group of five.

The important thing was to attack the camp from above. At the first shot the Chinese would run, downhill if they could, following the easiest lines of escape, then fanning out and collecting later at a prearranged rendezvous. Only an attack from above would drive them down into the Sergeant's cordon. To be sure of it the assault group should have taken a long detour and approached from the head of the valley. But there had not been time for that. Going up the right bank was the next best solution: it avoided the courier route and with luck would bring them between the camp and the sentry on this side. That at least seemed to have happened. The sentry was probably on the ridge.

But was this the camp? They had started to climb at first light: it was now nearly nine. That would mean they had covered three hundred yards. Or four. Certainly not more than five.

Pershing asked the Corporal. The Corporal said three, maybe slightly over.

Three hundred yards? Pershing pulled a plastic bag from his pocket and peered at the contents—a square of soggy paper, solid green with occasional blue veins. According to Special Branch the terrorist camp was "high on the stream," and according to the map the stream was a mile long. Maybe it was raining the day they did the survey; maybe Special Branch were wrong; maybe, for once, the Gurkhas were wrong. Consult the Corporal.

The Corporal came up close, putting his ear to Pershing's mouth. His skin was dry and hairless, the same smooth brown as always. Pershing's face was a mess of stubble and spots; normally pale, it was now spectral, blue eyes starting from the skull and streaks of lank yellow hair falling from under the floppy green jungle hat. He was a foot taller than any of his soldiers, six foot six, and to pull his broom-handle limbs through the undergrowth at the same pace as theirs was a cruel, punishing effort. Sweat was running into his eyes, dripping from his nose and chin, trickling down his chest to form pools above his belt.

The Corporal thought it was the camp. People don't wander about the jungle washing tins.

Pershing mopped his face with his camouflage net and without hope scanned the tangled greenery for a sign. He had been in this jungle, on and off, for a year. At first the look of it had filled him with enthusiastic awe, but now, after six months' almost continuous patrolling, he had come to loathe the place. Dank, secret, verminous, putrid, it could turn your skin green in a matter of weeks, and sometimes you wondered if your brain was going green as well. Each day you started out rational and in control, but it pulled you down, tripping you on its vines and sucking the soles from your boots, until you were grubbing across the forest floor with the ants, following the line of least resistance, too tired to remember why you were there or care if you got shot.

Before Malaya Pershing's image of war had been borrowed from the movies—charging over desert and mountain in polka-dot scarf and chukka boots; enemy lines over there, ours back here, and a hot-eyed nurse in Cairo. Instead it was this creeping about the undergrowth, this struggle to take a decision with a hopeless map and unreliable information.

Usually it didn't matter if you were wrong. The search would end at an abandoned camp, tracks would disappear. *But this time someone was there.* Suddenly Pershing's mouth was dry and a moth had began to flutter inside the walls of his chest. He tried to remember the rules. If this was the camp, they must move quickly. The Sergeant was laying his cordon too close; any minute the Chinese might hear him.

He raised his eyebrows at the Corporal and pointed down the hill. The Corporal nodded agreement. Leaving their packs behind, the section started cautiously down the slope, weapons held high, free hands gripping the tree roots.

As he started down, another thought brought terror to Pershing's heart. What if the noise had been made by one of the Sergeant's men? A mess tin or water bottle could have worked loose as they crossed the stream. On an OCS exercise in the Welsh mountains Pershing had once launched a charge against his own men. He could see the instructor now, pointing his stick into the wind and shouting to the other cadets: "Mark well, gentlemen—the ideal conscripts' mistake! You'll never see the like again."

That time they were using blanks.

The hands of the electric clock in the Sungei Siput Police Headquarters jerked to nine o'clock, and the District War Executive Committee took their seats around the table.

2

District Officer, District Special Branch Officer, Officer Commanding Police District, OC Home Guard, the Colonel of the Second Battalion of the Sixth Gurkha Rifles and his Intelligence Officer— brisk, neat men, competing for punctuality, the smell of their sleep overlaid with bay rum and after-shave lotion. They met at the same time every morning to discuss the progress of the war, and even when there was no progress, which was most days, managed to instill an air of urgency into their deliberations. It was their defense against the perpetual disappointments of a war of attrition. After ten years the state of Perak was one of the few still to be cleared of Communist guerrillas, and Sungei Siput was the worst district—since April it had been the target of a Federal Priority Operation, with almost no result. On the wall behind the DO's head hung a board, and on the board a hierarchical tree of little discs; each disc bore the name and photograph of a wanted guerrilla, and some were marked with a red cross, to show where a man had been killed or captured. In the last eighteen weeks not one new cross had been added. Keeping up the appearance of momentum had strained the committee's skill to the limit.

But that morning there was nothing false about the urgency. The information from Morgan had kept things humming since the previous afternoon. Morgan himself

7

had come up from Ipoh for the meeting, and the Brigadier had come down from Taiping.

The DO opened the proceedings.

"Would you run over the position again, Gareth, for the Brigadier?"

Gareth Morgan, Head of Special Branch, was the only man there who did not look as if he had just stepped out of a dry cleaner's. Belly bulging over his trouser belt, sweat stains on yesterday's shirt, dried clay on his shoes and above it all the face of an albino toad. The Brigadier considered it almost a criminal offense that a man should be in such condition at thirty, but he listened. Morgan was the best in the business, knew the Chinese like a brother; if they ever did any good in Sungei Siput it would be because of him.

Morgan lit a cigarette and leaned forward on the elbows of his white suit. "Well, sir, I don't want to raise hopes prematurely, but it does look as if we've found Chiang at last."

Although he knew very well what Morgan was going to say, the Brigadier went stiff in his seat at the mention of the name and he glanced at the topmost disc behind the DO's head. A youthful, smiling Chinese face, shiny black hair brushed straight back, white shirt open at the neck: Chiang Li-shih, District Committee Secretary of the Malayan Communist Party, alias "The Tiger of Perak." The fact that all the troops under his command could not put a red cross through that face was driving the Brigadier to the edge of a nervous breakdown.

Morgan noted the reaction—nothing of that kind ever escaped him—and continued: "Yesterday I got a call from one of our people in Simpang Jalong, a sandal-maker by the name of Ong Keng Kong. Reliable chap—we've had quite a bit of stuff from him. He said that this time the information was so important he would only give it to me personally, so I met him in my car at the seventeenth milestone. He gave me this."

Morgan opened his briefcase and dropped a sheet of pink paper, torn at the edges and covered in printed Chinese characters, in front of the Brigadier. It was a surrender leaflet, one of thousands dropped by RAF Valettas over the surrounding jungle: a terrorist found carrying one was guaranteed safe-conduct to the nearest police post, or instant death at the hands of his comrades.

"The penciled characters on the back are a message from a member of Chiang's gang. He doesn't give his name, but describes the location of their camp and says it's to be abandoned at noon today. The writer will identify himself to British troops by a tapper's orange headscarf worn around his neck."

The Brigadier fingered the leaflet. He did not read Chinese. "How was this message delivered?" he asked.

"Ong found it under the door of his sandal shop yesterday morning," Morgan replied. "According to him the whole gang had been in the village that night. Supplies had been falling off and Chiang thought the masses needed encouragement. That part of it seems to be true. We found a hole in the perimeter fence."

"The whole gang? What a bloody nerve." The Commander of the Home Guard started to offer an excuse for his men's lapse, but the Brigadier signaled for silence. No one cared about the Home Guard. "And you think the message is genuine?" he said to Morgan.

"Yes, for two reasons. You'll see from the numbers along the bottom of the leaflet it's from last week's drop on Gunong Kijai. That fits with the alleged location of the camp."

"I wouldn't set much store by that. What else?"

"Ong was found dead last night, not far from the road. The villagers must have followed him out there."

"Was he, begorra? Well, that's something." The Brigadier's fingers began to snatch at the bristle on his upper lip, a mannerism well known to the committee and normally the prelude to some kind of outburst. "Do you think the villagers found out what he told you?"

"I don't see how. He hadn't shown the message to anyone else. Normally they would have tortured him, but there was no sign of that. Someone had bashed his head in from behind. Killing a man as quickly and openly as that is not their usual form; it shows they're exceptionally nervous. Of course Chiang will get to hear of it, and as soon as he does he'll break camp—so we had to act fast."

"Yes, I see," the Brigadier said. "All a bit slender, isn't it? But the most we've had for a while." A new thought occurred to him. "It could be a trap, you realize. Chiang may be trying to lead us into an ambush."

Morgan looked bored. A man could grow old listening to the Brigadier's theories on Communist terrorist tactics. "True, but surely that's a risk worth taking."

Grunts of support from the rest of the committee.

"Yes. I agree. Thank you, Morgan, and well done." The Brigadier placed both hands, palms down, on the table and addressed the whole committee. "Now, gentlemen, what have we done about it?"

The Colonel of the Sixth Gurkhas, responsible for military operations in the district, spoke up, but only to apologize. "I'm afraid I just came back from leave last night, sir, so I'd better let my Intelligence Officer give you the picture."

Lieutenant Robert Duthie rose from his seat beside the Colonel and moved to the Current Operations map. The Brigadier looked at him with approval. Athletic build inside an impeccable uniform, fair hair cut short, straight eyes in an honest face—this was the sort of young man he understood and admired. "Carry on, Lieutenant," he said.

"We don't have much in the area, sir. According to the message Chiang's camp is here, high on the third tributary leading left off the Sungei Bemban. The contours show a steep valley, no flat ground anywhere, so it could be anywhere on the stream. Pity the terrorists don't carry our maps—they could have given us a grid reference." Duthie made a point of having a joke ready every morning to keep the committee cheerful and found the habit hard to break.

"All right. Keep it brief."

"Sir. The SAS are here, about four squares south. Too far down to make it in time, so they're spreading out on all the likely escape routes to the south. The only unit near enough was a platoon of ours, one square west—here." He pointed to a small orange pin on the map. "When they reported in yesterday evening, we got them to head east immediately. With luck they would have reached the foot of the valley before dark, and started the assault this morning."

"Landing zones?"

"Only one LZ anywhere near, sir. Here. Too near, in fact. Chiang would hear the choppers coming in."

The Brigadier stood up and squinted at the map as if by looking closely enough he could find Chiang himself.

"Is there a British officer with these Gurkhas?" A Nigerian company had once failed to come to his support in Burma, and the ensuing shambles had left him with a permanent distrust of native troops.

The Colonel, whose military service had been a long love affair with the warriors from Nepal, recognized the slight and answered huffily: "Yes, sir. Second Lieutenant Pershing, a national service officer. Been with us about a year."

"How old?"

"Twenty-two."

"Any good?"

"First class." In the Colonel's view Pershing was the crummiest officer Eaton Hall had ever sent him, but there was no point in making the Brigadier a present of that.

"All right. We must just hope for the best then. What about the follow-up?"

Duthie turned back to the map. "As soon as Pershing makes radio contact, two more platoons will be lifted in and cover to the north; they're standing by at the airstrip now. But so far we've planned nothing on the east or west."

"What about the Loyals?"

"Two companies, ready to go."

"Put them both in now along the east, at the edge of the trees. An ambush every hundred yards. When Chiang's in trouble he crosses the road."

"And the west?"

"As soon as you hear from Pershing, tell the Australians to lay a barrage down that side and to keep it up until they hear from me. That'll keep Chiang running east."

Duthie and the Colonel exchanged a glance of sympathy. Of all the weapons in use in Malaya, artillery was the least effective. A barrage in the west would tell Chiang there were no troops on that side, and he would march straight toward it. The chances of a hit were thousands to one. But the Brigadier was still on the road to Mandalay; no one had ever persuaded him to think small. As if to prove the point, he said:

"And call up the RAF. Tell them to have some thousand-pounders ready. All units to come under command of the Second Sixth until further notice. I'll get that little devil if I have to blow the whole bloody jungle up."

The meeting dispersed in a clicking of heels and grinding of chairs on parquet.

Gareth Morgan stayed at the table, the ash from his cigarette falling down his front. The ceiling fan was directly above his head—he was often first at such meetings to be sure of the place—and he saw no need to move from the gently stirring column of cool air. His part was over. All he could do was sit and wait, leave it to these military men in their starched olive-green and their steel-capped shoes, and hope they didn't make a mess of it.

The Colonel left Duthie to telephone the Brigadier's instructions and returned to his barracks at Ipoh. Sitting in the back of his car, he found himself muttering little prayers. The battalion badly needed a success; their kills-to-contacts ratio had already been overtaken by the SAS. If they got Chiang it could mean a Distinguished Service Order. It all depended on Pershing, and he wished he could alter that.

Waiting for the call to the RAF, Duthie stared glumly at the green spread of the Currrent Ops map. If only they *could* blow the whole bloody jungle up. That would solve everything.

At a signal from the Corporal in front, they stopped to listen once again.

3

Pershing picked a blood-fattened leech from the back of his hand. His sleeve had torn and thorns had pulled across his forearm until it looked as if it had been whipped; his legs ached from the effort not to lose his footing and all the water in his body was gushing from his open pores. The motion of his shirt had burst a boil between his shoulder blades.

A moment before he had had an odd sensation. Suddenly he had seen himself as a robot, without volition, deposited in this alien place and set in motion down a hill to kill people he knew nothing about.

The feeling was not new, but lately had recurred more often, more vividly, than before. It had started on his first day in Malaya. As he lay on his bed at the transit barracks in Singapore, fresh off the plane from London, it had struck him that for the first time in his life he was totally cut off from everything that had made him what he was. Now he could be any sort of person he liked, and no one would know he was different from the man who left England. From that moment every act would be a new decision. But when, exhilarated, he had looked for the inner Pershing, he had found an empty space.

Of course it was rubbish to say that he was there by no decision of his own. No one had given him a reason why these people should die, but he had never asked for one. Cothill, Harrow, Cambridge, Eaton Hall, Sungei Bemban —the orthodox progression. He could have insisted on the

Medical Corps, like that anti-Suez bunch from Trinity; but that would have been ostentatious, and for him insincere. He had chosen to be an officer in the infantry, and asked for service in Malaya. Why? To protect the rubber trade, to serve his country, to save the Malayans from Communism? In lucid moments Pershing knew that the answer was less inspiring. He had learned how to stay on the escalator, and never asked where it would carry him.

Not that all these thoughts passed through his head at the time. Some of them seemed clearer later than they did that morning. It was just that various remembered reflections coalesced at that moment to produce an especially strong attack of the robot feeling. . . .

A new sound in the forest.

Or rather no sound. Every animal and insect still.

The Corporal looked back and grinned at them, the cheerful Mongol face creasing like old leather. They all knew what it meant, and it was the best thing that had happened yet. An angry crowd was massing behind the ridge, then on the ridge, then advancing downward, voices rising to a roar. Wind, like the blast from an explosion, swept through the trees. And then the rain was upon them, pounding on the foliage a hundred feet up, reaching the ground in a trickle here and there.

They waited until the trickles had become a torrent, then started to advance again. All the Gurkhas were smiling, smearing the water over their faces and the backs of their necks. The terrorists would never hear them now.

Pershing forced his aching legs into motion.

*Extract from Special Branch Files,*
*Ipoh, 1957.*

4

CHIANG LI-SHIH.
Secretary, MCP District Commit-
tee, Sungei Siput.
("The Tiger of Perak.") Age, 29.

Father—Chiang Yi,
Mother—Hu Ching-ling,
Sisters—Chiang Meh-li, Chiang Ah
Ming.

1. Originally resident in Shanghai, where the father was a
wealthy merchant, the family fled the Communist revolution in 1950, taking refuge in Hong Kong. At the
suggestion of the father's brother, Chiang Chia-hsiang,
who had emigrated to this country some years earlier,
the family came to Malaya and took up residence in
Ipoh. The father became a partner in his brother's tin-
mining business, the Chemor Tin Company. In 1952
Chiang Li-shih also joined Chemor Tin, working as a
clerk in the sales department.

2. The company operates two mines south of Kampong
Rimba Panjang and the majority of the employees come
from Kantan Bharu New Village. Chiang, who resented
what he considered a betrayal of the new China by his
father, had secretly joined the MCP on arrival in Malaya
and now used his job with Chemor Tin to support the
local party, first organizing a levy among workers at the
mines and later rising to be Masses Executive responsible for finance in Kantan Bharu. After a series of arrests
in the village during 1953, he took command of the
organization and succeeded in rebuilding it in a matter
of months. In 1954 his activities were reported to us by
his uncle, Chiang Chia-hsiang, who had traced irregu-
larities in the company's sales accounts. Chiang fled to

the jungle, and joined Kantan Bharu Branch of the MCP Armed Work Force.

3. We believe that Chiang was warned of his impending arrest, but the source of his information was not discovered. Chiang Chia-hsiang suspected his brother, and a month later the partnership at Chemor Tin was dissolved, Chiang Yi becoming a silk trader in Ipoh. The family's social status was reduced considerably and Ah Ming, the younger daughter, was removed from school to assist in the new business.

4. Following Chiang's recruitment the terrorist activities of the Kantan Bharu Branch showed a marked increase. The Branch continued to enter the village frequently, keeping a tight control on the masses organization and gaining new recruits. On 1955 alone, 5 deaths were recorded among the local police and Home Guard, whose loyalty became suspect. The same year the Branch made two attacks on the premises of Chemor Tin, destroying the pumping station at each mine. Military operations in the area suffered from a lack of reliable information: two of the Branch were killed in chance contacts in 1955, but Chiang, who by that time headed the Branch, escaped on both occasions. Despite this year's amnesty offer there have been no surrenders.

5. In June 1956 Chiang was promoted to the Sungei Siput District Committee, and three months later was summoned by Chen Ping to receive the congratulations of the Central Committee. In January of this year an internal feud resulted in the death of Lan Fatt, District Committee Secretary, and Chiang succeeded to the post. Simultaneously Ah Ming disappeared from the family home in Ipoh. We have no evidence as to her current whereabouts, but she is assumed to have joined her brother in the jungle.

6. Following Chiang's promotion events in the Sungei Siput District have followed the same pattern as earlier at Kantan Bharu: an increasing number of incidents, improved recruiting and effective control of the masses organization. Breaking the usual security procedures,

Chiang is not afraid to visit the Branches and villages under his control, with the result that morale and loyalty are unusually good. Our attempts to recruit informants have been notably unsuccessful.

7. Since April of this year a Federal Priority Operation against the District, involving most of 28 Commonwealth Brigade, has produced only 3 contacts, 2 kills and no surrenders.

*Summary.* The elimination of Chiang Li-shih remains the principal objective of all security forces in the Sungei Siput area. The reward offered for information leading to his death or capture stands at M$12,000.

They advanced into the camp line abreast, firing as they went. After the Corporal's first shot Pershing heard a voice shouting ahead of him, then a shriek in the bushes to his left. He altered direction and advanced toward the sound. There was nothing in front but a wall of vegetation sagging in the rain. Then suddenly the leaves shuddered with animal panic, twigs snapping underfoot, whole branches heaving about; another shout, and two bursts from the bren away on the right, and screams, close, ahead of him, human screams and monkey screaming above, everything screaming and running and hacking to get out of his path. . . .

# 5

He fired.

He only half expected the thing to work, but it jumped in his hands with a flat, metallic bang. He fired again and walked toward the bushes, stopping to fire from the shoulder at every movement of the leaves.

He pushed the branches aside and found the edge of the camp.

Beds of palm leaves roofed with plastic, pamphlets scattered on the ground, an overturned pot of rice and a fire still smoking in the center. A Chinese in a white T-shirt had fallen into the ashes. At Pershing's feet a man in khaki was lying face down, both hands gripping an orange scarf.

He prodded the form with his carbine. Smoke still curled from the barrel, raindrops hissed on the hot metal. He was exultant, calm.

The man rose to his feet and tied the orange scarf around his neck. "Good morning, Lieutenant," he said.

Pershing stared at the emaciated face and the mop of spiky black hair. Trying to hold the carbine steady, he fished for the identification photographs in his shirt pocket.

The man smiled at the clumsy effort. "You needn't bother with photos, Lieutenant. My name is Chiang Li-shih."

Duthie slammed down the phone and picked up another. "Call the airstrip and get those two platoons in the air, then tell the Aussies to open up," he shouted.

Morgan, still sitting below the fan, looked up. "Well?" he said.

"Wow," said Duthie, then slapped the arm of his chair, jumped to his feet and danced twice around his desk, ululating like an Apache.

Morgan was unamused. "For God's sake, man, what's happened?"

"Hold your hair, Morgo, me old fruit. All will be made clear. Now where is that damn thing?" Duthie rummaged through a box on the desk, then, with a shout of triumph, held up a red crayon and advanced to the board of discs behind the DO's chair. He faced Morgan, beaming from ear to ear. "Pick the disc—the new game for all the family. Get it right first time and we'll give you a life subscription to *True Detective.*"

Suddenly the two men were eyeball to eyeball. In three swift strides, his fat face flushed with rage, Morgan had rounded the table and grabbed Duthie by the lanyard. "Tell me what has happened or I'll knock your flaming head off." The words came out one by one, meticulously pronounced in a whisper charged with menace, the Welsh accent rising to the surface.

Duthie was reminded that obesity was not the only affliction of Gareth Morgan; halitosis was another and sudden fits of temper in which the usual self-control disintegrated with such theatrical extravagance that it made you laugh—or would, if you weren't still worried about what the man might be capable of.

Without laughing, he raised his hand and put a neat red cross through the disc of Chiang Li-shih.

The flush faded from Morgan's face. "Dead?"

"Guess again."

"Dead, he must be dead."

"Chiang wrote the message."

Morgan's hand dropped to his side and he stood quite still. "Chiang? Surrendered? That's impossible." His eyes narrowed with suspicion. "How did it happen?"

"He wore the orange headscarf, just as he said in the message."

"Good God." Conviction acted like a stomach blow, crumpling the white heap of flesh into the nearest chair. For a moment neither man spoke, then Morgan looked up, shaking his head in bewilderment. "Chiang, of all people. *Why?*"

Duthie realized that Morgan was disappointed, and understood. Spend years of your life working to defeat a man, and you need to believe in him.

"Same old reason, I expect. He's tired, he wants to go home. If he turns in his gang, he's sure of repatriation."

"True; but what a mucky way to do it."

"Perhaps he knew he couldn't talk them into giving up. There're some tough nuts in that lot—three of them were in the jungle against the Japs. They wouldn't know how to live if they did come out, and certainly wouldn't stand for a new boy like Chiang telling them it's all been a waste of time. On the other hand if he'd come out by himself, he'd have had the risk of taking us back to find them. So not mucky, but very neat. Just his style, I'd say."

"I shan't believe it till I see him. What about the others?"

"Three dead—one in the camp, two on the courier route. The Sergeant's bringing them to the LZ now."

"Any women?"

"No. But Pershing's following a trail; there may be more to come."

"Quite a day for the Gurkhas."

"Best soldiers in the world, Morgo, always told you. It brings the battalion's score to 301. There'll be bubbly in the mess tonight."

"Yes, well, you tuck into your bubbly. My work's just beginning." Morgan stared into space, tapping his teeth with a pencil. The mask was back in place, and behind it the quick, professional mind was already two steps ahead of anyone else. "Six of them still on the loose, you say. Thanks to our ham-fisted Brigadier they'll almost certainly get away. But with luck they won't know how they were rumbled. If Chiang's going to help us find them, they mustn't know we've got him. I'd better take a van out to the airstrip and collect him myself."

Halfway to the door, Morgan hesitated. "Oh, Robert— sorry I blew my top. You haven't been after that man as long as I have. I think if we'd lost him this time I might have given up." He smiled, and hurried from the room.

Duthie stood looking at the closed door, and shook his head. Morgan's smiles were like pennies thrown to the poor.

The Alsatian slavered and panted through the bloodstained leaves. He was pulling his little Gurkha master up the slope like a steam engine. Pershing and two more Gurkhas scrambled behind, panting, questing like the dog. All had shot and none had killed: a lust to accomplish the act drove them on.

7

The trail had started in the bushes where Pershing had fired. They had followed it for twenty minutes and now it was getting warmer—whole rainpools stained a muddy pink, and the soil showing black where hands and feet had failed to grip. The rain had stopped, and now it seemed as if the only sound in the forest was their footsteps in the dead bamboo. Every few minutes they stopped to listen for their quarry; it was only a question of time.

Then they came to an open patch under the trees and there he was, a flimsy figure in khaki uniform, lurching up the slope about forty yards ahead.

Pershing, who was right behind the tracker dog, saw him first. In a flash the carbine was at his shoulder and he was firing, steady single shots at one-second intervals. His blood was racing but his brain was cool, controlling the movement of his hands, concentrated wholly on the act of silhouetting the foresight on the khaki torso, then bringing it down into the circle of the backsight.

The regular officers joked about the American M1 carbine. They called it a popgun, said that to stop a man you'd have to score a bull or empty the magazine—unlike the FN, which would fling a man ten yards uphill if it even winged him.

So he kept on firing. He saw the figure cartwheel down the slope, then rise again and stagger toward them hands raised. But he went on squeezing the trigger until the magazine was empty. When he looked up from the sights, the figure had vanished.

The Gurkhas stared at him blankly. None of them had fired a shot.

They walked up the hill, still cautious, and found the body face down in the undergrowth, full of small holes. When they turned her over they found she was still alive. One shot had entered above the breast and must have pierced her lung, because the moment she started to cry, blood came out of her mouth. A wave of it ran down her chin every time she breathed out.

Pershing knelt to inspect the damage. This brought the score to five. No point in chasing others. They could get her to the LZ in time to meet the helicopter. It had been a textbook operation. Almost, anyway. Standing instructions were to bring a terrorist in alive if possible. This one had tried to surrender: the Gurkhas knew it but would never say; Pershing knew it but closed his mind to the fact.

One of her eyes was swollen shut with a bruise, but now the other opened, and when she saw him bending over her the moans became screams—not just cries of pain or fright, but a word, repeated over and over again. She was pleading with him, shaking her head and plucking frantically at her neck.

Pershing opened the top button of her shirt. He did not care if she lived or died, but this noise must stop.

"Khembahadur, the medical pack."

One of the Gurkhas took off a first-aid kit and spread the contents on the ground, then looked unhappily at Pershing. "I dropped it in the assault, sahib." He pointed to the glass fragments in the field dressings and Pershing saw that every morphine syrette was broken.

So they cut down a pair of saplings and threaded them through a poncho cape to make a stretcher, and carried her down the hill. And the noise went on.

The platoon filed slowly into the clearing, shielding their eyes against the glare, like men coming out of a mine.

Already they could hear the familiar clatter of an RAF Whirlwind, rounding the hill, then rising to a crescendo as it came in low over the trees and headed for the yellow marker. The Sergeant marshaled it in and signaled to the pilot when his wheels were over a patch clear of tree stumps. As the blast of the downdraft hit them the Gurkhas laughed and held their hats. Crouched low to avoid the rotor blades, a white-suited civilian ran toward the trees where Pershing and Chiang were standing.

For a moment the three men looked at each other, the stretcher on the ground between them.

Then Morgan nodded appreciatively at Pershing, and bawled above the din of the engine: "You were right, it's Chiang."

Pershing pointed to the stretcher. "Who's she, then?" he shouted.

Morgan looked down, and a brief frown of disgust or compassion crossed his face. "She dead?"

"Yes."

"It's Ah Ming, his sister. Been with him about six months. Only seventeen."

"What was that?"

Morgan cupped his hands around his mouth. "I said she was seventeen."

Chiang stood by the stretcher; he did not look down. As

Morgan handcuffed their wrists together and led him toward the helicopter, his features were fixed in a smile.

Pershing watched them go.

"Ten minutes' rest, Sergeant," he said, "then we'll
march out. Tell the battalion to meet us on the pipeline."

The Sergeant walked to the other side of the landing
zone, where the signaler had strung his aerial between the
trees. The Gurkhas squatted together, talking softly, their
shirts steaming in the sun.

Pershing propped his pack against a tree stump, then lay
on the ground and closed his eyes. He covered his face with
his hat, and the light burning red through his eyelids
turned to darkness.

*Part Two*

# PEKING, LONDON AND CLEETHORPES

THURSDAY AND
FRIDAY
9 & 10 DECEMBER

In Peking Chiang Li-shih was shown into the Prime Minister's room by a plump, bespectacled girl whose pigtails were tightly tied with red ribbon. The room was empty.

1

In the nineteen years since his return from Malaya, Chiang had only been there twice. His own work was with the Party, and did not bring him in touch with the head of the Government. He remembered from the last time thinking that it must be the only office in Peking without a bust or portrait of the Chairman. In pride of place opposite the door hung a yellowing photograph of the Communist leaders at Yenan in the early forties. Mao was there, of course, in the center, first among equals, hardly distinguishable from his comrades. For the rest, the room was like any other important office in the People's Republic; the velvet chairs were dark red, the antimacassars spotless, on the table stood a huge vase down which a green and a yellow dragon chased each other tirelessly. Chiang stood by the window, looking down into the gray courtyard, wondering what it was that had caused him to be summoned to this office on a cold Thursday morning.

The Prime Minister came into the room without noise and shook Chiang's hand quickly and sharply. More than thirty years had passed since the photograph outside the caves at Yenan, but the man's striking good looks had hardly changed. The lines down from either end of the mouth were deeper, but the hair and eyebrows were still amazingly thick and black for a man in his late seventies, and the body in the black jacket and trousers was erect and trim. It was known that the Prime Minister had his uniform cut by an old tailor who lived down by the Temple of Heaven. Chiang felt young and ill at ease, feelings he thought he had long outgrown.

"Let us sit down," said the Prime Minister. "I will not detain you for long. I have sent for you to tell you that the Political Bureau has decided that the time has come to incorporate Hong Kong in the People's Republic."

No trace of surprise appeared on Chiang's face; he was too well trained for that. The Prime Minister went on. "An ultimatum to the British Government is being drafted at the Ministry of Foreign Affairs and will be delivered tomorrow by the Chargé d'Affaires in London. It will give the British five days to agree to leave Hong Kong. The Political Bureau has selected you to go to London to receive the British reply and to work out the practical arrangements."

The Prime Minister had stopped speaking, and Chiang groped for the right mixture of words, formal yet enthusiastic. "The Chinese people will be delighted at the decision to liberate Hong Kong, Comrade Prime Minister. As regards myself, I of course welcome the part assigned to me." He paused. "May I ask a question about the Political Bureau's decision? If the British imperialists refuse to accept the ultimatum, will the People's Liberation Army be authorized to use force against them?"

The Prime Minister frowned. "I will repeat the decision of the Political Bureau: the time has come to incorporate Hong Kong in the People's Republic. That should be enough for you. But I will also tell you that the Chairman attended the meeting, and was particularly anxious that the matter should not be mishandled. That brings me to another point. It is some years since you were directly concerned with the British. Are you satisfied that you are qualified for this mission?"

Chiang felt the sweat start on his palms at the thought of the Chairman, so old now that the peasants thought him immortal, rarely seen even by his former intimates, hardly ever emerging from his stronghold in the Imperial City, yet felt by seven hundred million people as a presence brooding over all they said and did. "I have continued to practice the language," he said. "For the rest I assume that the Political Bureau examined my record."

"They examined it fully. In particular the story of the Englishman. His help will be necessary on this occasion, and you will renew your contact with him. Indeed that is why you were chosen."

Chiang moved uneasily forward to the edge of the red velvet chair. "I cannot be certain how he will react."

"No, you cannot be certain. That is your problem." The Prime Minister smiled for the first time, then rang a small brass bell which stood on the table by his chair.

To Chiang's surprise the girl with the pigtails brought in a tray on which stood two small bowls of tea. He had not been served tea in a government office since the first years of the revolution. It was pale green in color and had a thin, astringent flavor. It reminded him of childhood meals at his grandfather's house by the lake at Hangchow; quite different from the thick orange stuff which was all his sister could find in the shops of Peking.

Chiang sipped his tea and wondered what was coming.

"It will be an interesting assignment," said the Prime Minister. "For myself I have always found the British inconvenient people. Not that I dislike them, or admire them, or find them particularly intelligent. It is simply that compared to, say, the Americans or the Russians, it is hard to follow the process by which they make up their minds."

"They will wriggle on the hook," said Chiang. "They will try to find some way of preserving their capitalist interests in Hong Kong. But it would be a contradiction for them to fight, since in a war those interests would certainly be destroyed."

"Certainly it would be a contradiction." The Prime Minister rose to close the interview. "You should go this evening to see Comrade Wang Yao-pang, head of the West European section at the Ministry of Foreign Affairs. He will give you details of your journey and of the ultimatum, and show you the latest reports from London."

He walked to the door and held it open, again an unusual gesture. As they shook hands he looked closely at Chiang and said: "How is your father these days? I remember meeting him in Shanghai soon after the Liberation. He helped to organize the first consumer co-operatives. Then, of course, he took you to Malaya. Is it true that he is now living in Hong Kong?"

Chiang's expression did not alter. "I have not seen my father for twenty years."

As he walked down the stairs to the little Skoda waiting in the courtyard Chiang passed through a mixture of feelings. It was disquieting that the Prime Minister should have chosen to remind him obliquely that those on high knew his father was in Hong Kong. But as a Communist he was pleased to discover that until that last remark he had not thought of his father at all in connection with his new task. Hong Kong liberated would mean ruin, perhaps death for the old man; but the idea had not entered his trained revolutionary mind.

2

Mrs. Harvey sat at one end of the table peeling a pear and thinking about Christmas. At the other end her husband was stabbing absentmindedly at his shepherd's pie with the fork in his right hand. His whole attention was given to the blue paper on the other side of the table mat. Every now and then he would mutter crossly, abandon the fork and scribble on the paper with his fountain pen.

Three years ago Mrs. Harvey had complained bitterly about this bringing of work to the table. There had followed a short period during which her husband had come to lunch without papers, eaten silently and very fast, and hurried back to his study across the corridor. That was the road to an ulcer, and she had given way. Now she wondered over the pear how she could get him to Blewbury for Christmas. The cottage which they had bought there lay empty and unused except by an occasional niece or cousin. The charwoman dusted every week, and every week the dust returned. It was always Chequers or Downing Street, and both she loathed. At Chequers it was noisy servants and bad food, both beyond reform. From the bedroom windows of the cottage at Blewbury you could see the beginnings of the Berkshire downs, bare, clean slopes, fit for the silhouettes of the racehorses which trained nearby.

A louder mutter than usual came from the far end of the table, and Patrick Harvey's foot pressed the buzzer beside him. There was a pause before Joynson appeared.

Nominally Bill Joynson was the Press Secretary; in fact he ran the Prime Minister's staff.

"For God's sake, Bill, the FO get sloppier every day. Look at this. They've left Ian Smith out of the list of people coming to the Commonwealth Conference."

"That's my doing." Joynson had stubbed out his cigar before coming in, but there was a mess of ash and sandwich crumbs down his front. "He hasn't said definitely he's coming and it would be much better if he stayed away."

"Nonsense. Last year's settlement is the best thing we've done since we got into power, and it's working well. I want him to come and explain it to the African PMs, be photographed beaming with them at Marlborough House, that sort of thing. We might even make him a Knight of the Thistle, if you can find him a Scottish grandmother."

"There'll be trouble if he comes. The Left have been after him for too long. Even if he filled his Cabinet with blacks, there'd still be placards and bloody noses outside his hotel, just for old time's sake."

"No, I want him here. Put him in the Ritz, not Claridge's; you can't have much of a riot in Piccadilly with all that traffic."

Harvey pushed aside the shepherd's pie and finished his lager. Joynson made a move to go, but Harvey took another paper from the table and waved it in the air. "The agenda," he said; "it's much too long. We'll be at it till Boxing Day. Look at this, item twenty-three, review of the situation in Hong Kong."

"What of it?"

"It's quite unnecessary—who put it in?"

"It wasn't in the Commonwealth Secretariat's first draft agenda, but the Foreign Secretary was keen on it. Bennett said he wanted Pershing to report to the Conference on the recent riots and the threat from China."

"That's nonsense. The Communists have left Hong

Kong in peace for years. They won't make serious trouble till the lease of the New Territories runs out, and by 1998 we shall all be dead or demented. Hong Kong's worth too much to them as it is—carries the cash into China from all over Asia. They want the golden eggs more than they want the goose. Ryder Bennett's an alarmist, and I'm not going to wreck my Christmas so that he can scratch at his worries."

Mrs. Harvey, half hidden behind the bowl of pink and blue hyacinths in the center of the table, leaned forward at the mention of Christmas, then thought better of it.

"Go on, get the Secretariat to scratch it out. And the next one, number twenty-four, on Fiji, that can go too; there could be a bad row over that. I'll talk to Bennett on the Front Bench this afternoon." Harvey got up. "Now where are the answers for today's questions? That figure for the railway deficit looks fishy to me. . . ."

Mrs. Harvey watched the two men leave the room. They did not say good-bye to her because they did not really know she was there. Wearily she prepared for her afternoon. Selfridge's was cheaper than Harrod's, but Oxford Street was intolerable in December. She hated the windy pedestrian platform with the traffic roaring beneath. She took the list of Christmas presents out of her bag; it ran to three pages.

Jack Kemble threw into the fire the last half inch of the Punch Corona which he had brought back from the restaurant. He was experienced in such evenings and knew this one was near the turning point. The glow of the food and drink and easy chat at Nick's Diner was beginning to fade. Jane had put a Brandenburg Concerto on the phonograph and given him a glass of whisky mixed too weak for a newspaperman. Neither music nor liquor would be enough to keep up the impetus.

3

"I like that," he said, pointing at the wall. "Where did you get it?"

It was a scroll painting of a magpie perched askew on a branch which sprouted vivid sprays of red blossom diagonally across the parchment.

"Pershing gave it to me for Christmas. He said he bought it in Peking when he was there *en poste*. Those characters down the side mean it was painted by someone call Liao at the age of eighty-six."

*En poste*, thought Kemble, that sums up the girl; even her private vocabulary is Foreign Office. He looked at her as she stood changing the record; long, admirable legs, a gray and green patterned dress with high neck, a thoroughly nice, nondescript face, good eyes, unimaginative brown hair set neatly that afternoon. He had met her the year before at a memorial service for Alan Selkirk, a mutual friend, and they had seen each other often since. At times he had thought of marrying her (like many confirmed bachelors Kemble was always mentally rushing to

the altar on the slightest of pretexts) but she would be
too earnest, too set to improve him, too nice. She would
look better without any clothes on, but he was not sure he
would get that far without offering marriage. Of course,
there was another reason for keeping up the friendship.
As chief editorial writer of the *Globe* and TV pundit on international affairs, he had a professional interest in the
Private Secretary to Laurence Pershing, the Minister of
State for Asian Affairs at the Foreign Office.

"What's Pershing really like then?" As he spoke Kemble
swung his legs onto the sofa and drained the weak whisky.
Jane moved over to him and for a moment knelt by his
side to collect the glass. The edges of her hair shone
against the firelight. He raised his hand and lightly touched
her cheek, but she carried the glass back to the drinks tray
as if the gesture had not been made. The siphon squirted
as she answered his question.

"He's the best kind of young Tory. Not interested in
ideas, but quick and absolutely straight. He's ambitious,
works hard, masters his subjects thoroughly and hates in-
efficiency. What more can I say?"

"Social conscience?"

"Oh yes. Sometimes talks as if he's in the wrong party.
But I'm never sure how deep it runs. Questions of right
and wrong seem to make him uneasy; he just gets on with
the job."

"That makes him a member of the club. Is it true he's
nerving himself to leave his wife?"

Jane's anger never came fast. This time she had time to
fill her own glass before the color rose in her face. "Jack,
why do you keep on and on about Pershing? Don't you see
what it makes me think?"

The bottle of Valpolicella, the brandy and now the second whisky were slowing Kemble's mind. Also he was con-
scious for the first time of sitting in a draft. "No, honey,
I don't," he said.

Jane came again to stand over the sofa. His black hair was thinning badly, and middle-aged flesh was beginning to swallow up his chin. The stomach beneath the bright blue shirt strained against the top of his trousers, although the top button was already undone. His shoelaces were not a pair. Altogether, at thirty-two, he looked a mess. Why then did she find him so attractive?

"Every time you ask about Pershing you make me feel I'm just Kemble's smart way around the Official Secrets Act," she said.

"Don't be soft."

"It's true!"

He was pulling a face, laughing at her. When she was four, she and her brother had been forbidden to eat sweets. One day her brother had found a shilling, brought a box of lollipops and eaten them all in front of her, daring her to join him. That was Kemble all over. An arrogant, self-indulgent man, of deeply contagious vices. She lost the fight to keep her voice even; it shot up out of control. "My hours of work are ten to six-thirty. If you want to ask me about Pershing, just call extension 605 and save yourself the price of a dinner!"

In Kemble's half-blurred brain the light flashed green. The turning point was past, the way forward clear. He pulled her down onto the sofa beside him.

"Jane, Jane, Jane. Ten to six-thirty, that's a third of your life, and you spend it in the company of an attractive man. Am I supposed not to worry about that?"

What a preposterous fraud you are, Jane thought. She laughed out loud, but the thought stayed unspoken.

As she found his arm around her shoulders, her heart bounced against her ribs in one violent leap of panic, then settled down to a steady throb. Forgotten nerve ends stirred to life, asking to be touched. A long time since she had felt like this. Not since Oxford. You would think that by now the glands or whatever they were would have dried up. . . . She sat still and let his hands pass over her, until the moment for protest was well and truly past, then leaned forward and pulled his mouth to hers.

When she opened her eyes, the empty armchair the other side of the black hearthrug seemed to reproach her; she remembered the many young men who had sat there in the last years, slim, well-mannered, handsome young men, good for intelligent talk about everything that interested her, good for a quick kiss at the door and a polite good night. And here she was at the end of it all, about to be seduced by a paunchy journalist with a second-rate mind and thick lips.

Kemble thought of last year's girl. She had been an Ambassador's daughter and had slapped his face so hard at Victoria Station that even he had taken the rebuff as final. But she had known her way around his shoddy, enjoyable world better than Jane Richardson could ever manage.

Looking at her as she sat on the other side of the brazier, Chiang wondered again why his elder sister was so stupid. He himself was far from stupid, their parents were notably intelligent within their own bourgeois framework, and as for their younger sister Ah Ming, everyone said that if she had lived she would have been a prodigy. But Meh-li was as stupid as she looked. They had just come back to their own little house from the communal eating place at the end of the street. The food had been good, but Meh-li was always hungry, and she was now heating chestnuts in the brazier, munching them noisily in the intervals of their argument. The plump cheeks wobbled as her jaws moved, and her wiry, graying hair escaped untidily from the bun at the back of her head. The husks of the chestnuts she had eaten lay unheeded around her feet.

"I don't see why I cannot go to see them," she said for about the sixth time that evening. "Our father is already seventy; he may fall ill and die at any time, with no children near. I have the money for the train. I will simply go, stay about a week and then come back."

It was infuriating that his sister should bring up the old nonsense about visiting Hong Kong on the very day he had been told about the ultimatum and the part he would play in it. Of course, he had said nothing to her, simply that he would be going abroad for some days. She had asked no questions, for he had long ago deterred her from showing any interest in his work.

"Don't you understand," he said, "it was our father who left us? We owe him nothing. He gave up the new China, gave up his children, just to live in comfort with the capitalists in Malaya, and now Hong Kong."

He saw that as usual this line of argument would fail. For him the return to China had been a new incarnation: for Meh-li a separation from their parents.

He tried a new approach. "In any case your Bureau would never let you go." Meh-li worked in a bureau of the Ministry of Scientific Research which handled foreign contacts; she was not a responsible cadre, simply a translator and interpreter, in and out of English.

Meh-li rose to feed the brazier with coals. Despite the padded jackets she was always complaining of the cold, and sometimes in his irritation Chiang thought that the attraction of Hong Kong for her was simply that it was warm. Returning to her chair she said: "Last year my friend Liao Chang took her leave in Hong Kong because her brother was ill. He works there in the Bank of China. The Bureau gave her permission to go."

Chiang was getting angry; only his sister could rile him in this way. "Can't you see the difference between a brother who works for the People's Republic in the Bank of China and a father who is a capitalist, an enemy of the Revolution? In any case the British wouldn't let you in. They are much stricter since the last riots. They're only interested in spies and people with money, or peasants with food. Luckily you don't have enough money to be interesting to them, and in your Bureau there are no secrets worth selling. The British would turn you back even if you did have permission. Get it into your head that you can't go, and don't let me hear any more about it."

Meh-li sat munching chestnuts as though she had heard nothing. This had been one of her maddening habits even as a child, to compensate for her stupidity by cutting herself off from the argument raging around her. But Chiang knew that she absorbed what he said, because later she twisted it and turned it against him.

Not for the first time he regretted the big, bare, modern apartment which until the year before he and Meh-li had shared with five other officials outside the old Western Wall. There in the evening there had been joint activities—reading, singing, political discussion—and brother and sister had not been forced into each other's company. They had got on better in those days. But after his promotion in the Party the Peking municipality had offered him this old-fashioned house, four big rooms around a courtyard in the Chinese City south of the station, and he had accepted it as better suited to his new grade. One of the few mistakes he had made: the quiet and his sister's constant presence irritated and depressed him. He broke off the argument and went to bed.

An hour later he was awakened by the sound of crying. His own room was separated from Meh-li's only by a partition of fretted wood and noises passed easily between the two. This was not loud sobbing, just a steady drizzle of misery. After listening for a few minutes Chiang left his bed and tiptoed in his underpants into his sister's room. Meh-li was kneeling by the bed, face hidden in her hand, shoulders heaving. Chiang had often seen her like that, trying to remember she was a Christian, trying to bring God somehow into her trifling sorrows, but ending up always as the same fat, stupid, middle-aged woman alone in a society which she did not understand.

She heard her brother come in, and started up, expecting him to be angry. But he spoke softly. "Meh-li, I told you I was going abroad. If you want to write to our father and mother, and promise to tell no one, I will take your letter and post it when I am in a foreign country."

Meh-li turned her blotched face to him. Until a few years ago she had written to her parents in Hong Kong

every week; then the Party had warned her brother un-
officially that this correspondence, artless though it was,
looked odd on his file, and he had forbidden her to write
anymore.

"Thank you," she said. "That would be kind. I will
write tomorrow."

Chiang went back to bed, and lay awake for some time,
while his sister's sniffing turned into a gentle snore.

It was Friday morning, so fish for lunch and had been inevitable. Pershing had left his untouched and slaked his appetite with the brightly colored vegetables. Fish, prunes and rice reminded him of school, and he hated them all.

It was that sort of day. At the last moment Moira had refused to come to the lunch, saying it was all business and no concern of hers. Pershing had explained that his wife had a headache, the seating had been hurriedly rearranged and Mrs. Thatcher had sent up a bottle of codeine. Everyone was very concerned; no one believed a word of it.

Moira Pershing hated politics, an attitude for which she produced every reason but the real one: her husband was better at it than she was. To this she added that degree of English-style snobbery which only foreigners achieve. Neither fault mattered much until she crossed the borders of the constituency, and then she was dynamite. Recognizing this, Pershing had struck a bargain: no joint constituency visits on condition she came to the Association's annual lunch and ball. Now he wondered whether that too might not be better managed without her.

He stood by the window, pulling at a damp cigar. The Aurora's dining room window was a single sheet of plate glass looking onto Cleethorpes' seafront, designed to exploit the view and the sun. Today there was neither. The tide was out and a waste of sand or mud, dotted with lonely seagulls, stretched from the promenade to the limits of vision, merging into the mist and the gray waters of the Humber. He tried to come here as often as he could, but since his appointment to the Foreign Office, it had not been so easy—a fact which he tried to believe he regretted. The previous Member had been a good constituency man, but never held a government post. In choosing his successor the Association had looked for a change: Pershing's youth and good looks, his degree, his Military Cross in Malaya and success in the Diplomatic Service had marked him as a likely candidate for office. Now they had what they wanted, but Pershing was not sure they all still wanted it. His eyelids began to droop.

"When are we going to get that bridge then?"

A square, red-faced man took him by the elbow. Roger Bamberg had been Chairman of the Association since 1973. The only political issue he could be persuaded to talk about for more than two minutes was the Humber bridge, a preference not wholly unconnected with the fact that he was the biggest building contractor in the area.

"Not just yet, Roger. I saw the Minister on Tuesday and they're still waiting for the committee's report."

"But that bloody committee has been sitting for six months!"

"Yes, I'm afraid I can't do more."

Pershing suspected that the Chairman was one of those whose enthusiasm for him was on the decline, and it was so. Bamberg had lived in this northern corner of Lincolnshire all his life, and loved it like a brother. The fish docks at dawn, the football, the windy wolds and the flat, rich farmland—he could not have put it into words, but at the bottom of it was the feeling that this was a place for men, where the jokes were as rough as the weather, and the business rougher than either. Looking at the pale young politician beside him, eyes fixed on the sea, mind somewhere else, Bamberg knew that he would never fit and therefore wondered if he were quite a man.

The silence between them was interrupted by the agent.

"Laurence, Mrs. Thatcher would like a word with you about Hong Kong. Her boy's out there with the Blue Funnel line, and she's worried."

"In that case Mrs. Thatcher's an alarmist."

"I know, but she gave her house for the fete. You'd better speak to her."

Ten minutes later Pershing had thanked his hosts and retreated upstairs. The bedroom faced the sea and the windows were white with a film of salt, but inside it was gay —three different flower patterns competed over carpet, bedspread and curtains—and comfortable. And hot. Moira liked it hot.

She was sitting cross-legged on the bed, reading *Harper's* under a portable hair dryer. She said the smell of lacquer in the local salons made her sick. For a woman who had borne three children she was still remarkably slim and pretty, with perfect teeth and large brown eyes set wide apart in a slightly tense face.

"I thought you were never coming up," she said.

"I was talking to Mrs. Thatcher."

"Lucky Mrs. T. What about me, friend? I didn't come to this dump to sit by myself all afternoon."

She called him "friend" when she really meant trouble, and as petulance escalated to contempt, her English would falter—the plummy accent washing away in a flow of muddled abuse. She was Swedish, only child of two professors at Uppsala University and Pershing had met her during a tour at the Paris Embassy. She was supposed to have had some high-powered job at UNESCO; the impression created was of the international community in despair at the loss of a brilliant young administrator, but over the years it emerged she had only been a secretary. Because she said she would die if she did not work, he had agreed to an au pair; but she did not work and had not died, and the au pair had stayed.

Without warning the door opened and a waiter appeared carrying a plate of spaghetti and a Coke. He put the tray on her knees and she smiled in his face.

"Thank you, Ottorino. Could I have some ice in this?" In case anyone should mistake her for a provincial Briton she liked to speak to foreign waiters in their own language, but her Italian was not so hot.

"Of course, madam."

The waiter was back in half a minute, at the trot, with enough ice for a cocktail party. As the door closed Pershing said: "Ottorino. What a bloody ridiculous name."

"Oh, I don't know."

Pershing closed his eyes and listened to the spaghetti. It had been an exhausting morning; for him the hardest part of politics was winning and keeping votes. He used to wonder what drove him on, but now considered such questions dangerous. For instance, if you asked yourself whether it was worth getting to the top for your wife, you might be driven to the answer that with your wife getting to the top was a necessary consolation. He thought about Jane Richardson.

He was half asleep when he felt her lips in his face. She had brushed her teeth.

"Oh—hello. I was just dropping off."

"I thought you liked doing it in the afternoon."

"Usually, yes."

"Well then."

When it came to that she was a genius. Afterward she said she felt much better and what a marvelous husband he was. Pershing said it was mutual and fell asleep, suppressing the thought that the waiter would have done as well.

Ryder Bennett, Foreign Secretary, found that more and more often he was in a bad temper by five o'clock. And by five o'clock on a Friday evening his store of unvented malice was such that the slightest spark was enough to ignite it—in this case the sight of his newest and youngest Private Secretary.

# 6

"Why the hell can't Pershing see him?"

He saw the young man wilt. Personnel Department had been enthusiastic about Glossop; Ryder Bennett would make them regret it. When would they realize that to be a good Private Secretary you needed more than a quick brain, a Rupert Brooke profile and a good tailor? You needed to enjoy the company of poltiicians, and to judge from his air of slightly fastidious deference, this young man didn't. Ryder Bennett tried to calm himself.

"Look here, Glossop, it's not your fault, but see it my way. You put me down to see the Chinese Chargé d'Affaires. Then the Department serves me up with a brief, too long as usual, which says in effect they don't know why he's come, and can't find out. For God's sake, man, he's probably come to complain about the drains in Portland Place. We keep a Minister of State exactly for this sort of thing—7,000 pounds a year he costs. And Pershing knows about that part of the world; for all I know he can talk about plumbing in Chinese. So shunt the man down the corridor, will you, and let me get on with these papers."

"I'm sorry, sir, but the Minister of State's not here this afternoon."

"Not here? Where is he then?"

"I'm sorry, sir, but I don't know."

"Well, find out. No, no, wait a minute—what's the name of that Private Secretary of his, the girl who helped us unravel the Rhodesian business? Jane Richardson, that's right. Ask her to come in at once, will you?"

"Of course, sir, but the Chargé d'Affaires is already in the waiting room."

"What are waiting rooms for? Give him the evening paper, and say I won't be long."

Left to himself, Ryder Bennett thought for a moment about Pershing and the next reshuffle. It might come any day now. Harvey had more or less promised Ryder Bennett the Treasury, but the move had been stuck for lack of a good Foreign Secretary to succeed him. The Home Secretary, Broom, was the obvious choice; he worked hard, pushed harder, smiled at everyone but remained wholly unlikable. Ryder Bennett wanted it to be Pershing, who knew the Office already, and was liked in the party. But there was his bitch of a wife, who was apt to foul things up. And Ryder Bennett never knew quite what Pershing really believed. He was always a little on the defensive, as if hiding an unfashionable opinion.

Jane Richardson came in quietly and the Foreign Secretary, who liked girls pretty and remembered her as plain, was pleasantly surprised by the way she walked toward his desk, and the color in her cheeks.

"Come in, Miss Richardson—Jane, isn't it? Look, what's happened to your master?"

"He had to go up to his constituency this morning."

"But my dear girl, he's got the biggest majority in Lincolnshire: why on earth does he have to butter them up on a Friday? Are they thinking of throwing him out?"

"No, sir, but it's the Association's annual ball tonight, and apparently there's always a big lunch with the officers the same day."

"He shouldn't let himself be bullied. It's a bad example for us all." Really, the girl was quite attractive, and if her skirt had been a bit shorter, she would have looked just right. "Well, I suppose I can't get out of it. Go and tell Glossop to bring the Chinaman in. And stay yourself to take the record. My Private Office are illiterate, and anyway it will be useful for you to give Pershing a firsthand account."

Jane took a chair by the big table, opposite the windows overlooking St. James's Park. Today was an unreal day. Half of her felt slightly ill and the other half much better than ever before. She wondered when she would see Jack Kemble again. She wondered whether she could concentrate enough to take the record. Luckily she had brought her bag, and took out of it the pen and the sizable piece of blank paper, which like all experienced Private Secretaries, she carried wherever she went in working hours.

The door opened and Hsu Teh slid into the room, a tall, slim man of about fifty, with gray hair brushed smoothly back from the gray face of an intellectual. He seemed to know that the dark blue Chinese jacket and trousers which he wore were too large for him. As Ryder Bennett shook hands he saw that the man was nervous. His hand was moister than the central heating in the waiting room would justify, and there was sweat on his forehead. The Department's brief said he had been a poet in his youth.

With an inaudible mutter Hsu Teh handed over two sheets of paper. The top sheet was covered with elegant black characters and at the bottom a square red seal. Behind, fastened with a paper clip, was a translation into English, badly typed on scruffy paper. Ryder Bennett skimmed quickly through the translation.

The Chargé d'Affaires of the People's Republic of China has been instructed to make the following communication.

The Chinese people have long watched with admiration the gallant struggle of the masses in Hong Kong against the illegal colonialist regime. They have looked forward to the day when the colonialists would be expelled and the people of Hong Kong joyfully reunited with their comrades in the People's Republic of China. They have prepared themselves eagerly for that day, confident that the collapse of imperialism would not be long delayed.

In recent months the provocations of the colonialist regime in Hong Kong have become intolerable. Progressive elements of the population have been ruthlessly suppressed by the Fascist police. The conditions of work of the masses have continued to deteriorate as a result of unbridled capitalist exploitation. The harbor of Hong Kong has been increasingly used by units of the notorious Seventh Fleet. Agents of the reactionary clique formerly led by Chiang Kai-shek make no secret of their counterrevolutionary activities in Hong Kong, tirelessly directed at subverting the invincible Chinese revolution.

All these maneuvers and provocations having been exposed to the light of day, the Chinese people cannot stand idly by. They are resolved to bring to an end once and for all the sufferings of the people of Hong Kong at the hands of the British colonialists.

The Government of the People's Republic of China therefore request the British Government to agree within five days to the following just demands:

1 The unequal Treaty of Nanking and all subsequent treaties affecting Hong Kong to be declared null and void;
2 Hong Kong to be incorporated forthwith in the People's Republic of China;
3 All British armed forces to be withdrawn within a period of three weeks.

Chiang Li-shih, a high cadre of the Government of the People's Republic, will arrive in London to receive the British Government's acceptance of these demands and to make the necessary practical arrangements.

If at the expiry of five days, that is by 12 noon British

time, Wednesday 15th December, no satisfactory answer
has been received, the People's Liberation Army will be
instructed to take possession of Hong Kong.

Jane Richardson noticed the Foreign Secretary's fingers clench on the paper, so that it shook slightly in his
hand as he passed it to her. She felt the thrill which comes
to the diplomat who after weary years finds unexpectedly
that something dramatic is happening.

The strain showed in Ryder Bennett's voice when he
spoke, poking through the frozen courtesies like the tip
of an iceberg.

"Mr. Chargé d'Affaires, I have some comments of procedure and of substance which I ask you to report to your
Government. Your communication seems to have been
drafted more as a manifesto than as a Diplomatic Note,
but I will let that pass. I will consult my colleagues and
give you the reply of the British Government. My question of procedure is this: is it the intention of your Government to publish this?"

Jane could not understand why Hsu Teh was so unhappy. He was shifting his weight from foot to foot, and
the sweat was still forming on his forehead. When he replied in perfect English his voice was high and fast; in
fact he gabbled.

"My Government does not propose in present circumstances to publish the note immediately, but reserves its
position should circumstances change."

Ryder Bennett gave less than a smile, then turned away
from the window, moved behind his desk and sat down.
Jane noticed for the first time the freckles standing out on
his fair skin. Jack Kemble had a birthmark on his back.

"Now I have a comment of substance," Ryder Bennett
said. "When we took possession of Hong Kong in 1841 it
was a barren rock sheltering a few families of fishermen
and smugglers. Now it is one of the greatest cities of the

East. How has that happened? Not by our doing only, though we take pride in it. It is the doing of millions of Chinese who have chosen to pass their lives and exert their talents under our flag. We British can take our men and our money elsewhere if need be, we shall survive and flourish. It is your fellow Chinese whom you are threatening with a way of life which most of them have already plainly rejected."

Daughter of a professor at Ruskin, herself a surreptitious, evenings-only Fabian, Jane could not help a silent inward cheer.

To her surprise Hsu Teh made no attempt to expostulate but began to shamble out of the room. At the door he stopped and stood forlornly, his long arms in the even longer sleeves drooping by his side. After a moment's hesitation Ryder Bennett crossed the room and opened the door to show his visitor out. As the two men stood together in the open doorway Hsu Teh jerked into action as if an electric current had struck him. He raised his fist, thrust it in Ryder Bennett's face, and began to shout furious, high-pitched sentences at a range of less than a foot.

"You will come to no good end, you and your bloodthirsty imperialist colleagues. Your hour has struck! Nothing can prevail against the unshakable resolve of the Chinese people. May the Chairman live ten thousand years!"

Instinctively Jane ran toward the door, fearing that Hsu would actually strike the Foreign Secretary. She reached the scene of action just in time to see a Chinese face appear around the half-open door of the waiting room opposite. There was a flash and the door closed again. Hsu Teh gave Bennett a last furious look and walked quickly along the corridor and down the stairs, followed at a short distance by two Chinese who scampered out of the waiting room.

Ryder Bennett wiped a blob of Chinese spittle from his cheek as he walked back to his desk.

"What a frightful man!" said Jane. "He was so quiet in here, I felt quite sorry for him, then suddenly he was almost murderous."

Ryder Bennett smiled. "You've never served in a Communist country, have you, Jane? I should have let him open the door himself. Now the *People's Daily* will have a fine front-page picture of him ranting at me with his fist under my nose. I expect they taped it too; that last Chinese had something bulky under his coat. The worrying question is, when will they publish?"

His mood changed and the smile snapped off. He took the ultimatum and wrote TOP SECRET on it in red ink.

"Take that at once to the Far Eastern Department and tell them to send it Most Immediate to Washington, Peking and Hong Kong, marked personal for heads of post and Governor only. Warn the Permanent Under-Secretary and the Under-Secretaries concerned that I shall want to see them after I've talked to the PM. And tell Glossop to get me the Prime Minister on the telephone at once."

Ryder Bennett watched her skirt swing around the long trim legs as she left the room. Yes, Glossop would have to go. Then his eye was caught by the brief prepared by the Department for the interview just ended.

". . . Anglo-Chinese relations are at present smooth, and we may legitimately expect the recent improvements to continue, particularly as regards the problems of Hong Kong. . . ."

That Friday night Chiang returned home late and chilled to the bone. The Skoda car which was usually at his disposal had broken down, and he had been forced to take a pedicab. The driver had a rough fur rug slung across his shoulders, but Chiang suffered unprotected from the wind blowing from the hills. After such a wind there might be snow, the first of the winter.

7

As he entered Chiang noticed the warmth of the living room; the brazier had been lit for some time and its crackling fire had almost burned through to the few black coals remaining on top. Then he noticed that Meh-li had taken one of their old blue and white bowls out of the chest in the corner, and filled it with bronze chrysanthemums. He put his briefcase down near the door and shouted through the partition to the kitchen: "I'm here, Meh-li. What is this, a holiday? It's not the New Year yet!"

Meh-li came out of the kitchen, followed by a noise of sizzling and an unmistakable and delicious smell. "You are going away tomorrow morning," she said smiling, "and who knows when you will return? And it is too cold to go out, though we are not yet at the Day of Little Snow. So I thought we would not eat at the People's Restaurant tonight, and I am cooking a duck I found in the market as I came back from the Ministry." Chiang was pleased that Meh-li was not in one of her grizzling moods, and though he disliked the extravagance, the duck smelled promising.

As usual they ate without saying much, but the silences were almost companionable, not, as sometimes, heavy with reproach. As Chiang leaned forward with his chopsticks to prise away a final slither of duck and wrap it in a pancake with soy sauce, the bell of the outside door pealed harshly. He crossed the courtyard to open it, and found outside a government messenger, the collar of his dark blue raincoat raised against the wind. The note which he carried was short: "There are some new telegrams which you must see before you go. Take my car." It was signed by Wang of the Foreign Ministry.

The messenger pointed down the lane to the point where it widened into a crossroads. The Ministry of Foreign Affairs used cars more lavishly than the Party, and Wang, though as a mere head of department he was junior to Chiang, had a big Russian Zim at his disposal, too wide to enter the lane itself. Chiang went back into the courtyard to shout to his sister that he had to go out again.

As the car slid smoothly through the streets, he wondered about the new telegrams. They might be from the Chargé d'Affaires in London, or from Hong Kong itself, where the New China News Agency was under instructions to send daily confidential reports to Peking. Instinctively he drew the white net window curtains with which all official cars were furnished, as if to trap the warmth and savor of the meal which he had just abandoned.

Left to herself, Meh-li walked into the courtyard. Its high walls kept out the bitter wind, and she always found it easiest to think in the open air. She had been told that day at the Ministry that she would be needed tomorrow as interpreter at the Agricultural Machinery Fair at Canton, and she had taken her decision. She would slip away from the Fair and take the train to Hong Kong, and she would not come back.

As soon as she had made up her mind the whole thing seemed easy and obvious and she could not think why she had hesitated for so long. She could speak Cantonese and had old clothes in which she could pass without trouble as a peasant woman, going to sell fruit or eggs in the market on the British side of the frontier. There was nothing to hold her in Peking. The duck had been a sacrifice to the past, to the time when she and her brother and her dead sister had been part of one family, sharing pleasures and troubles in her father's big house in Shanghai. But that was long ago, and she and Chiang Li-shih had taken different ways.

Meh-li touched the grotesque little mountain of twisted rock which served as ornament in the center of the courtyard. When the house had belonged to one of the old Manchu families before the Liberation a fountain had spewed water over the rock, and in the basin below you could still see the wire to hold in place the lotus which had flourished there.

One remark of her brother's was scratching away at the back of her mind. Chiang had said that the British would not let her into Hong Kong unless she brought in money or information. She wondered if this was true. She had not heard it before, but in her experience her brother did not tell unnecessary lies. Nothing would be worse than to be reunited for a few hours only with her parents, and then bundled back by the British authorities to meet her punishment in China. . . . Meh-li looked up reproachfully at the clear winter stars. She had no money to speak of, and no secrets. Her brother had plenty of secrets, but he never talked to her about his work. She did not even know where he was going tomorrow.

She sighed and went back into the warmth. As she started to clear the table something glinting in the corner of the room caught her eye. It was the metal lock on the dispatch case, the home of Chiang's secrets, lying where he had left it on first coming in. But it would be locked, or if not locked, empty; he was always so careful. As a young girl Meh-li had been brought up a Catholic, and though she had forgotten the names of the saints, she appealed to them collectively in moments of stress. Her lips moved as she put the case on the table under the lamp and tried the catch. It sprang open. Inside was a small pile of papers.

Meh-li began to read, then broke off to fetch a pencil and a pad of paper. Laboriously she copied out some of the sentences which she read. As she read further she became agitated. In any case she had never been quick with a pen, and some of the characters were in the new simplified form which she did not yet know well. But the saints and Comrade Wang were kind, and by the time Chiang returned, his sister was asleep, the dispatch case back in its corner and the pad hidden under the bowl with the K'ang Hsi mark at the bottom of the chest in her bedroom.

The air in the conference room at Chequers was stale with the smell of after-lunch cigars; Harvey noticed that the ashtrays had not been emptied.

8

"The rise in the Health Service estimate is wholly out of proportion. . . ." From the slight change in his voice it sounded as if Broom was rising to his peroration. Why, thought Harvey, didn't the man realize how much he lost by talking to his colleagues as if they were a public meeting? ". . . There is a market for medical services as for any other commodity. We must let the demand find its own level by the free play of the market."

Ignorant claptrap, and catching a sardonic look from across the table, Harvey saw that the Chief Whip agreed. Broom desperately wanted the Foreign Office, but it really would not do. Farther along the table Ernest Clapburn, Minister of Health, nibbled his moustache in nervous fury. If his estimates were cut Clapburn might resign. Suddenly Harvey had had enough. It was already dark outside; in the light thrown from the main porch he could see the black army of official cars parked in the drive. They had been at it since lunch and tempers were fraying. Harvey ignored Clapburn's attempt to catch his eye.

"I expect some of us will want to comment on Broom's interesting thesis," he said, "but I think that should wait until tomorrow morning. We can finish off our discussion of the Health estimates before we go on to Defense. If we adjourn now we shall have time for a glass of sherry before dinner."

Harry watched them troop out through the double doors at the end of the room, each as he chatted to his neighbor unconsciously slipping back into the ordinary words of private life after four hours submerged in the vocabulary of politics. He opened a window and looked out onto the dark lawn; a thick night without stars. They were not a bad bunch, he thought, though some of them visibly tired after three years in office. Particularly the Chancellor, whose chin had jerked up and down after lunch in a losing battle against sleep. The old man would have to go soon, and Ryder Bennett take his place. But would Pershing do as Foreign Secretary? Ryder Bennett said yes emphatically, the Chief Whip doubted; Harvey was not yet ready to make up his mind.

The telephone on the sideboard under the portrait of Asquith jangled. Harvey moved quickly and pressed the scrambler button. The switchboard operators were the most efficient section of the Chequers staff. Their instructions were to put through calls to the conference room only in an emergency.

Harvey listened to Ryder Bennett's story without interrupting. His disciplined mind turned to think of what needed to be done first. British Governments had lived with the threat to Hong Kong for twenty-five years; there was no point in getting emotional now it was coming true. He tried to check the dramatic tone in Ryder Bennett's voice.

"Well, you'd better come down here at once, don't you think? We can talk after dinner. Milton's here, of course; we're taking the Defense estimates tomorrow morning. Tell your press people I've asked you down to explain the FO aspects of defense expenditure." He thought for a moment. "The main thing, Ryder, is that this shouldn't leak until we've made up our minds. Who knows about it already? . . . Well, I suppose they had to be told, but no one else. . . . And bear in mind the Chinese may leak at any time, so we must aim to have a Cabinet decision by Monday morning at the latest. . . . All right then, we'll see you about nine."

As he left the room Harvey noticed the doodle lying beside Broom's place at the table. The Home Secretary had drawn two bombers above a city of skyscrapers. Blobs of flak were bursting about the planes, but they were getting their bombs away; two skyscrapers were burning, and crude little human figures lay spread-eagled in the streets. Harvey went through to claim his sherry.

A dull day for Jack Kemble, a non-day. The only glimmer of interest was quickly petering into nothing. He decided to try once more before putting the telephone down.

9

"So you don't deny that Ryder Bennett had a fracas in the corridor with Chinese this afternoon?"

A touch of exasperation in the voice from the News Department: "As I've explained already, we've absolutely no comment to make."

That was it then. The Chinese and the FO had both refused to talk; the story could not be printed without corroboration.

"Thank you, mate. You know, you really ought to do something about those lips of yours. Next time you get a cold you'll suffocate."

Kemble did a vee-sign at the receiver as he put it down.

He had been to the Foreign Office that afternoon for a briefing to "trusty" correspondents on the new British disarmament proposals. Bored and impatient, he had left before the others, saying he had to see a man about a TV interview. As he came into the corridor at the bottom of the main staircase by the bust of Ernest Bevin he had heard a high voice shouting indistinctly near the top of the stairs, just outside his range of vision. Then three men, unmistakably Chinese in their dark blue uniforms, had clattered down, rushed past him and around the corner toward the Park Door. Kemble was no longer able to break into a gallop at a moment's notice, and had been held up by a slow, grizzled doorkeeper in a frock coat, who told him that journalists used the other exit. By the time he had sworn his way over the obstacle and reached the Park Door, the Chinese had disappeared, presumably in the black car accelerating along the edge of the Horse Guards toward the Mall.

By then the doorkeeper was not in a talking mood, and the pound note visible in Kemble's hand merely increased his dudgeon. But Kemble knew his Whitehall geography, and was sure the original shouting had come from Ryder Bennett's office. Was the Foreign Secretary involved? What did it mean? The Foreign Editor had given him a free hand. Ten years ago he would have hammered at the mystery until it cracked; now it was past six and he was thirsty.

Besides, he had other things on his mind. Jane Richardson was the kind of girl who would expect last night to lead somewhere. He knew the type. She would hate to be thought possessive, but could not help wanting to take possession. Already in her mind she would be sorting out his diet and his clothes. She would expect him to call her that night, and if he did not she would call him, or even come round to his horrible little flat in Chalcot Square. But he was not ready to decide about Jane Richardson; so for the moment he must avoid her.

He started to tidy his desk, pushing odds and ends of papers into drawers, wondering which pub to drown his joys in. A piece of cardboard fell to the ground and gave him his answer. "His Excellency the Ambassador of the Albanian People's Republic requests the pleasure of your company at a reception on the occasion of the visit to Britain of the Minister of Defense. . . ." That would do; the drinks would be odd but strong, and Jane, bless her, would not be there.

It was only as he waited for the lift to take him downstairs that Kemble saw the beauty of it. An Albanian diplomatic party meant Chinese diplomatic guests, and in as genial a mood as they ever managed. Perhaps after all he could get a story out of the rumpus at the FO that afternoon. It had been a dim twenty-four hours in the newsroom, and if there was a story it might rate the front page in the later editions. Kemble straightened his tie in the mirror of the lift, glad to find his professional spirit still alive.

The Albanians, having resumed diplomatic relations with Britain only in the early nineteen seventies, had lost out in the postwar rush for agreeable Embassy premises. After months of camping at Claridge's they had finally accepted a gloomy house in Kensington, whose only diplomatic asset was a minor ballroom built out into the garden by an Edwardian owner whose South African speculation had thrived.

Kemble entered the room at the end of a long line of guests, shook hands with the Ambassador and chose an almost colorless drink from the tray in the belief that it would be pure spirit. Still choking he found a Corinthian pillar behind which he could survey the scene. The Albanians, perhaps suffering from the impact of Claridge's on their budget, had not redecorated the ballroom, which remained the shade of dirty cream-yellow now seen only in southwest London. Trestle tables under white cloths lined one side of the room; the dishes of food were still covered.

Looking around him, Kemble realized that this was a party from another era. Eastern Europe had changed, and the Communist diplomats one met now were smooth-tongued, well dressed and usually on their way to give lunch to a machine-tool manufacturer at the Mirabelle. But gathered at this party were the backwoodsmen, faithful to the age of Stalin; squat, sour men in black suits cut wide about the legs, with mountainous wives in cheap bright colors looking hungrily at the covered dishes. The English guests were equally dated. A member of the Protocol Department of the Foreign Office was talking to a titled lady who went to all diplomatic receptions with a handbag large enough to take sandwiches. An elderly Labour MP in a spotted bowtie was lecturing the visiting Albanian Minister on disarmament. And there, standing alone in a corner with an orange juice in his hand, was the Chinese Chargé.

Kemble grabbed another glass of Albanian firewater and made for his quarry. He came up so fast that Hsu Teh had no time to get away. This was no moment for finesse, or even strict accuracy.

"Excuse me, Mr. Hsu Teh, I'm Jack Kemble of the *Globe*. We're printing a story tonight about the row you had with Ryder Bennett in the Foreign Office this afternoon. Would you care to comment?"

Hsu Teh clutched at his orange juice in alarm, as if he had never seen a live journalist before.

"No, I have nothing to say. Excuse me." Slipping around the back of the trestle table he made his escape at full speed. Kemble watched him head for a group of Chinese standing by themselves in the middle of the room, and speak earnestly to a fat man in a light gray uniform. Kemble swore at all diplomats and began to look for a final glass of comfort. But almost at once a young Chinese detached himself from the group and marched toward him; he looked about fourteen.

"Excuse me, but the Chargé d'Affaires of the Chinese People's Republic wishes to have a word with you."

Wondering, Kemble allowed himself to be led to the center of the room. Hsu Teh had recharged his orange juice but looked no happier. It was the fat Chinese, his forehead glistening with plum brandy, who spoke; as if Hsu Teh knew no English.

"The Chargé d'Affaires would be interested to know if you have ever visited Hong Kong, Mr. Kemble?"

"But I was talking to him just now about today's—"

"Precisely. Perhaps the two things are connected. The

Chargé d'Affaires hopes you are aware of the struggle of the valiant people of Hong Kong against the colonial regime. He suggests that you keep next Wednesday free of engagements. That is all the Chargé d'Affaires has to say, Mr. Kemble."

Kemble spoke direct to Hsu Teh. "This is ridiculous, Mr. Chargé. I asked you a straightforward question. You can answer it or not, but it's no use your friend here feeding me with riddles. What's all this about Wednesday?"

Hsu Teh answered in a flat, official voice: "I have nothing to add to what my Counselor has said, except to wish you good night."

Kemble turned angrily away. As he left, the waiters took the covers off the dishes and the guests surged across the room like an army entering a long-besieged city. The Chinese stayed aloof, and for the first time Kemble saw Hsu Teh smile. Feeding time for the barbarians.

Now, damn and blast, he would have to ring Jane and take the consequences. She worked for Pershing, and Pershing was the FO Minister for Asian Affairs, so she was the only person he knew who could solve this puzzle. The story had a grip on him now. He must get to the bottom of it even though he wasn't yet ready to talk about life and love. He rang her number from a kiosk, once, then again; no answer. He called the FO in case she was working late; but she had left at the usual time.

Now he was really mad. What right had she to gad about the town as if last night had never happened? Women, diplomats, newspapers, God rot them all. He kicked at the door of the kiosk and one of the bottom panes splintered. What could that fat Chinese have meant about Wednesday?

At Chequers dinner had gone
cheerfully. They had been unable
to escape the Ministry of Works
Burgundy, but Harvey had found
it was the Minister of Education's
birthday and produced his own
champagne with the soufflé. The
Minister, who was the only lady
present, giggled skittishly during
his little speech, and by the time
they moved to the big drawing
room for coffee and bridge the ran-
cors of the afternoon were forgotten.

# 10

Harvey had tried to keep Hong Kong well at the back of
his mind. There was no point in thinking about it until
Ryder Bennett arrived. He knew his own instinctive reaction, and wanted to test it against Bennett's before telling anyone else.

He took his coffee quietly into his study, meaning to
search the Health estimates again for a compromise. He
usually found it easy to concentrate his thoughts there—it
was the only modern room in the house: plain white walls,
black sofa, black desk and chair, abstract paintings tend-
ing to orange and purple, a few favorite books on history
and economics—but this evening he could not fix his mind
on the statistics massed before him. Ryder Bennett might
not arrive for an hour yet. Too long. He pressed the button on his desk marked Chief Steward.

"Would you ask the Minister of Defense to bring his
coffee in here please?"

A minute later a stocky man with a brown, lined face
and white hair marched into the room. Well-pressed pin-

stripe, glowing black brogues; undoubtedly the best-dressed member of the Cabinet.

Sir Rodney Milton had held his post for fifteen quiet months. After a solid career in the Navy he had retired as Rear-Admiral and found a safe south-coast seat. His promotion from the back benches to the Cabinet in 1975 had been a surprise. Unimaginative, said the papers, but that had been the point. After the stress of the Rhodesian crisis the services needed time to convalesce; no excitements, no reforms, a safe man at the top. And so up to now it had proved.

His first reaction to Harvey's news was to call for a second brandy and an atlas. Sitting down gingerly in the angular armchair, he frowned for a second at the orange abstract, as if he had spotted an unauthorized stranger in the room and was wondering whether to have him removed. Deciding against it, for the next ten minutes he pored intently over the atlas. Every so often he took a propelling pencil from his pocket and did sums across the Pacific. Like a schoolboy working out a magazine competition, thought Harvey. (Was that an *arrow* pointing into Manchuria?) Outside the rain began to fret against the window. Why the devil was Ryder Bennett so late?

He was about to ring the Resident Clerk at the Foreign Office when he heard a car brake outside, locked wheels sliding through the loose gravel. The melodramatic touch was recognizable as a trademark. Two minutes later the Foreign Secretary was in the room, brushing the rain out of his hair. Not for the first time he reminded Harvey of a brisk, friendly terrier.

"Sorry to take so long, Patrick. Got stopped for speeding in Amersham. Breath test, the lot. I started to argue, but that just held me up longer."

Harvey let out some of the irritation which had been building up inside him.

"Do you mean to say you drove down here yourself? Why on earth didn't you take an official car?"

Ryder Bennett grinned, showing his uneven teeth. "I'm a real twentieth-century man. My brain thinks best when part of it is driving a car."

Harvey pressed the buzzer on his desk. "Bring up the sandwiches I ordered for the Foreign Secretary please, and a bottle of whisky with three glasses."

Ryder Bennett put his feet up on the sofa. A crisis, however gloomy, brought out the buccaneer in him; this evening he felt full of bounce.

"What a frightful room this is, Patrick," he said. "I hear the Ministry of Works threw a fit when you told them what you wanted."

Harvey was in no mood to be teased. He sat down behind his desk, and something in his manner caused Ryder Bennett to swing his legs off the sofa. The Minister of Defense drained his brandy. The meeting was thus silently called to order.

"You'd better show us the exact text of the Chinese Note, Ryder," said Harvey.

Ryder Bennett took from his wallet the translation which Hsu Teh had given him and passed it around.

Sir Rodney colored as he read it. He looked like a man who had been insulted, which was indeed the way he felt. "This is an arrogant load of rubbish, and should be treated as such. The Chinese know of course that Hong Kong isn't militarily defensible, but we've planned for exactly this situation. You both saw the paper which our Joint Services Mission agreed with the Pentagon last year. Operation Peak, it was called. I've just been refreshing my memory with the atlas; can't recall the details, but the gist of it was that an attack on the colony would be met within forty-eight hours by a strike from the Seventh Fleet—tactical nuclears against the Chinese army attacking Hong Kong and several Poseidons on Canton, with Hankow as an additional option."

"But that was a contingency plan," Harvey said. "The President made it clear to me beforehand that he could give no commitment."

"Surely that was just a technicality." Like most service-men Milton was impatient of any technicalities except his own. "The Americans couldn't stand by and see Hong Kong taken over."

Ryder Bennett intervened. "Rodney, you don't under-stand, the Chinese have thought this one through. The President's a lame duck now, he's just hanging on till Lind-say takes over in January. He's lost everything except his formal power. Is he going to expose himself to humilia-tion by asking Congress to help us defend Hong Kong? The Chinese are betting against."

Harvey was anxious to get on. He disliked doing business after dinner in armchairs.

"There's not much time," he said. "In theory the Chi-nese have given us till Wednesday to make up our minds. But they may leak the story or it may get out from our side, and we mustn't be caught unprepared. We should be ready with an announcement for the House on Monday afternoon. That means a Cabinet Monday morning. So the White House must let us know by Sunday night whether they're prepared to announce that if Hong Kong is attacked the Seventh Fleet will mount Operation Peak."

"The telegram's gone to Washington already," said Ryder Bennett.

"Good."

Now that the first small decisions had been taken, Har-vey felt better. He even found a box of cigars and offered one to each of the others. "What about our Polaris subma-rines?" he said to Milton.

Sir Rodney shook his head sadly. "Two are on operational patrols, but one's in the South Atlantic, the other off Spitsbergen."

"I thought one of them was in the Pacific."

"Yes, that's the *Revenge*. She's there for six months with a supply ship. We're doing a joint exercise with the Americans."

"Could she be made operational?"

"I'm not sure. Some of her missiles are armed, certainly."

"Do you know her position? I mean, could she be within range of China by Wednesday?"

Milton began to look thoroughly alarmed. "I could find out. But surely, without the Americans—"

Harvey cut him short. "Never mind. That's all I wanted to know. I think that'll do for tonight. We'd better call off the Defense discussions here tomorrow morning, so that you, Rodney, can get back to London and concert in detail with the Chiefs of Staff before the Cabinet meeting. Unless you'd rather go tonight?"

"No," said Milton hurriedly. "Tomorrow first thing will be time enough." He believed in weekends and hated changes of plan. The room was warm, the brandy had been good and the thought of driving back that night to his cold bachelor flat near the Albert Hall was repulsive.

"Right. Now is there anything else the Cabinet will need to know before it makes up its mind?"

"Yes, I think so." Ryder Bennett bit the end of his cigar and, to Milton's dismay, lit it with a Zippo lighter. "We must know what the feel is in Hong Kong. How much trouble can the Communist unions make? How reliable are the police? How many guns and bombs are around? No use putting the Gurkhas in to fight on the frontier and whistling up the Seventh Fleet if the place is going to slip out of our grasp in a few hours of rioting."

"Do you want the Governor to fly back?"

"Too risky. Things might go wrong while he was away.

No, I want Pershing out there. If he goes tonight he can talk to the Governor, size things up and report back by Monday morning."

Harvey smiled. Ryder Bennett gave newcomers the impression of impetuous no-nonsense, but in fact he was as skilled a politician as any. He wanted Pershing to succeed him at the Foreign Office and was thrusting him forward deliberately. But it was a good idea.

"Right, but where is he? You should have brought him with you."

"Doing the tango up in Lincs."

"What?"

"Association Ball. Can't think why he bothers." Ryder Bennett spoke with the scorn of a man with a very safe London seat. "But I've sent that nice Richardson girl up to smoke him out. You remember, the tall one with good legs who knows your daughter. If you agree, they can both be on a plane to Hong Kong tonight."

Harvey stood up. He had been peace-making among his colleagues all day, and a wave of exhaustion momentarily submerged his brain. "I agree about Pershing. Well, that will do for the moment. Let's sleep on it, and have breakfast together before you go, Rodney. And of course nothing at all to be said to anyone except the Chiefs of Staff and those in the FO who already know. The colleagues will have to take this at one gulp."

"They'll splutter a bit," Ryder Bennett grinned, and looked thirty instead of forty-five. Sir Rodney Milton wished that he was back in the Navy, where people didn't make simple things sound complicated. All said good night but Ryder Bennett lingered for a second after Milton had left the room.

"It will be hard going, Patrick," he said.

"Of course. Do you think we can get the Chinese to withdraw?"

"There's a chance."

"And if they won't?"

Ryder Bennett took out his white handkerchief, held it out to Harvey for a moment and blew his nose.

"Yes," said Harvey slowly, "I'm afraid you're right."

But after Ryder Bennett had gone Harvey picked up a red telephone and pressed a button which connected him instantly to a Vice-Admiral in a concrete bunker under the suburb of Northwood. The two men could talk to each other at any minute of any day, as easily as if they were Siamese twins, but had never met.

"Good evening, Admiral," he said, and they went through the usual identification procedures. "I'd like to have a word about the *Revenge*. . . ."

In the sixteen years since the end of the Malayan emergency, fate had been kind to the Brigadier. Labour's army reduction program had twice grazed his ear and finally toppled him; but on the very day this happened he had received another letter to say that he had inherited his brother's business. The business was a private detective agency, and in a short time he had, by the vigorous application of military methods, turned it into one of the most reputable and effective in the trade. In which capacity he had caught the eye of Bemand Remington, Harvey's Paymaster-General, who saw in this combination of upright soldier and mechanized snooper the ideal candidate for a post he was trying to fill.

11

With relief the Brigadier returned to public service. A discreet change of office address; muttered explanations to friends about a new weapons research unit. While contemporaries died or turned to their gardens, he still caught the morning train to Victoria. Though now in his middle sixties, he seemed to grow younger; he had given up smoking and acquired a new manner, brisk as before but more relaxed. He looked like a man who was doing well.

Which he was. From his office in the faded mansions the Brigadier (he was never known to his staff as anything else) commanded a group of men of whose existence the press and public knew nothing. Founded in the aftermath of Profumo, their job was to maintain security in the highest echelons of government—ministers and top civil servants. Liaison with MI5 was only at the highest level and although for the purpose of estimates their budget came under Defense, they reported direct to Downing Street. Only the Prime Minister, the Foreign Secretary and the Paymaster-General himself were excluded from their scrutiny. Their official designation was the SSG, or Special Security Group, but Remington, who was rather a wit, called them the Shadow Cabinet.

At eight-thirty that Friday evening the staff of the Group had been summoned from their homes and now, thirty minutes later, all fourteen of them were sitting around the Brigadier's desk, modest-looking men in Burton suits shiny at the elbows, ex-policemen mostly, talking of whooping cough and emulsion paint while they waited.

At five past nine the Brigadier and Morgan arrived. The two men had walked from Remington's office in Downing Street and their noses were pink with cold. They sat down and the Brigadier counted heads.

"Right, gentlemen, sorry to spoil your evening. I'm afraid there'll be no weekend either. We're doing a twenty-four-hour watch until next Wednesday noon.

We've cut the list of targets to eleven, but that's as low as we can go for the moment, so no one's going to get much sleep. I shall stay here to coordinate and Gareth has kindly agreed to join the men in the field. Harrison, Lane and Furber will do relief shifts till Monday. Now Gareth will give you some of the background to this."

Gareth Morgan's appearance had hardly changed since 1957. Not that he now looked young at forty-nine; he had just looked old at thirty. In fact he was slighly slimmer these days, but the skin had been stretched too long to contract, and now hung from him in folds. A few years before he had started growing his hair long at the sides to sweep it over the bald patch on top; in a few more years it would not be worth the effort. His clothes still seemed an afterthought, but were obviously the sort that only a bachelor could afford. Over the years, all traces of the Welsh accent had disappeared. But by and large he was the same man: very healthy, very permanent. No one doubted that he would head the SSG when the Brigadier stepped down.

"It concerns Hong Kong, gentlemen," Morgan said. "But before I go into that let me give you a little back history. As you know, since 1971 we have suspected a high-level leak in this country on Chinese affairs. There have been three incidents in all. The original complaint came from the Americans, who convinced themselves that some-one on the British side had passed information to the Chinese during the Southeast Asian Security Conference. On that occasion there were too many in the know, both here and in Cambodia, for us to narrow it down, and the same thing applied to a lesser extent in the two subsequent cases. We now, however, have a new issue, only a few hours old, very seriously affecting this country's relations with China. All the details have already received the highest classification and are known only to a small number of people. So we have a much higher chance than before of detecting and, I hope, preventing any lapse of security. . . ."

The Brigadier listened to the succinct but unhurried briefing with admiration. When his previous deputy had retired he had known immediately whom he wanted for the job. He owed his success in Malaya to the Ipoh Special Branch, and had not been surprised to discover that its former head was still in Intelligence. After a long battle with the people down the road, Morgan had been drafted to the SSG.

". . . As I say, this time it concerns Hong Kong. I'm afraid this is one of those cases where I can't give you the full picture. All I can tell you is that a number of deci-sions have to be taken about the future of the colony be-fore next Wednesday noon, and the Chinese will certainly want to know about them. The main decision will prob-ably be taken in Cabinet early next week, and it's after that that we can expect our friend to make a move. As the

Brigadier has told you, we're rather stretched on this exercise and he will be coordinating. I'll be helping the FO
detail. You'll find your targets and relief times on the
board in ten minutes. Get started as soon as you can.
That's all."

The streets of Cleethorpes were empty, so they stopped at a fish-and-chip shop to ask the way, and Jane ran in. Two youths were leaning on the counter, hoping that Friday night still had a card to play. They looked her up and down, looked at each other, broke silence.

## 12

"Hello, darling."

"Looking for mummy?"

"No, for my boss." The level voice killed Friday night stone dead, but the smile which followed said that she understood, and was sorry. "He's at the Winter Gardens. Can you tell me how to get there?"

"Turn right at the promenade, keep on down to the end."

"Tell you what, sweetheart—we'll come with you."

"Thanks, I'll be all right."

The smell of the fat reminded Jane that she hadn't eaten since breakfast, and she bought some chips for herself and the driver. She shook the vinegar with a practiced hand and wrapped the newspaper tight. "Good-bye, and thank you."

"Ta-ta."

"Mind how you go."

A parade of shuttered shops and empty amusement arcades passed by the windows of the car; bingo, hot dogs, bed and breakfast—the paraphernalia of once fashionable holidays, handed down to the poor like used clothes. Jane had never been to such a place before, and for a moment saw very clearly the difference between a politician and a civil servant.

At the end of the promenade cars huddled around the ballroom as if for warmth. The doorman had gone off duty. Jane ran under the striped awning, then stopped to swallow the last of the chips. The cheap carpet was wet underfoot and the canvas walls were flapping loudly in a wind which must have come non-stop from the Arctic; the sea sounded surprisingly close. As she turned inside she wondered if anyone would offer her a drink.

They didn't. Feeling conspicuous in her tweed suit, she stood at the edge of the floor and searched the dancers swaying uncertainly in the pink light to the rhythm of a tenor sax. Pershing was always the tallest man in the room.

A dinner jacket introduced himself as Pershing's agent. "The FO told us to expect you. They want you to ring them back. I'll show you where the phone is, then find Laurence."

Jane followed him into an office by the cloakroom and phoned the FO Travel Section. She was still copying the flight times on the back of her checkbook when Pershing came in. His hair was disarranged and he was mopping his brow. The whole building now shook to the beat of electric guitar and drums. Nothing stuffy about the Tories.

"Hello, Jane. They told me you were coming. What's the flap?"

"It's about Hong Kong. The Chinese Chargé paid us a visit this afternoon. They're demanding we give the colony up by next Wednesday, or they use force. The Secretary of State wants you out there straightaway to sound out the position, and suggested I go with you."

"When do we leave?"

Jane approved. No time-wasting incredulity, just the basic questions. "Tonight. There's a QANTAS flight leaving Foulness at one and we can catch a connection at Nottingham at twelve-twenty."

Pershing looked at his watch. "Can we make Nottingham in time?"

"The driver says he can do it. Everything's still under hatches, you see—the Chinese haven't published the ultimatum—so the PM thought we should use commercial flights."

"Very sensible. I'm always walking out of balls and catching planes in my dinner jacket. What could be more normal?"

They both laughed. "It's not quite as desperate as that," she said. "You can snatch five minutes at the hotel now and the Office have asked your au pair in Chelsea to pick you out some clothes. They're collecting her in a car and taking her to my place to do the same, then bringing her out to the airport. I hope she's sensible."

"My dear Jane, she's Swedish, and if they had a Nobel Prize for stupidity, she'd get it. But tell me, are we to stay in Hong Kong until it's blown over?"

"No. They want you back for a Cabinet on Monday morning. The Chinese are sending a special envoy to London to handle the thing."

Pershing's professional interest was roused. "What's his name?"

"Chiang Li-shih."

For a moment Jane thought Pershing was going to faint. His eyes widened, and the color drained from his cheeks and lips. He gripped a table for support and stared at her as if afraid that the moment he stopped seeing her face he would drop dead.

"Are you all right?"

"Yes, yes. Thank you. It's been a long day. I'll just go and pay my respects to the Chairman and tell Moira what's happening. Will you pick up my coat? Here's the ticket."

But neither went immediately to his task. Jane bought herself a large whisky, and Pershing was sick in the lavatory. Before coming out he carefully restored his appearance—washed and dried his face, reparted and brushed his straight yellow hair, straightened his bow tie, pinched his cheeks to bring back the color. Now he would go through the expected motions and no one would guess a thing. But inside he knew that he was finished, climbing only to fall from a greater height. Chiang's arrival in London could mean only one thing.

*Part Three*

# HONG KONG

## SATURDAY
## 11 DECEMBER

The Concorde came booming out
of the low cloud, banking steeply
to avoid the hills which surround
Hong Kong, and floated down onto
the new extended runway of Kai
Tak Airport. To Jane, stiff with
fright in her seat by the window,
it seemed as if the sea was lapping
at the very wheels of the plane. For
the first time it was a comfort to
have Langton, the taciturn ex-po-
liceman who had joined them as
bodyguard at Foulness, sitting beside her; clearly the only
thing that bothered him was how long he would have to
wait before relighting his pipe. As the plane taxied toward the terminal they joined Pershing in the first-class
compartment (since the economic troubles only Ministers
and the loftiest officials had been allowed to travel first
class) and moved to the door ahead of the other passen-
gers.

The cool air which flooded into the plane was refreshing but a surprise; they had all expected blazing heat. At
the top of the steps Pershing paused to see what was waiting on the tarmac—the Chinese army, a rioting crowd, a
sea of journalists, or at least the Governor in plumed hat?
But it was just the normal civilian noise and bustle, out of
which quickly emerged a handsome young man in civilian clothes pressed too well for a civilian's.

"Captain Okeshott, sir, ADC to the Governor. His
compliments and he thought you would prefer to come in
quietly without ceremonial. He is waiting for you at Government House. The launch will take us across the harbor."

And quiet it proved. There were policemen in the terminal building, dotted about haphazardly among the
bookstalls and inquiry booths, and a police officer caught
the ADC's eye for a moment as they passed. Jane walked
a yard behind Pershing, trying not to match her stride with
his; she had never learned the art of carrying both her
own handbag and the regulation black FO pouch, particularly when as now the pouch was bulky with documents.
She felt large and dowdy and stuffed with QANTAS food.
It was too late for the Governor to offer a second lunch,
but there was sure to be cream tea. . . .

Joe Allott, the man from the *South China Morning
Post*, took her by surprise, but she had her answer rehearsed: "Pershing, that's P-E-R . . . Minister of State for
Foreign Affairs—purely a routine visit, just a day or two,
yes, staying at Government House.

Joe Allott slouched back to the bar. He spent all day
every day at the airport, watching for comings and go-
ings, a sad, alcoholic man in a baggy white suit. The faint
curiosity which he had felt when he recognized the ADC
was quickly quenched; just another bloody joy riding politician. But it being a dull day at Kai Tak Airport he stirred
himself a drink or so later to ring his office and give them
Pershing's name. They were disappointed; someone had
said that Terence Stamp would be passing through.

The train jogged interminably through low green hills, their tops blotted out in mist. Meh-li looked at her watch. Almost four o'clock: if they were on time they would reach the frontier village of Shum-chün in twenty minutes. And of course, this being the People's Republic, they were on time. She peered out at the tiny, sodden fields, but her view was partly barred by the enormous posters stuck on the windows: "The Chinese people welcome the foreign guests to the 25th Canton Agricultural Fair."

## 2

Meh-li looked down the coach to where the British guests to the Fair were drinking beer around a small bamboo bar rigged up in one corner. During the time she had served as interpreter to this group she had grown fond of them. They were physically unattractive, like all Europeans, with bodies which in warm rooms smelled intolerably, but their simplicity put her at ease. She had long ago accepted the verdict of her family that she was a stupid woman, but among these British manufacturers of tractors and fertilizer she felt wise and subtle, ready for the great thing which she had to do.

One of the businessmen detached himself from the bar and came over to her with a more unsteady step than the movement of the train required. A small, stout, middle-aged man with a black moustache; he had won a contract for a million pounds' worth of pesticide, and was standing most of the drinks.

"This is a bloody fine carriage you've found for us, Meh-li." From the way he looked around him Meh-li saw that this was meant as a compliment. Swearwords were a notorious pitfall for interpreters out of English.

"We are not yet a rich country, but we like to do our best for our foreign friends." The regulation answers came quickly to her tongue.

"Bloody marvelous, I call it." He looked around at the marquetry paneling, the individual blue leather seats which could be adjusted like a dentist's chair and the ornate mock-stone carving over the doors (so that one plunged into the lavatory as into a Chinese grotto). Meh-li knew that the coach had been built in the twenties to the order of a warlord who for a short time ruled a couple of provinces in the north of China. Three slots for a tripod in the floor by one of the windows marked the site of the machine gun which had encouraged the loyalty of his subjects.

"But then this is a marvelous country," the pesticide man went on. "No dirt, no crime, and everyone working hard and looking happy—and when I think of all those whores and beggars in Hong Kong!"

For a moment, looking up at the flushed, friendly face, Meh-li was tempted to talk to him about the China of her own life, the China which lay behind the sights which she had so often shown to foreigners. It was odd to think that if all went well she would never again hear Young Pioneers with red scarves around their necks chanting the songs of the Chairman, explain the soaring graphs in the office of a model agricultural commune. . . .

The pesticide man asked her to join the party at the bar, but she refused politely. She heard the loudspeaker in the next carriage interrupt its reading of the leading article from the *People's Daily* to announce that in ten minutes they would be at Shumchün. She looked up at the rack above her seat; it carried a shabby black suitcase which she had bought the day before in one of the markets

of Canton. Perhaps the case was too shabby for her purpose. For the first time she felt afraid.

Meh-li had left Peking with no clear idea of how she
would cross the frontier. She had sewn into the lining of
her blue cotton jacket the papers which she had copied
from her brother's dispatch case. She had been told that
Cantonese peasants crossed the border in considerable
numbers each day to sell their produce on the British
side; she had hoped to pass herself off as one of them. She
had even bought in Canton a big basket, several catties
of lichees and sweet potatoes and one of the cone-shaped
straw hats which the peasants wear in those parts.

But then she had gone to see old Madame Lu, as she
usually did on her official trips to Canton. Madame Lu's
husband had been the Canton manager of the tea business owned by Meh-li's parents. She had been a great lady
then who gave parties for Europeans in a big house with
lawns running down to the river and a bandstand with
dragons on the roof. In those days Madame Lu had smelled
deliciously of perfume and a silver box in her house had
been full of hard, sugary pastries cut into animal shapes
for the children of her friends. The Communists had shot
her husband and turned her out of her house to starve; but
somehow Madame Lu had smuggled out a camphorwood
chest with part of her husband's collection of jade. Now
she was eighty and the chest was almost empty, but in her
tiny suburban hovel she still behaved and talked as if
she was queen of Canton. She even had a small circle of
old friends who came and sipped tea. Meh-li was amazed
that the authorities let her alone. In Peking she would not
have been able to sell her jade and would long ago have
been swept into some dingy hostel as an indigent nuisance.

Madame Lu was the only person in China to whom
Meh-li was ready to tell her secret; but the old lady had
stamped firmly on the idea of crossing the frontier as a

peasant. A son of a friend of hers had thought of doing it that way; but you needed a special pass from the Kwang-tung Provincial People's Government and these were impossible to buy, steal or forge. In her high, thin voice, Madame Lu had explained that the best way now was through Macao. Entry into Macao was an easy business and after that you hired a junk which would put you ashore by night on a beach in British territory. It was risky, of course, as the junks could show no light and the channel was dangerous. Madame Lu had a cousin in Macao who might do the job for two thousand Hong Kong dollars paid in advance. She had mentioned the figure wistfully, knowing that it was far beyond Meh-li's means, and Meh-li had walked sadly back to her hotel.

But there, in the hotel lobby, watching a group of visitors to the Fair leave with their luggage, Meh-li had had her own idea, so simple that she was amazed not to have thought of it before. She went upstairs and ate most of the lichees which she had bought in the market; they would not be needed now, and she disliked wasting food. The next morning she volunteered to escort the British group back to the frontier at Shumchün, and bought the small black suitcase.

Now the train was drawing slowly into Shumchün. Meh-li recognized from a previous visit the building which served as a hostel for those unlucky enough to be stranded at the frontier overnight. It was an ungainly whitewashed hulk of a place, quite out of proportion to the mud huts and small wooden houses which made up the rest of the village. If her attempt failed she would be taken to that building for interrogation. She shivered; her plan was too simple, a hundred things could go wrong with it, she should have stuck to her first idea. . . .

For a moment Meh-li was in a panic at her own boldness. Jumbled names of saints came unbidden to her lips. One or two of the British businessmen were still finishing their drinks, but most of them were already out on the platform. Although the railway line crossed the frontier, there was no through train to Hong Kong. You had to leave the Chinese train at Shumchün, walk a hundred yards across the railway bridge which spanned the frontier stream, and then you were at the British post of Lowu, and your British diesel was waiting to take you on the short journey through the New Territories of the colony to the twin British cities of Kowloon and Hong Kong.

She stepped out onto the platform, which was almost empty except for the knot of businessmen. The loud-speaker was blaring a medley of Party songs, one cheer-ful, monotonous chorus after another. The businessmen began to move toward her uncertainly, wanting to say thank you and good-bye. The man from Massey Ferguson, who had not been to China before, was fumbling in his wallet for a tip but one of the others spoke to him and he put it quickly away. Meh-li assumed her most brisk and bureaucratic manner.

"I will now escort you to the frontier officials for the final formalities. I hope that you have all enjoyed your visit to the People's Republic of China and that we will be able to welcome you again before long."

She led them down the wide, empty platform, past the posters, past the man selling nuts and beer, to the barrier at the far end. Two soldiers in green uniform manned the barrier; no badges of rank, but Meh-li could see that the burly northerner was the one in charge. The cap with the red star was too small and perched uneasily on the back of his close-cut head. Beyond him four sentries with rifles watched the entrance to the bridge.

"This is the British delegation from the Canton Fair," she told him. "You will find their exit permits are all in order."

"Let them fall properly into line, comrade," grunted the big man.

Meh-li chivied her businessmen into a queue. One by one their passports were examined and stamped and they were allowed through the barrier onto the bridge. The bridge had a roof, and the rails running across it were in deep shadow, but at the far end she could just see where the drizzle was falling onto the steel. This was the hardest moment. She was convinced that she would fail. . . . The last man through the barrier was her beery pesticide friend; he turned and waved to her before beginning the trudge across the bridge.

Suddenly, though she had made no final decision, Meh-li found that her legs were carrying out the plan over which her brain was wavering. She was walking slowly back, back into China, down the platform, past the posters again and the man with the trolley, back up the steep little stairs into the carriage. For a moment she stood staring at the black suitcase on the rack, the suitcase she had bought the day before. Then she snatched it down, jumped out clumsily and trotted back along the platform toward the barrier. She felt the sweat burst through the skin of her face and arms. She thought of nothing. She did not realize she had reached the barrier until she saw the big northerner's moon-face above her, and the red star on his absurd little cap.

"One of the English businessmen left his case in the train. I must take it to him at once."

The moonfaced soldier took the case and tried to open it. It was locked.

"You cannot cross the bridge without an exit permit."

This was it. Meh-li, back in control of herself, called on all her experience as a servant of the People's Republic. She showed her badge from the Ministry of Scientific Research.

"Comrade, you must understand, this is a serious matter. I am speaking to you as a responsible cadre of the Ministry of Scientific Research. When that businessman finds he no longer has his case, he will say that it has been stolen in the People's Republic. He will make a slanderous accusation which will damage the good name of our people. It is possible that he deliberately left the case in order to be able to make this accusation. It is your duty, comrade, as a vigilant member of the proletariat, to frustrate this slander before it can begin."

Meh-li could almost see the slow northern mind engage with the new idea. It was irregular to do what this female comrade wanted, but it was even more irregular and dangerous that there should be a suitcase without an owner. And the talk of theft made things worse; in the new China theft was a greater crime than murder. The big soldier doubted. . . .

Meh-li forced the pace. "There is no time to lose, comrade. The British train will soon be leaving for Hong Kong."

The soldier looked at Meh-li. Large, earnest, untidy, with no makeup, sweat on her forehead, baggy jacket and trousers, the red badge pinned on her front: she was the very image of China. He shoved the suitcase at her and turned to the sentries who stood across the track at the Chinese end of the bridge. "Let her pass," he shouted, and to Meh-li: "You'd better run."

Meh-li ran. Through the sentries, out onto the bridge, under the metal roof. Panic was on her again. As she stumbled over the ties the wet rails seemed to come up toward her. She recovered and ran on. Suddenly there was a strange sound in her ears. A hollow rumble, getting louder and louder—filling the air, making the whole bridge tremble; her brain refused to analyze it. . . .

Animal instinct pushed her to one side as the diesel locomotive passed her. "Sir Alexander Grantham, Made in Australia," she read on its side. She had forgotten that. The British engine had to shunt across the bridge and back again.

Now Meh-li was on the British platform, shouting in English to the khaki shorts and black belt of the colonial policeman: "Suitcase—businessman!" He stood aside, more surprised than assenting, and Meh-li ran on, the ugly black case still in her hand. She saw some steps and scampered up them. Now she was in the British train, charging down the corridor, colliding with an elegant old Chinese lady, bumping a child's head with the suitcase. There was no metal platform between one coach and the next, so she had to jump the gap. . . . At last, in front of her, the sign she was looking for: FREE.

Four final minutes of waiting, locked in the lavatory, the saints again on her lips; waiting for official steps, the wrench at the door, the peremptory shout, the misery of the march back across the bridge. Instead a jerk—then another—and the train was moving. Slowly, then faster, and faster. Out of the window Meh-li saw brown-skinned soldiers in green berets, propping their rifles on sandbags; behind them a white hut and a flag with strange, messy stripes which she remembered from Malaya. She began to cry.

Shortly after Pershing and his party had left the airport a tall Eurasian in a blue mohair suit detached himself from the crowd and walked quickly toward the exit of the terminal building. He was halfway across the lobby when a loud voice hailed him from the bar.

"Well, well, look who's here!"

A brief twitch of irritation crossed the Eurasian's face, which was as smooth as his well-oiled hair. Revealing immaculate teeth in an affable smile, he turned to face the man at the bar and beckoned him into the center of the lobby.

"Over here, Joe, If you can make it."

"Yes, yes, boy, I can make it, if you'll just stand still. . . ."

Joe Allott shambled from the bar, still clutching his drink, and shook the Eurasian's hand, more for support than anything else. "Well, well," he said again, "and what brings Robert Foo to the airport on a Saturday afternoon?"

"Business as usual."

"Don't you boys ever relax?"

"We never close."

"Well, there's nothing doing here. Except I did see Kim Philby going through customs."

Allott's guffaw ended in a racking smoker's cough. The Eurasian put an arm around his shoulders and guided him toward the exit. The glass doors hissed open at their approach and Allott did a mock bow; as they walked through he could be heard saying, "Wonderful tennis party you gave last week, meant to write to your wife . . ."

They discussed the tennis until they reached the center

of the car park, when the Eurasian, without any change in his jovial expression, lowered his voice and said: "One of these days, Allott, you're going to get so damn drunk you'll say something stupid."

"But half the bloody colony knows what you do."

"All right, but you know the rules of the game as well as I do."

"I was hoping you might have another little job for me."

"Our connection is purely social."

"Come off it, Bob."

"If I want anything I'll contact you, at the right time and place—and that is not the airport bar on a Saturday afternoon."

"Well, don't hold out too long, the *Morning Post* hardly keeps me in fag money."

"I'll let you know."

The Eurasian gave Allott a cheery wave and drove away. Allott watched him go, then drained his glass and dropped it into a litter bin.

Robert Foo parked his car in the basement of a building opposite the Law Courts and took the lift to the top floor. A group of men standing in the corridor followed him into his office and gathered around his desk. He took a paper from his in-tray and handed it around. "A message from Morgan," he explained.

"Who's Morgan?"

"You remember Morgan. Fat fellow. One of our best men. He's stuck in London now—runs a thing called the SSG. Keeps a watch on Ministers."

"And he's interested in Pershing?"

"Must be. He's got an SSG tail on him, posing as a bodyguard. Name of Langton. I've just been out to the airport to watch them come in."

"So what does Morgan want us to do?"

"Double-check. Watch everything Pershing does. Every move, every visitor. Langton can't keep track of him all the time without blowing his cover."

"And we report to Morgan on Monday?"

"That's right, then we keep a watch on all the top brass till Wednesday. Let's get to work then."

Could this be the right place?

She had expected a lively Chinese hotel of the kind she remembered in Malaya, a flashing line of electric characters outside, washed clothes hanging from every balcony, people always coming in and out, a cheerful Cantonese chatter everywhere. But the Bowring Hotel, Kowloon, was not like that at all. Steps up to a faded cream portico, a chipped plaque with the name in English only, the glass of the front door opaque and impenetrable and a bow window looking out from the dining room, where English women and their children sat eating boiled eggs at tables set with pink and blue plastic flowers.

For the second time that day Meh-li's courage suddenly left her, and she sat miserably down on the hotel steps. Her parents might have died or disappeared.

She had walked from Kowloon station, asking her way from time to time; people had glanced curiously at her shabby blue jacket and trousers. She had no other clothes and was not at all sure that she could change the few Chinese yuan she had brought with her. There had been a great argument on the train before the ticket inspector had accepted a large Chinese note for her fare. Now it was early evening and the streets were crowded with jostling traffic. The bargaining shopkeepers, the shouting and laughing, the women's dresses, the rickshaw men, the smells, the flashing advertisements were all Chinese, and they stirred in Meh-li sharp memories of childhood. But

4

how could she live in a colorful, unscrupulous place like this after so long in a different world?

Her wits had by a great effort brought her to Hong Kong, but as she sat exhausted on the scrubbed hotel steps she knew she could not survive the next round of dangers alone. She had always relied on her family. Now she had let go of her brother; unless her parents caught her she would fall.

She rose slowly to her feet, still clutching the empty black suitcase, and pushed through the opaque front door. Inside an Englishwoman with straight black hair and a disagreeable expression sat at a desk hemmed in with a wooden barrier. Her face sharpened when she saw Meh-li.

"I'm afraid we have no rooms at all," she said curtly. "We are full up with British service families." The emphasis on the word "British" was just noticeable. Behind her a notice on the wall read: "On weekdays high tea will be served from 5:30 to 6:30 P.M. only. Guests are particularly requested to be punctual."

Meh-li felt even more sure that she had come to the wrong place. She was too tired to say anything except: "My name is Chiang Meh-li. I am the daughter of Chiang Yi."

After a moment of surprise the sharp lines of the woman's face softened into neutrality. Her voice became less genteel.

"Oh, well, that's different. I didn't know they had a daughter in Hong Kong, but then I've only been here a month. You'll find them in their usual room."

She pointed to a door with a brass handle at the end of a short passage.

Meh-li went in. It was getting dark outside and the room was already lit by two big lamps with cheerful red characters of long life on their paper shades. By one her mother was sewing a piece of brocade; she had seemed old at thirty, and looked no older now. By the other lamp sat her father, turning a green celadon bowl forward and backward in his hands. It was a habit she remembered. He did not look at the bowl, his pleasure came from the feel of the glaze on his fingers. He was bent and shrunk, and the dark gray gown which he wore was stained with food.

Meh-li's mother put down her brocade as the door opened and stared for a moment. Then she stood and opened her arms for Meh-li, her lined brown face cracking into a smile.

"It is Meh-li," she said to the old man, and to Meh-li: "He is getting a little blind."

The old man rose painfully, supporting himself on a stick, and peered at his daughter.

"You are welcome, Meh-li. Is Chiang Li-shih also with you?"

When the dishes had been cleared away, Meh-li said for the sixth time that evening:

"But you *must* go. It will not be safe to stay."

So intent had she been on reaching her parents she had almost forgotten that this could only be a respite. If her brother's papers had told the truth, within a few days the power from which she had escaped would reach out and swallow up Hong Kong. The smells, the noise, the slit skirts, the color would vanish into the People's Republic. And so, if they stayed, would she and her parents. She was now a criminal, and there would still be a file in Peking on her father. But luckily they had money; it would be easy to fly at once to Taiwan or back again to Malaysia. This had seemed the least of her problems. It had not occurred to her that they would refuse.

Her mother was obdurate. "We could not sell the hotel in time."

"But when the Communists come there will be no British wives to stay in your hotel, and the Government will take it anyway."

"Maybe the Communists will not come. Maybe my son meant you to read those papers and carry a false report to Hong Kong."

"But Mother—he did not know I was coming!"

"He could have guessed. And anyway, this is a good time of year for us. I have just arranged for the Gloucester Hotel to send on to us the tourists whom they cannot take. There are six Americans coming tonight. They will pay in U.S. dollars. It would be foolish to throw all this away."

In the old days her mother would never have taken the lead in such matters. It was clear to Meh-li that there had been a palace revolution. It was her mother, not her father, who ran the hotel, hired the disagreeable English-woman, organized the plastic flowers and the high tea. But surely the old man had not shed all his authority. Meh-li made her last appeal to him.

"Father, you know what the Communists are. You saw what happened in Shanghai when they came. How many of your friends were shot? You tried to work with them, but after two years you had to go. It will be the same here, they have not changed. Do you not value your old age? I am no longer a stupid girl, Father. I have come to say that you must go."

The old man blinked and his shriveled hands moved aimlessly in his lap. For a moment Meh-li thought he had heard nothing. Then he turned toward her, and in the dim, ancient face his eyes were intelligent.

"I forget many things, Meh-li. In what year were you born?"

"In 1926, Father."

"Then you were a baby, you will not remember. It was the spring of the next year that a friend came knocking in the darkness, as you knocked just now. He said that Chiang Kai-shek had broken with the Communists and was com-

ing to settle accounts in Shanghai. I was a Communist
then, young and full of new thoughts and new talk. This
friend of mine went from house to house that night, warning all the Communists to find boats and go up the river
quickly to our comrades at Hankow. I would not go; I did
not believe him. But most of my friends took his advice.
They found a small junk and went away cheerfully, singing the songs of the Russian Revolution. My friends were
right and I was wrong; it was true that Chiang Kai-shek
had turned against us. But who won the argument? There
is a point twelve hours up from Shanghai where the channel of the Yangtze runs under steep bluffs. It was there
that Chiang Kai-shek's machine guns found my friends. I
stayed in my house with my wife, and you, my new baby,
and became one of the richest men in Shanghai."

"Yes, but Father, in the end you lost it all. You had to
leave Shanghai."

"I left Shanghai and built a new life in Malaya. Then
your young sister was killed, and I came here. Another new
life to be built. Now you come with your stolen papers
and say I must leave again." The old man was getting
angry now, and his wife plucked at his sleeve. He pushed
her away. "Three lives in one lifetime is enough. I cannot make another. And besides, Meh-li, you have forgotten
one important thing."

His wife spoke to calm him. "What is that, Chiang Yi?"

"She forgets that when we left before, first from
Shanghai, then from Malaya, our son was too young, he
could not help us. But now Chiang Li-shih is strong, he is a
great man in Peking. It is certain that he will protect us."

The old man sank back in his chair exhausted. Sweat
stood in tiny drops on his forehead. His wife tried to stop
the argument. "He is tired and must go to bed. We can
talk again in the morning."

But Meh-li was as obstinate as her parents, and infuri-
ated at their blindness. "But you do not know Chiang Li-

shih, he is not your son now, he is a Communist, not just on top like so many, but right through to the heart."

"What nonsense is this?" The old man was querulous. "Of course he is my son!"

Meh-li was driven on by love, weariness and jealousy. "Do you remember the boy with the lock falling over his forehead? Huan Hsing-yu was his name, and he was my brother's friend at the school in the International Settlement. You remember when he saw the section Chief of Police take a bribe, and told the local Kuomintang headquarters? They found him in the river two days later; my brother and their friends dragged him ashore on the Bund with boathooks. His tongue had been cut from his mouth."

The old lady remembered. "After that Chiang Li-shih would not speak to us for a week."

Meh-li swept on. "You remember the girl he danced with in the evenings, the daughter of the schoolmaster, and how the thin American came from one of the big ships? For a time they all three ate and danced and were friends, and then the American disappeared with the girl, and two envelopes came for Chiang Li-shih from the Astor Hotel on the same morning—a poem of farewell from the girl and from the thin American an envelope full of dollars."

"He threw the dollars in the fire," said her mother, still surprised after thirty years.

"So you see why I say he is a Communist to the heart," said Meh-li.

But her father had not listened. He had his own memories, of characters painfully studied by the firelight, of kites flown side by side in a spring wind, of roasted chestnuts shared at street corners. What should clacking women know of a father and his son? He began to move on his stick toward the door, and his wife rustled quickly to help him. They did not look at Meh-li as they passed her chair.

In the passage outside her father muttered something, and Meh-li heard her mother reply:

"You are right. If there is to be trouble he will surely come."

"With respect, I don't care a bloody damn what it says in the contingency plan."

Lieutenant-General Sir Hugh Lamont, Commander British Forces Hong Kong, a lean, angry man whose face seemed to be permanently looking into a high wind, disliked politicians. Pershing watched him pull at his whiskey. He had been drinking heavily all evening, at first from habit, but now, Pershing thought, as the facts of the Chinese ultimatum sank in, to steady his nerves. A bad sign when generals start to swear.

"It may say forty-eight hours in the plan, but I tell you, if their punch comes with the right power in the right place they could be through us in thirty-six or less. The Gurkhas will go on fighting in those hills for as long as they're told to, but even if they fight to the last man, I can't guarantee you forty-eight hours."

The big bay window of the drawing room at Government House gave directly onto Victoria harbor. The mist which had swirled around the house that afternoon had retreated up the Peak, and the four men were looking down on the lights of the ships at anchor, then beyond to the dazzling brightness of Kowloon, then farther again to where the city lights gradually gave way to the darkness of the New Territories. Pershing thought of his old Gurkha comrades stationed in those hills, the sentries and patrols staring northward year after year for some sign of the sudden onrush which so far had never come. He turned to the Governor.

"But is thirty-six hours enough for your evacuation?"

Lord Maltby fiddled with the carnation in his white dinner jacket. One of the last acts of the Wilson Government had been to raise Ronald Maltby to the peerage and send him to Hong Kong. The choice was not entirely bizarre, for as a socialist MP Maltby had been known to speak fervently about sweated labor and housing conditions in the Colony. On arrival he had arranged for a housing estate already under construction to bear his name, and for the rest had been content to rely on the advice of his subordinates and enjoy to the full the honors and comforts of Government House. His first reaction to Pershing's announcement of the ultimatum had been to send for his Commissioner of Police, who now made the fourth of the group in the window, the only one not in a dinner jacket, the only one sitting in an upright chair, the only one without a glass.

"Tell him about the lists, will you, Fane?" said Lord Maltby.

Alec Fane, Commissioner of Police, had been exceptionally handsome ten years before. Now the skin had drawn tight on his skull, and his face was pale as if the blood found no space to enter between skin and bone. Dedication to his job had consumed all surplus tissue.

"List A is those British officials and service personnel who would not be required to stay to the end. List B is British businessmen who we think would want to leave. List C is senior Chinese who have worked with us. List D is well-known Chinese who have worked with the Nationalists to the extent that their lives would be at risk. How many we can evacuate by sea will depend on what ships are in port at the time. But assuming no ships, we reckon that by requisitioning the civil planes based on Hong Kong and calling up troop transports from the UK and Australia we could get out A, B and C within thirty-six hours. Women and children first, of course, and to keep the planes turning around we'd do the whole lift to Formosa; we can worry about final destinations later. The Nationalist Government would have to deal with list D, and we have calculated on giving facilities within reason at Kai Tak for whatever planes they put in."

Pershing made a note on a little pad which clever Jane Richardson had remembered to give him: "Coordinate with Nats as soon ultimatum public." The Governor seemed to be thinking of something else. Down in the harbor the pattern of lights shifted as the Star ferry bustled across from Kowloon to Hong Kong. Those lights spread before them equaled four million people, and God knew how many million pounds; would they still be bright in a week's time? Pershing glanced at his watch. Like all weathered politicians, he knew the value of sleep; he must speed up his questions.

"The Cabinet will want to know about internal security. Could you keep Hong Kong quiet once the Chinese ultimatum was known?"

The Governor simply said "Fane," but Fane was already speaking.

"As soon as the ultimatum becomes known the Communist unions will strike and riot. They will be joined by plenty of non-Communists who will think they've spotted the winner. But provided Peking can control the local Communists we can control them too."

Pershing looked at the man sharply: police officers didn't often deal in paradoxes. Fane explained.

"We've always assumed that Peking will need Hong Kong unscorched—airport, factories, banks, Government House, the lot. So they won't want big riots and big damage, and they'll keep their own people in check as far as they can."

"And if they can't?"

Fane answered each question briefly, but Pershing recognized the controlled tension in his voice. Here was a man who preferred even disaster to routine. He reminded Pershing of Ryder Bennett.

"It can only be a guess, but I think my police can keep on top until the Communists actually cross the frontier. After that they'll stop being policemen, they'll be Chinese, each with his own calculations to make. A few will stick, but it won't be a force anymore. The General is letting us have two companies of Gurkhas for security duty in the last stages: that means mainly looking after the perimeter of the airport and mounting patrols to collect the people down on our lists for evacuation."

"Steady, Fane, it's not as bad as that yet"—the Governor could not get away from the feeling that to raise such unpleasant facts after a fine meal in his fine home was bad manners—"and I'm not at all sure—"

But Pershing brushed his host aside.

"What you're saying, Fane, is that you can hold things here even after the ultimatum becomes known, unless the Chinese actually move in. So if the ultimatum is a bluff, you can handle the colony. Can I tell the Cabinet that?"

Fane turned his chair to look out of the windows. Rifles, bombs, sticks of dynamite, lying concealed by the ton in the city glittering beneath them. Junks without lights nosing ashore in a deserted bay just before dawn, with cargoes full of trouble. Sleek, trusted men in high positions, perhaps his own officers, bribed or terrified from across the border, showing their falseness only at the moment of crisis. These were the facts of Fane's life, and he savored them for a moment before replying.

"Yes," he said quietly, "we could manage."

But the Governor, standing with his back to the window, had had an idea. He made a politician's gesture, and the glowing end of his cigar swept the night sky; it might have been the light of an airliner rising from Kai Tak. "We're all forgetting the political side," he said expansively. "What is our real asset? Not Fane's police, not the

General's Gurkhas. Our real asset," warming to his theme, "is the anti-Communism of the people of Hong Kong. In my view we should hold a referendum at once. A simple question: are you for or against the incorporation of Hong Kong into Communist China? No doubt about the answer. And then the Chinese couldn't move without turning the whole of world opinion against them. It would be a master stroke. After the referendum we could go to the Security Council. That's your report to the Cabinet, Pershing—couldn't be simpler."

Lord Maltby turned happily away to refill his glass. He hadn't had a better idea since he made them christen that housing estate Port Maltby. He fiddled proudly with the carnation in his dinner jacket.

Pershing's fatigue showed for the first time.

"If one thing is clear from Chinese history, Imperial, Nationalist or Communist, it is that they've never cared a damn for world opinion. It would be odd if they started now. And anyway, Fane, what would be the result of such a referendum?"

"A high poll, and ninety per cent for incorporation."

The Governor was outraged. "But Fane, you've always said—"

"I've said, sir, that three quarters at least of the people of this colony are anti-Communist, Of course they are, that's why they're here. But if you ask them to vote on it, that can only be because the Communists are putting on the pressure—and they'll draw only one conclusion from that, whether the ultimatum has been announced or not. They'll run for cover."

The Governor was ready to argue, but Pershing had had enough. There would be a formal meeting in the morning, but he had the truth of it in his head already. He got up.

"Thank you very much, gentlemen. We can discuss all this in more detail after church tomorrow. If you will excuse me, Lord Maltby, I think I'll go to bed." As he shook hands with Fane, he said: "You'll be at the meeting?"

"Of course."

In the hall the ADC was waiting, spruce as ever, with an important question. Pershing chose kippers for breakfast.

Ten minutes later, alone in a stately double bed under the royal arms, Lord Maltby poured himself a final whisky and settled down to write the daily installment of his private notebook. This was to be the foundation for the memoirs to be written when he retired in a year or two. *From Engine Driver to Excellency* or *From Hornsey to Hong Kong*, he was not sure which had greater pith. He was a fluent writer, and within five minutes the notebook was safely back in his personal safe, under the basin where he shaved each morning. His duty done, Lord Maltby slept.

As usual when he was mentally tired, Pershing found it difficult to sleep. He took a pill but it did not work. Images raced through his brain: the lights of the city, Fane's dramatic face, Maltby's cigar against the darkness, Jane Richardson carrying the FO pouch, Moira in bed in the Cleethorpes hotel, Moira raging at him, blotchy face, clever tongue. . . . Jane again, her frank smile and kind eyes, capable hands with the nails cut short, holding the scarf on her head as they walked from the plane. . . . Chiang, tying the orange scarf around his neck. . . .

He switched on the light and got out of bed. Suddenly he knew what he must do. Sitting at the desk by the window, he pulled a wad of the Governor's notepaper from a drawer and started to write, slowly at first, in civil service style, then more quickly, his pen flying across the pages. He was still there when the butler brought the kippers.

*Part Four*

# CAMBODIA
# 1971

Tonight I feel compelled to record an episode in my life of which I have told no one, and the memory of which I have systematically deleted from my mind for the last five years. What makes me want to record it now? Partly the simple urge to unburden myself, partly the suspicion that it may soon be public knowledge (my supposed "bodyguard" here is, I am sure, a security man); but mostly the certainty that Chiang Li-shih's arrival in London is a consequence of it, and will present me with a choice. Perhaps by writing an account of what happened before I shall see more clearly what to do next.

*Confession of Laurence Pershing, written at Government House, Hong Kong, on 11th December, 1976*

It happened in March 1971. At the time I was a member of the Diplomatic Service, seconded from my post at the Paris Embassy to serve on the British delegation to the Southeast Asian Security Conference in Phnom Penh, of which we and the Russians were co-chairmen. The Chinese were there, of course, and among them Chiang Li-shih. Officially he ranked as their No. 3; in practice, as representative of the Party, he was the most powerful man on the delegation. The fact that I had already crossed swords with him in Malaya was rated a feather in the British cap.

The object of the Conference, it will be remembered, was to find a stable formula for the area following the end of the Vietnam War. The solution favored by the British, and which seemed to have Russian support, was international guarantees for the Thai-Laotian border and a guaranteed neutrality for Cambodia, with a revived International Control Commission. The Chinese wanted none of it, but could find no excuse to wreck the talks. The Americans were not opposed to the Conference, but had no confidence in the Anglo-Russian formula. Having decided to cut their losses in Laos and Vietnam, they were determined that Cambodia should not go the same way. They did not believe in neutrality, guaranteed or otherwise, and were deeply suspicious of Sihanouk. In their view the only stable solution was a hard and fast line between Communist and non-Communist states, backed by defense pacts of the Warsaw and NATO type.

For the first ten days all went well, and our proposal seemed to be winning general favor. Then in the middle of the second week the Americans informed us in confidence that they expected an early Communist coup in Laos; they would not oppose this, but intended to match it with a right-wing military takeover in Cambodia. With the map thus redrawn and the uncertainties removed, the Conference could resume and work toward a durable settlement.

To us this seemed a drastic mistake, certain to alienate the Russians, and we were considering ways of dissuading the Americans from it. But the opportunity never arose. On the Monday of the third week the Chinese broadcast the American intentions to the world, and three Cambodian generals fled the country. The Chinese added the charge that the British and Russians were privy to the plan; both Governments denied it, but neither believed the other. The result is well known. The Conference broke up and was never resumed. Sihanouk took Cambodia into the Communist camp, China's domination of Indochina was secured, Britain and Russia withdrew from the scene discredited and America was left, alone once again, supporting an increasingly unpopular regime in Thailand.

Most of this is already in the history books, the rest in

official documents. What is not known is that it was I who told the Chinese about the American plans for Cambodia.

Why did I do it?

It's a question I might often have asked myself if I hadn't been so determined to pretend that it never happened. As it is, I have no ready answer. An act out of character, or a self-assertion in a life out of character? An act of madness perhaps. I don't know.

Certainly it was not the result of any political conviction. True, I disapproved of American policy; along with most orthodox, history-trained British diplomats I thought that China, like the other great powers, deserved her sphere of influence. But I believed then, and still believe, it would have been better if that conference had worked. If I could see myself as responsible for the present situation I should feel crushed by guilt; but I can't, and don't. I look at the map now, and cannot, even in my present mood of honesty, believe that it was my doing. The course of history is not altered by spies.

Whether that is true or not, my motives for that act were not political but personal; they derived from my state of mind at the time.

A prolonged state of dissatisfaction is perhaps the best way to describe it—relieved occasionally, but still with me, and reaching a pitch during those weeks in Cambodia. A lifelong search for a motive for action, or perhaps just identity. Whatever it is I have never found it, and no longer expect to. But five years ago I still hoped for an answer, and the knowledge that time was running out had brought an almost frantic urgency to my search.

One thing at least I had been able to decide: I must leave the Foreign Office. The triviality of diplomatic life, the sheer crushing ennui of the cocktail circuit were simply aggravating my condition beyond endurance. A few weeks before I had announced my intention of going into politics, and now it looked as if I might get a chance to fight the Louth by-election later that year. But in Phnom Penh even this latest enthusiasm withered. I walked the treelined boulevards of the French town (my abiding memory of that city is of rats: a purge was on, and the streets were littered with their bloated corpses) and as usually happens when I find myself alone for any length of time, dissatisfaction turned to despair.

It was Moira who held me up. I'd had to leave her in France with the children, but a letter from her arrived by every bag, so that I was never out of touch for more than three days. Once even this was too long and I put a call through to Paris, but she was inaudible. I just felt that if I could keep my mind fixed on her I would come through to the other side.

That has always been a weakness of mine: never having found a self to rely on, I rely too much on other people. Their approval becomes a reason for action, their pleasure sufficient reward. Take them away, and I'm lost. A bad weakness in a politician maybe, but a fatal one with women, for whom my upbringing left me singularly unprepared. I had hardly any contact with them until I was twenty and reached the age of thirty-two with nothing more than a few platonic affairs to my credit. And then, shortly after I was posted to Paris, I had met Moira. For a time that was enough: I believed I had found my cause. Now, after three years of marriage, something had gone, but something was left, enough to keep me going, and I clung to that.

So far then a state of depression, a low point in my life: not much of an excuse for treason. But two things happened at that conference to push me over the edge.

The first was the presence of Chiang Li-shih, day after day, across from me at the conference table. I recognized him at once. Sitting rigidly in his seat, never speaking, he seemed to watch me for long periods, but never gave the slightest sign that we had met before. Soon the strain of this began to tell in the way I feared, and perhaps he knew, it would: I began to dwell on the death of Ah Ming. After fourteen years that old scar—first anesthetized, then healed, then forgotten—began to tear at the edges and finally split open. I could think of nothing else. What did it matter, I asked myself, if my life lacked a cause, so long as it concerned only me? But in the name of this no cause I had killed this man's sister, a girl of seventeen. I was in no state to be reminded of the fact.

The second event occurred at the end of the second week. The Conference had adjourned on Friday evening and on Saturday morning the British delegation held a long meeting at the Embassy to discuss our reaction to the Americans' revelation. After lunch I retreated to my room at the Rajah Hotel, where I found a large envelope, sealed but unaddressed, lying on my bed. Inside was a set of photographs—about a dozen prints in all, quarto size, and considering the circumstances, remarkably clear. They showed Moira in bed with a man from the Quai d'Orsay.

The next day the Ambassador had arranged to take the whole delegation swimming, but I had asked for a car to take me to Angkor. One of the Third Secretaries had volunteered to come with me, but at the last moment, to my profound relief, he begged off. I left while it was still dark with an agreeably silent Khmer driver.

I remember that dawn well, and the mood which came with it—an odd exhilaration, and a feeling of total irresponsibility. I had sealed myself in that soundless air-conditioned hotel room all Saturday afternoon and finally, exhausted by misery and dizzy with drink, had slept for twelve hours. Now I felt fresh, stripped, light-headed. And in particular, *detached*. As if somewhere in that long sleep I had died, and awakened in a new incarnation. All the clutter of my old life—ambassadors, telegrams, draft resolutions, Chiang and Ah Ming, Moira and her Frenchman—was far behind, irrelevant. Daylight came, and the feeling grew. The car bounced on through wooden villages on stilts and patches of stringy palms, until even these were left behind, and the road in front cut straight across acres of bare rice paddy, flat and deserted under the dead light. The endless alluvial plains of the Mekong—I wanted to drive across them till I vanished in a puff of dust.

We reached Siam Reap toward midday, a tired little town on a canal about a mile from Angkor. The driver parked the car by the French hotel, and I took a walk. I remember an ox pulling a waterwheel as slowly as his feet would carry him, and an old man trying to sell me a tigerskin. Two or three times as I wandered through those dusty streets I had a feeling I was being followed, but when I looked around no one was there. Returning to the hotel I bought myself a picnic lunch and drove on to the ruins.

Angkor Wat came into view at last: a mountain of gray stone rising above the trees, ringed by its wide green moat. A group of small boys were playing at the water's edge, their voices carrying across the stillness. Not another tourist was in sight. For perhaps an hour I walked through the monument, climbed the steep stairs to its lotus towers, strolled along its cool galleries, trailing my hand along the bas-reliefs. Except for an old priest in saffron robes I seemed to be completely alone. Sometimes I thought I heard other footsteps, but they resolved into an echo of my own. Out of the shade the heat was fierce, and walking back along the causeway which crossed the moat, I felt slightly faint.

After that I got the driver to take me down the road to the Bayon, then dismissed him for the afternoon, telling him to pick me up at four. And it was there that it happened.

But first I had this odd premonition. I felt on the edge of something. The cocoon of amnesia which had enveloped me all that day seemed about to crack, and I knew I was not ready for that. I thought I might go mad. Perhaps it was the heat.

Or perhaps it was the place. The Bayon, like Angkor Wat, was built by the ancient Khmers as a temple-monument to their King—a sort of shallow pyramid cut into terraces, and these terraces covered every few yards with square towers, each side of every tower carved into a gigantic face. A forest of faces, then, about eight feet high, and each one identical with the next; faces of the God-King, the Living Buddha, staring at the four points of the compass for eight hundred years. Eyes half closed, thick lips curving in a smile, they watch you from every angle. An easy place to go mad in.

I climbed to the top and sat in the shade below one of the towers. Walking from the car I had been accosted by a beggar—a woman, carrying a baby. She had followed me all around the temple, plucking roughly at my sleeve and moaning through swollen lips. Mother and child had the same disease, dreadful lumps deforming their faces, squeezing their eyes to watery slits. I had given her my lunch and she had shuffled off into the trees without a word.

I wondered if she was a leper. The God-King was said to have died of leprosy, and now the lichens were corroding his monument, creeping like a plague over all those hundreds of faces.

I closed my eyes and stretched out on the terrace, listening to the throb in my head, and beyond it the sounds of the jungle, birds and monkeys in the trees all around. Those sounds, and the hand of the beggar woman plucking at my sleeve, finally broke the spell. I was pulled back to Malaya, to the jungle above Sungei Siput and the clutch of another hand, small and white, life ebbing from the fingers.

The worst moment of all was just after we had got her on the stretcher. The noise she was making had us rattled, even the Gurkhas were frightened. We were in such a hurry we did not do the straps properly; and then we dropped her. At the bottom of the first hill there was a steep patch, slippery from the rain and tangled with roots. Each of us had a hand on the stretcher, trying to bring it down level, and I was in front when I fell. All four of us rolled down the slope, the stretcher cartwheeled over our heads. She ended up face down on top of me, her hands clawing weakly at my shirt, the blood from her mouth slipping warm over my face. And the noise never stopped.

I lay there on the hot stone and let the memory bang through my head.

And at that moment Chiang appeared.

A slight scuffing on the stone made me open my eyes. He was standing over me, one hand on the huge stone nose above my head, his face fixed in that familiar bland smile. Without speaking he backed away a few paces and sat down, wiping his brow with a clean white handkerchief. For some time we sat like that, looking at each other.

I remember some parts of the conversation which followed better than others, but I will reconstruct it as best as I can. His English was slow and stilted, but correct; unlike most Chinese he had no trouble with the consonants.

His first words were: "A great waste."

I asked him what he meant, and he waved a hand at the surrounding masonry.

"The talents of the Khmer people, wasted on a thing like this. They ruled all of Indochina but wasted their strength on stone temples. Their city was built of wood, and was burned to the ground by the Thais. A great people, destroyed by their religion. . . ."

He went on in this vein, delighted with his interpretation of the guidebook, until I said: "I see you're still a good Marxist."

The smile faded abruptly and he turned to face me. "Of course," he said. "And you, Pershing, what are you?"

"Obviously a capitalist bloodsucker."

"And what would you call yourself?"

He was looking at me intently, waiting for an answer. Harpooned by that iron stare I felt a lump of blubber. All sorts of flippant replies flicked through my head, but I knew he would not be satisfied. In the end I said the only thing I could think of: "A democrat, I suppose."

"A good one, as you say I am a good Marxist?"

I took the cue. "I suppose my greatest service to the cause was to kill your sister."

He nodded, and released me from the stare, as if he had the answer he wanted. "So it was you. I often wondered."

"Yes."

"All those bullets were yours?"

"Yes. They gave me a medal for it."

"They were right."

"Right? She was just a girl."

"In our country women are treated the same as men. Ah Ming was a good Communist, and therefore a danger to you."

And now I saw another cue. "Yet you betrayed her," I said.

"I? Betrayed?"

"Yes, you." I struggled to capture the image of Chiang as I had first seen him: the thin tousle-haired figure in khaki uniform, face down in the mud, clutching the orange scarf. "It was your message that brought us to the camp. You had the tapper's scarf."

This seemed to catch him off guard. He looked away,

frowning, mouth slightly open, then turned back and said: "I sent that message because I knew we had lost the fight in Malaya. The British were offering to send back to China those who surrendered, and I decided that we should accept that offer. My sister was foolish. If she had obeyed me she would have lived. When the attack came I shouted to her and the others to lie down, but they were too afraid. When Ah Ming saw the others running she ran too. I tried to hold her but she escaped."

"Why did you leave it so late? You could have told them sooner what was going to happen."

"Some of those men had been in the jungle many years; they did not believe the British offer. I understood the Brtiish better, I knew they were speaking the truth. But I was a young man—if I had tried to explain to them they would have killed me."

"So you were the only survivor. And when you got to Peking, were they pleased with what you had done?" (This rapid rise of Chiang's had puzzled me since I first saw him at the Conference; as far as I knew, every other repatriated Malayan terrorist had sunk without trace.)

"I had many friends in the Party," he replied. "They had written to me in Malaya, asking me to come back; I did not need to prove my loyalty."

A long silence followed, while Chiang just sat and looked at me. A friendly, neutral, appraising look. Then in a quiet voice he pursued his previous train of thought. "It was right for me to go to China. The Communists in Malaya were stupid, they turned their own people against them. It was a bad place for my sister to die."

The trick worked perfectly. We began to compete for the blame. "Right or wrong, she believed in what she was doing," I said.

"She was there because of me," Chiang replied.

"What about me?" I protested. "If you'd asked me what

I was doing in that jungle, I couldn't have told you. At least you and your sister were there by choice."

"The choice was mine, and it was a mistake."

Chiang had dropped his head to look at the ground between his legs. His arms were resting on his knees, hands clasped together, fingers twisting slowly. Suddenly I wanted to reach out and touch him.

"She need not have died, you know," I said. "I think she was trying to surrender when I shot her."

I shall never forget the look on his face when his head came up. The penitence had vanished, and in its place was contempt, triumph, fury, loathing. "You *think*?" he hissed.

I began to jabber nervously. "Well, her hands were in the air, she was running toward us, it was difficult to tell, you remember how it was."

"But you fired just the same—not once, but many times. You did not give her a chance."

"We were trained to shoot automatically, on a reflex, you know that."

Chiang scrambled to his feet and stood over me. I tried to get up but he pushed me back. He was shouting savagely. "So, you are a murderer after all. She was no danger to you. She was just a young girl trying to surrender. She never even learned how to hold a gun! How does that feel then, for a democrat, to be a killer of children?"

I looked up, and the sun scorched my eyes. I thought he was going to hit me, but slowly he leaned forward, blotting out the light, and spat in my face.

That was the moment when I might have resisted. Any small memory could have done it: my father coming to take me out from school—Moira smiling weakly as she was wheeled from the delivery room—even that poor old Ambassador in Phnom Penh, working through the night on dispatches no one would read. . . . But nothing came to my rescue. I was alone in the jungle, enmeshed in blinding vegetation and the lives of this Chinese family I did not begin to understand. The brother's saliva was running down my face, just as the sister's blood had done, and the monkeys were shrieking with laughter.

"I am sorry." They were the only words I could find, ritual words used in the nursery to avert disaster.

But Chiang was not to be appeased.

"Ah, yes, your Christian conscience is at work, and you are sorry. But what use is that? I have seen how it is done. You say a few words, the priest lifts his hand, and it is as if nothing had ever happened. I don't believe that, Pershing, nor do you. You killed a girl, you had no reason and there is nothing, nothing at all, you can do to make it good. Your life is rotten, useless, and nothing can restore it."

I am not a hating man, but I hated Chiang at that moment. I hated him most for the certainties of his life. Everything he said seemed right. I wanted nothing more than to prove him wrong.

"You are wrong," I said, but he twisted the knife again.

"How can I be wrong? I find you again after many years, and what are you doing to make amends? You sit at the conference table day after day, giving stupid men intelligent things to say. Then you drink and laugh and sleep in an expensive hotel, and soon you will go back to Europe and your beautiful wife. That is a pleasant web you are caught in. Why should you break out of it because you killed my sister fourteen years ago? No, there is nothing you can do."

The Frenchman was fat, and there was hair on the back of his shoulders. Ah Ming's limbs were almost weightless; at the end we lifted her, thinking it would help her breathe, and she died like that, her head sinking against my chest.

"Nothing, nothing at all," Chiang repeated, and turned away.

The sun was pitiless, and the Living Buddha leered from every side. I shouted so loud that a parrot clattered out of the masonry above us.

"You are wrong, I can prove you are wrong!"

The parrot flew into the west; the monkeys chattered in alarm, then stopped. Everything seemed to stop.

Chiang turned back. Quietly, professionally, I proved to him that I could make amends. And quietly, professionally, he listened.

Afterward a feeling of great relief, of desire satisfied, swept over me and I felt incredibly tired. As soon as Chiang had gone I lay down and slept.

And when I woke I was myself again. The fever had passed, leaving only a cold horror at what I had done. On the journey back I tried for a time to fit that act into the pattern of my life. What had made me do it, what would the consequences be? But as the sun went down over the ricefields and the car approached Phnom Penh, the mood of that morning was reversed: it was Angkor which began to seem unreal, a dream, nothing to do with my ordinary life at all. Knowing it was the only way to survive, I shut the episode out of my mind.

For a time there was plenty to remind me of it: the diplomatic flurry following the breakup of the Conference and the probing of the security men. When I got back to Paris Gareth Morgan was there, and for three days he hardly left me alone. It was a bad time. Since Malaya he had always been on the fringe of my life, turning up all over the world in obscure intelligence jobs, and he knew me uncomfortably well. Now he was working for MI5, and obviously the Americans were on his back. He didn't seem to know that Chiang Li-shih had been at the Conference, and when I let it drop that seemed to rub salt in the wound. He's a clever, determined man, and watching me still, I am sure, but he could find no evidence against me, and soon the fuss died down. I heard no more from the Chinese, and within a few months I could almost believe it had never happened.

I stayed with Moira. I destroyed the photographs, and never tried to discover who had sent them. I won the by-election and prospered in my new career. That, as expected, did not bring peace of mind; but I had learned my lesson. I stopped asking myself the old questions, and settled for success.

And now the reckoning has come. Chiang is in London and I am in Chiang's power. How will he use that power? He will soon find a way to tell me.

*Part Five*

# HONG KONG

## SUNDAY 12 DECEMBER

Lieutenant-Colonel Robert Duthie, Commanding Officer of the Second Battalion of the Sixth Gurkhas, arrived at the Sha Tau Kok Observation Post before first light. The platoon could hear his Land Rover whining up the steep track a mile away, and by the time he reached the barrack hut, climbing the last hundred yards on foot, they were dressed and standing by their beds. Greeting the Gurkha officer and the Sergeant with a brisk salute, Duthie walked slowly down the line of short, erect figures under the weak electric light. But inspection was a formality; they had heard that previous evening of the General's visit and had sat up half the night polishing everything that could be polished.

"All right, Sergeant. Stand down."

"Hazur."

Followed by the Gurkha officer, Duthie walked on to the Observation Post, a small concrete pillbox dug into the crest of the ridge sixteen hundred feet above the frontier. From here on a clear day you could see fifty miles into China. Here no one slept.

As Duthie entered two of the three men on duty snapped to attention. The third, as was the drill, stayed at the embrasure, watching northward through the infra-red binoculars, scanning slowly from left to right, right to left.

Using a pen-torch, Duthie glanced through the logbook, where every movement on the Chinese side was recorded the moment it was seen. But it was just the usual list of frontier patrols. Nothing to interest the General.

A figure appeared in the doorway, holding an enamel mug.

"Chiyar, sahib?"

"Thank you, Tambasing."

Sipping the sweet tea, Duthie moved to the embrasure. Yesterday's clouds had cleared, and the slowly lightening sky was spattered with stars. It was going to be a fine day. The Gurkhas watched unmoved, their breath condensing in the cold air, as the darkness lifted: it was an old film they had been forced to watch too often. But Duthie, who came here perhaps once a month, never failed to be stirred by the sight.

To the east the flat gray waters of Mirs Bay, sprinkled with sampans hardly seeming to move as they brought home the night's catch; on the shore the jumbled rooftops of Sha Tau Kok, divided village; in the valley below, running from east to west, the frontier—two roads winding parallel with a high wire fence between; and beyond, stretching northward to infinity, the bare, wrinkled hills of China.

When the light was strong enough Duthie asked for binoculars and examined the whole length of the frontier. On the Chinese road a solitary sentry was stamping his feet in the cold. Two armored cars of the 15th/19th Hussars, the sound of their motors lost in the distance, cruised slowly down the British road toward Man Kam To and were recorded in the logbook. The Chinese sentry watched them pass, then disappeared around a bend. Nothing stirred on the barren hillsides.

Duthie reached for his tea, but it was cold. He noticed with surprise that fifteen minutes had passed, and no one had spoken. Dawn was bogey time at the Observation Posts. In that half-lit moment of unverified shapes and sounds you could just believe the impossible—divison after division, massed under cover of dark, sweeping up the hill in an irresistible khaki tide. . . .

Handing back the binoculars, Duthie said in Gurkhali: "You know, lads, I'm beginning to think they'll never come."

The tension split in shrieks of Gurkha glee. Sometimes Duthie thought the best thing about the Gurkhas was the way they laughed at his appalling jokes. Chuckling softly, he walked down to the landing zone.

The General's introduction was drowned by the failing wheeze of the helicopter, but was superfluous in any case. After a punctilious salute, Duthie stood gripping Pershing's hand and smiling delightedly.

"Larry! This is a surprise."

"Bob! I'd no idea . . . Thought you'd be in a bowler hat by now."

"No, soldiering on."

"Guarding the Empire."

"What's left."

The General, who had found Pershing hard going, was piqued by Duthie's familiarity. "You mean to say you two know each other?"

"Yes," Duthie replied, "we were together in Malaya in the fifties."

"I see. Well, I'm sorry I couldn't tell you I was bringing the Minister with me. We want his visit to look as routine as possible, so I thought we'd slip in the New Territories while the press boys are still asleep."

Duthie wondered what was not routine about the visit, but knew better than to ask. He led them up the hill and showed them around the Post. The Gurkha officer remembered Pershing and Pershing pretended to remember the Gurkha officer. He said a few words to the men, who stared blankly ahead while Duthie translated. Faced with their smartness, Pershing felt ill at ease in his thin shoes and rumpled suit; he was the only one to be winded by the climb up the steep path.

Duthie tried to keep the atmosphere jocular and seized every opportunity for reminiscence; but the General continued to refer to Pershing as the Minister, and gradually an immovable embarrassment settled between the two younger men—like school friends returning from the holidays to find that one has been made a prefect.

As they left the barrack hut, the General said to Duthie, "Would you mind waiting here while we have a private word?" and led Pershing away to a vantage point on the ridge.

Watching the tall figure stumble on the rocky ground, steadied by the General's hand, Duthie's resentment evaporated and he suddenly felt unaccountably sorry for the man. Pershing had been a success at everything he had done—had even, to the envy of the regulars, picked up a Military Cross in Malaya—but it did not seem to have brought him joy. There was a slightly sad, dissatisfied air about him. Wife trouble, maybe; or perhaps politics was just like that.

When they were out of earshot the General said to Pershing: "We'll fly over the positions later, but this is as good a place as any to give you the general picture. We have three posts on the frontier itself—Sha Tau Kok, which you see down there—that's where they had the trouble in sixty-six—and over to the west, out of sight from here, the road bridge at Man Kam To and the railway at Lowu. Behind them and commanding the whole frontier, we have a string of these OPs. Of course we should never attempt to hold this line. The job of these forward parties would be to pass back an accurate assessment of the strength and direction of the Chinese attack, and then to hold them while our other units get into position."

"Would they be allowed to retreat?"

"Their instructions are to delay the Chinese as long as possible. They are mobile, with plenty of automatic weapons, and each post has a series of prepared fall-back positions between here and the main lines. They could in theory lay down quite an awkward fire. But of course they can't expect any air cover, and the Chinese artillery will have the range of these positions off by heart. I would not expect many of them to make it."

"I see."

Both men fell silent for a moment, and Pershing glanced back to where Duthie stood chatting to the Gurkhas. The sound of their laughter echoed across the valley. I envy you, he thought. The General thinks I feel sorry for you, but I envy you your lack of choice.

The General put his hand on Pershing's back and pivoted him toward the south.

"Moving away from the frontier, you can see it's flat, open ground for several miles. Rice paddies mostly. We'll blow all the road and rail bridges on that stretch, but there's not much else we can do. Just have to let them come across. Of course, if I could have air cover, we could do them a lot of damage there."

"But Kai Tak will be busy with evacuation."

"Precisely. So unless the Americans help, the only planes we can use are jump-jets. If I could have some Harriers out here before Wednesday, it could give us a few more hours."

Pershing made a note on his pad. "I'll mention it."

"Thank you. Now, you'll see the rice paddies end in a range of lowish hills spreading right across the peninsula. That's where we make our first stand. We have prepared positions there, commanding all the lower ground—mines, wire, tank traps, trenches. Of course, it's all been there for years. I expect General Kung could show you around it better than I could. Still, it's better than nothing."

"How long could you hold it?"

"A few hours maybe, maybe the whole of the first day—depends how determined they are. At that stage I would hope to see the RAF bombers from Darwin; they might be able to knock out some of the Chinese artillery, which would help. But either way I shall lose half my men there."

The General glanced upward to check the weather, as if the bombers were due any moment, then stared morosely back at the brown hills. How much more did this young man want to know?

But Pershing was inexorable. "What then?" he said.

"We withdraw what's left to our final positions. You'll see that behind those first hills there's a much higher one. That's Taimo Shan—three thousand feet. The peninsula narrows there, so the only easy approaches to the colony are along the narrow coastal strips either side of the mountain. We'll hold them there as long as we can, then Bob's your uncle."

"Tell me, General, how many men have you, all told?"

"About ten thousand. When we pulled out of Malaysia and Singapore the strength here was increased. I now have the whole Brigade of Gurkhas, an armored car regiment, the Volunteers, some tanks and artillery. And by the grace of God, two naval ships in port."

"And what would you expect the Chinese to put against you?"

"I try not to think about it. As you know, the total strength of the Chinese army is three million. General Kung Shihchuan, who runs the Canton region, commands two hundred thousand men."

Pershing felt his first twinge of sympathy for this rather unlikable man, but went on: "Last night you said they could be through you in thirty-six hours or less. How much less?"

At this some barrier seemed to burst in the General, and his tone became passionate—part angry, part pleading. Turning to face Pershing, he said: "Look—our whole conversation this morning and last night has assumed that the Chinese plan a frontal overland attack, which would leave the city unharmed and allow enough time for the evacuation of hostile elements. But I want you to understand, Pershing, and I want the Cabinet to understand, just what a risky assumption that is. If they come by sea or drop paratroops on the race course, it could be over before we're out of bed. If they bomb the harbor and Kai Tak, no one can get out, whatever we do. If they give the word to the local Commies, the city will be burned to the ground and the Governor hung from a lamppost. You and I know there is only one way to defend this place. Frankly, I would rather not be responsible for defending it any other way, and I strongly recommend against it. Better to ask for a reasonable period for evacuation, then let the bastards have it. Hurts me to say it, but that's the truth."

"You mean to say you would resign if we decide to fight?"

"Resign? Of course not. But you're not telling me the Government means to make a fight of it? Hell's teeth, man, that lease of the New Territories runs out in twenty years' time in any case, so what's the point?"

"I can't foresee what the Cabinet will decide."

"Well, you tell them from me it's hopeless. Bloody hopeless."

Now Pershing understood the General's fear—it was not the battle, but the risk of chaos and humiliation, the mockery of the world. Lieutenant-General Sir Hugh Lamont paraded in his underpants before a jeering Chinese mob. . . . The memory of Singapore 1942 was not far below the surface.

"Well, thank you, General," he said. "You've made yourself very clear. Is there anything more I should see here?"

"No, we can move on now."

"Good. If you'll go and wake the pilot, I'd like a final word with Colonel Duthie."

Diminished by his outburst, the General meekly accepted the order.


Standing together on the ridge, Duthie and Pershing finally caught a whiff of their old camaraderie.

"I thought Generals wore red hats," Pershing said.

Duthie laughed. "Not when they're under the eyes of the People's Liberation Army, they don't." Then, looking quizzically into Pershing's face: "I shan't ask you what's going on, but to judge from the old man's complexion it's not too good."

"It's pretty serious. I just wanted to tell you that I'll do my best to see that you and the Gurkhas get out of this all right."

Duthie smiled sadly. "Yes, I'm sure you will, Larry. But you know it's the end of the road for us, whichever way you look at it."

"How come?"

"Either we fight for the place and end up as fertilizer for those rice paddies, or we evacuate—in which case the Brigade will be disbanded. There's nowhere else for us to go."

"I hadn't thought of that. I expect you'd almost prefer to have a final scrap."

"Mind reader."

"Well, good luck."

"And to you."

As the helicopter soared high over the Gurkha camp at Fanling and headed toward the first line of defense works, Pershing looked back to see the hills of Kwangtung rimmed with gold by the sun, like enormous waves bearing down on the colony.

That Sunday was a beautiful day, one of the finest the old hands could remember. A deep blue sky with clouds like exploded bombs on the horizon, a light breeze to ruffle waters of the harbor, warm sun for the bathers at Repulse Bay; in the canyons of the Chinese town the deafening *passeggiata* of the poor, dressed in their holiday best, and on the Peak the flats and villas of the rich, shining pink and white against the green of palms and banana trees. At matins in St. John's Cathedral the voices of the hatted ladies rang out shrill and true.

For Pershing such style and confidence merely added to the stress of the occasion: like being in the first-class lounge of the *Titanic*, knowing what was going to happen.

After the service the leading British officials, Pershing in the chair, met behind closed doors at Government House; a calm and orderly conclave, moving quickly down their prepared agenda—evacuation lists, rallying points, destruction of confidential papers, maintenance of essential services, bomb drill, procedure for those taken prisoner. . . . A working lunch, a short summary from Pershing, and it was over. To have met for longer might have excited comment. The officials had dispersed to their families, Fane had gone water-skiing, the General had invited unit commanders (not yet in the picture) for a drink at his house that evening, Pershing and the Governor had taken to their beds. Not a flicker of abnormality crossed the public face of the colony.

But somehow a rumor had started. No one knew where

—some said the original spark came from the Bowring Hotel—but by midafternoon it was spreading fast through central Kowloon. Not many believed it; at least one such scare swept the city every month; but there were some whom it suited well. On instructions from the Hong Kong Anti-Persecution Struggle Committee, meeting on the fourth floor of the Hua Feng department store, a group of unemployed dockers began to roam the streets with cargo hooks, and just as a warmer, beat up a policeman behind the Majestic Theatre.

Pershing woke from an exhausted sleep to find that the sunlight slanting through the shutters had softened to a warm gold. There was no reason to move, so he lay on his back in the cool bedroom listening to the sounds of early evening—the muted rumble of trams, a sprinkler on the lawn, birds in the frangipani tree outside his window. How pleasant it would be, he thought, to lie in this quiet room to the end.

But at 8 A.M. tomorrow the returning Concorde would scoop them up from Kai Tak and whisk them across the world, annihilating time, to arrive in London at precisely 8 A.M. the same morning. London, decisions, Moira and Chiang.

In the next room the drone of a girl's voice and the clacking of a typewriter. The tireless Jane, sifting his notes, dictating a draft report for the Cabinet to the Governor's secretary. . . . What a marvelous girl! Even had a Bible ready, with the place for the second lesson marked, when I got back this morning. . . . A girl in a thousand. Not pretty, but gentle and womanly and dignified. Sometimes I look into that face, with its small hints of disappointment but not a line of bitterness and want to tell it everything. I believe I may be falling in love with her. . . .

"Are you awake?"

"Jane!"

"I knocked, I thought you answered."

"No, but come in." Pershing sat up, heart pounding. She must know. "What time is it?" he said.

"Half past five."

Banalities. Timidity, the curse of the English lover. "Half past five! I was out to the world. Is there anything new?"

"There's a Chinese woman asking for you at the gate."

"A what?"

"A Chinese woman. Normally I wouldn't have bothered you, but it's rather odd—she says she's the sister of Chiang Li-shih."

"His *sister*, did you say?"

"Yes—is anything wrong?"

"No, go on."

"Her name is Meh-li."

"Ah, Meh-li. I remember."

"She says she has an urgent message for you, refuses to speak to anyone else. Shall I send her away?"

"No—I must see her. Send her up to the terrace; I'll be down in five minutes."

Pershing sat on the bed, fingers fumbling at his shirt, face white, then flushed. Jane stood at the door, puzzled, solicitous. "I wonder—" she began.

"Yes, Jane?"

"Are you sure this is wise? I mean, we know nothing about her. It could be dangerous."

"Nonsense. She may have something interesting to tell us. I'm curious."

"Let me wake Langton. He can keep an eye on you, hide behind a hedge or something."

"No! Not Langton. Definitely not. If we're going to get anything out of this, it'll have to be delicately handled— I don't want any blundering coppers around. You leave Langton where he is."

"Right, I'll go and get her then."

Door closes. Jane's footsteps on the tiles of the hall. The feet of time catch up with you in the end.

Pershing dressed, wide-awake now, the instinct for survival sharpening his wits. A moment of truth: after all, the thing he wanted most was to be Foreign Secretary. Cunning and nerve were all he needed.

Circling to keep out of range of the
sprinkler, exchanging pleasantries,
they crossed the lawn to the gazebo
which Lord Maltby, a sun-hater,
had had built in the corner of the
garden. Pershing was walking in a
sort of fixed stoop to catch what
Meh-li was saying. Jane smiled as
she watched them from the terrace.
They were so opposite as to be
comic—the thin, almost absurdly
tall Englishman with his pale gray
suit and yellow hair (she always thought of Pershing's hair
as yellow; he put something on it which smelled nice but
dulled the color) and the short, plump Chinese woman
with her close-fitting black silk dress and gray-black hair
pulled tight into a bun. For some reason Jane had expected a lean and ferocious woman, ready to assault
Pershing with words or fists.

The gazebo was screened from the house by a thick
clump of bamboo and had absorbed none of the afternoon's
warmth. It smelled of damp wood, and as Pershing and
Meh-li entered, two cockroaches scuttled for cover. Clearly
not one of the Governor's cleverest ideas.

Pershing closed the door and pulled up two canvas
chairs.

"Please sit down, Miss Chiang."

"Thank you."

"Not a very welcoming place, but we shall be quite
private here. Now you may tell me why you have come."
There was a pause, and Pershing had to speak again. "You
live in Hong Kong?"

3

"No, I have been living with my brother in Peking. I arrived only yesterday from Canton."

So this was Chiang's messenger. Pershing looked at the puffy features rising from the high black collar: a kind face, he would have said, perhaps the face of a school-teacher—she must have continued to use her English since Malaya. . . . He must be on his guard. She was still apologizing.

"I was afraid that you would not see me."

Pershing smiled warily. "But I still don't know what I'm going to hear, do I?"

"No, I am sorry. I must explain myself." Meh-li rearranged her pneumatic limbs in the uncompromising chair. "Mr. Pershing, you know why my brother is in London?"

"I cannot really discuss—"

"It does not matter. I see that you do. I also know. He is there to make you surrender Hong Kong to his Government."

A brightly colored bird was fluttering in the bamboo. As if trapped.

"He told you that?" Pershing said softly.

"Oh no," said Meh-li, with an air of mild surprise, "he would never tell me anything. I discovered it for myself. You see, I wanted to visit our parents, who live in Hong Kong, and he was opposed to it—he said that in any case the British would never let me in unless I gave them secrets. So I took some secrets from my brother's papers. That is how I know of the ultimatum."

Pershing clung grimly to his caution. "You mean you came here against your brother's will?"

"Yes."

"He doesn't even *know* where you are?"

"No, though he soon will. He will be very angry."

The bird escaped from the bamboo and soared out of sight. Pershing's spirit soared with it, singing with relief. It was an absurd story, but looking at Meh-li, he did not doubt it for a moment. "Miss Chiang," he said, "you amaze me. What made you do it?"

"I should have to tell you the history of my family."

"I should like to hear it."

"Very well, if you wish. Then perhaps you will understand." Meh-li looked gratefully at Pershing. Her father had once said that at heart the English were a gentle race, and perhaps it was true. Certainly she felt at ease with this man. "Our first home was in Shanghai, where my father was a tea merchant. In those days we were very happy. Then the Communists came and my father was forced to leave. He took us to Malaya. We were all happy to go except Chiang Li-shih, my brother; he was a young student then and had already joined the Communists. The Kuomintang had killed his best friend, and he hated them. And he hated the foreign businessmen who came to our house. He kept his Party card hidden in the mattress of his bed."

"But your father forced him to go to Malaya."

"They had a great quarrel and my brother said he would not go. Then a few days later he suddenly gave way. When we came to Malaya we understood why. He began to work secretly for the Communists there, and when the police found this out, he joined the fighters in the jungle. My parents were disgraced and the police asked them many questions. My father was very sad—Chiang Li-shih was the only one he cared about. But my younger sister and I used to help our brother in little ways—carry messages, collect food, things like that. It was a game at first, but then it became too dangerous. We did not see him for so long we began to forget him. Then my young sister Ah Ming wanted to marry a young man who worked for a British bank in Ipoh, and said she would not help Li-shih any more. Li-shih was furious—every day men would bring letters from him, threatening many things. But she laughed and tore them up. Then one day she could not be found, and Li-shih wrote to say that she had joined him in the jungle. My parents were sad and afraid, but also they were pleased that Ah Ming preferred her brother to the Ipoh boy. So I could not tell them the truth."

Pershing sat quite still. Eyes fixed on Meh-li, he said: "And the truth was your brother *forced* your sister to go into the jungle?"

"Yes, she did not care about politics. She liked silk dresses and jade. She had a camphorwood chest full of pretty clothes. Even I knew more about political things than she did."

"After that what happened?"

"Ah Ming sent a message to the Malayan police."

"She did what?"

"Li-shih told me about it later when we were in Peking. One night they were inside a village and Ah Ming left a message with a man who was working for the British. The next day the villagers saw this man talking to the police; they killed him, and sent a courier to warn my brother. Li-shih still did not know who had betrayed him, but when the British soldiers attacked the camp, he saw Ah Ming lie on the ground and tie an orange scarf to her head; he guessed that the scarf was a signal to the British."

"What did he do then?"

"He took it from her. She ran away, and was killed."

Screaming at every bump of the stretcher, clutching his hand as he tried to hold her on. Voice fading to a gargle, eyes rolled back. Choked in her own blood a hundred yards from the landing zone.

"I'm sorry," Pershing said.

"I do not blame the British. The soldiers would not have fired if they had known. No, it was my brother who killed her, and I have never forgiven him for that. He told me that after he had taken the scarf he tried to keep Ah Ming with him, but I do not think he was telling the truth. You see, he knew that if the British believed that he himself had written the message, they would spare him and send him back to China, which was what he always wanted. So he took the scarf and let Ah Ming run away, knowing she would either be shot or lose her way in the jungle."

Pershing said nothing. Meh-li pressed her fingertips to her temples, closed her eyes and went on. "Anyway, that is what happened. Ah Ming died and Li-shih was able to pretend that he had surrendered. In his confession to the police he told them that I too had helped the Communists, so I was sent to China with him. We have lived together in Peking ever since. My parents left Malaya and bought a hotel in Kowloon. They are old now, and my father does not understand very well."

Pershing read her thoughts. "Is there nowhere else you can take them? Formosa, Singapore? It's not too late."

"My parents think there is no need. They refuse to go, they believe that Li-shih will save them. They do not know that for him they do not exist. When the Communists come, others may live, but we shall be destroyed. That is why I came to you today—I knew that you were the only one who mattered. I thought I could help you, and then you would help me. You could make them go."

Tears rose in Meh-li's eyes and flowed down her fat cheeks. Pershing looked away until she had composed herself. Still looking out of the window, he said: "I'll do what I can, I promise you."

Do what I can. The politician's let out.

"Excuse me," said Meh-li, "I cry very often."

Pershing stood up. "Let's walk in the garden a little. It's a beautiful evening."

"Yes. Thank you."

They walked together in silence on the gravel path, the sunset nourishing their thoughts. To Pershing the gathering darkness in the east was a cold reminder of the night to come and the day to follow. To break the spell, he said:

"Miss Chiang, just now you said you could help me. What did you mean by that? I already know of the ultimatum."

"But I found something else in my brother's papers."

"And what was that?"

"There is a spy in London working for the Chinese Government."

Pershing had relaxed too far, and could summon back no defense against the wave of terror which swept over him. "A spy?" he said hoarsely.

"Yes, he has a high position in the British Government, and Li-shih is to make contact with him. The Communists think this man will make it easy for them to take Hong Kong."

In the harbor below the ribbed sail of a junk was passing slowly along the side of a destroyer, like the fin of a prehistoric fish.

Pershing cleared his throat. "Do you know this man's name?"

"No, only that his code name is Polo."

"Polo?"

"Yes, and he has helped them before."

"Any details?"

"Some—not many. I had so little time. Here, I have written it all out in English."

They paused under a flame-of-the-forest tree, their feet crunching on the pods of black seeds.

Meh-li took some folded sheets of rice paper from her purse and passed them to Pershing, who read them through carefully twice. The huge copperplate reminded him of his daughters' Sunday letters from the school at Sunningdale. Hilarious to see Comrade Wang's portentous minute thus translated. The whole situation was hilarious. . . . The last strands of his control snapped. He burst out laughing.

Meh-li looked crestfallen, but there was no surprise in her voice. "I have made some mistake?"

"Oh no, Miss Chiang, no mistake. It's all here, everything. No, I laughed because I'm so pleased you came to me." Pershing folded the thin sheets of paper and put them in his breast pocket. "If you don't mind, I shall keep this. And I'm very grateful to you."

"I hope it will help."

"Indeed it will." Try as he might, Pershing could not remove the idiot smile from his face; but the realization of a fresh danger succeeded where willpower had failed. He looked sharply at Meh-li. "You've destroyed your original copy, I hope?"

"Yes."

"And you've told no one else of this?"

"No. I have told my parents of the ultimatum, but—"

"Just the ultimatum?"

"Yes, I wanted to—"

"I understand. Now, here is what you must do. Whatever happens in the next few days you must tell no one of what you found in your brother's papers. No one, you understand?"

"Yes."

"Say nothing about the ultimatum, and above all, nothing about the spy. Do not even mention that you came to see me today. You wanted to help, and that is how you can do it."

"I understand."

"Now I shall take you back to Miss Richardson. I shall tell her that you live in Hong Kong, and have not seen your brother for many years. When you saw in the papers that he was in London, you hoped that I would have news of him. I asked you a lot of questions about him, and promised to take him your good wishes. If anyone asks you, that is all we discussed. Clear?"

"Yes."

"Good. And I will see that your parents are put on the first list of those to be evacuated. You can tell them that is the order of the British Government. Now let's go up to the house."

Jane was waiting on the terrace with Captain Okeshott. She told Pershing that the draft report was finished; the Captain had volunteered to take her on a tour of the island; she had been cooped up in Government House since they arrived and would love to go.

Pershing agreed, and asked them to take Meh-li home on the way, then went up to his room, where he found Langton searching the walls. Having shown the man briskly from the room, he allowed two minutes to pass, checked that no one was in the corridor and locked the door. Sitting on the bed, he pulled Meh-li's document from his pocket and read it through again, then took it into the bathroom, burned it and washed the ashes down the drain.

After that he lay on the bed and tried to relax, but the effort to suppress his high spirits was too much; suddenly he laughed out loud and pressed the bell for a drink.

Captain Okeshott was a likable young man. Not bright, but never glum, and full of the boyish public-school charm which only survives in army officers. He looked younger than twenty-six. His wrinkle-free face was deeply tanned, darker than the fair hair which fluffed up long above his ears and stayed flat where the band of his cap had been; he wore a beige tropical suit and chukka boots. To Jane a slightly ridiculous figure, but without doubt beautiful to look at. She could see he thought her a bit of a bluestocking, which made it all the nicer of him to take her out.

He explained that he had only been in Hong Kong six weeks, so the tour would be rather "scratch"; Miss Chiang would make a better guide. But Meh-li held up her hands in protest and said she could never find her way in a car. Thus elected leader, he took command with gusto: settled them in his brand-new, bright red Cortina GT, put on racing driver's gloves with holes in the back and drove them down to the city.

Meh-li said she was in no hurry, so he took them first to what he called the Suzy Wong district and they watched the crowded houseboats for a while, listening to the soft slap of the water against their hulls. Then, for Jane, a detour through the tenements of the Chinese quarter, teeming like a disturbed ants' nest, loud with the clatter of wooden sandals and the strangest-sounding human speech she had ever heard; a pause to watch a game of mah-jongg, which Meh-li tried to explain above the noise of a jukebox belting out plaintive song; and then a cruise through the smart section, down streets lined with vertical neon, past shops heaped with silk, jade, gold and the riches of the free world—Minox, Remington, Sheaffer, Rolleiflex, Durex and Omega—to the center, where the Communist and capitalist banks soared to the sky in opposing cliffs of granite and glass.

"Super place, isn't it?" he said.

"Such contrasts," said Jane, unable to think of anything better.

"In 1950 there was none of this," said Meh-li.

Meh-li's remark struck Jane as odd, but she was too absorbed to work out why, and let it drift into her subconscious.

"I think it's the most super place I've ever been," said Captain Okeshott, and took the car through the harbor tunnel, completed the year before, toward Kowloon.

"I should love to *buy* something," said Jane on an impulse, "—a piece of silk for my mother, or something. I suppose it's impossible on a Sunday?"

But the Captain had a solution. "I know this Indian chap, Rai Sing—has a shop in an arcade off Cameron Road. Place is chockers with silk. We could try him."

"Do you mind, Miss Chiang?"

"No, I should like to come. I can help you choose; not all the silk is good."

They managed to park the car in Cornwall Avenue, and a small crowd collected. The papers carried a picture of the Captain almost every day, hovering at the Governor's elbow at some function or other, and he was often recognized. Jane noticed how thin the people were, their bodies curving back from their jutting hipbones, teeth decayed and several eyes white with cataract. One man was carrying a steel hook sharpened at the point.

Shepherding his companions along the pavement, Captain Okeshott led the way to the arcade. Rai Sing was there, a fat, slow man in a pink turban, asleep in front of his shop. Without enthusiasm he let them in and began to bang flat rolls of silk on the counter, giving them a quick twist first to reveal about a yard of material. Meh-li fingered the iridescent silks, explaining to Jane what she ought to like; she became almost chatty. When he saw that he was dealing with an expert, the Indian perked up.

The Captain's job was done. "If you'll excuse me, ladies, I'll go and keep an eye on the auto. Didn't do much of a parking job. See you there in about ten minutes." They nodded and waved him away, and went on with their business.

After ten minutes they settled on seven yards of an all-blue silk, which Rai Sing wrapped in brown paper. They left the arcade and walked back to the car, Jane carrying the amateurish parcel.

Meh-li was the first to react. As they rounded the corner into Cornwall Avenue, she grabbed Jane by the arm and pulled her into a shop doorway, then pointed down the street.

The Cortina seemed to have sunk into the ground. All its tires had been slashed, and little boys, shouting with laughter, were still hacking at the wheels with penknives. About a hundred people stood around the car, hooting and jeering as the Captain tried to maneuver it out of the narrow space. Jane and Meh-li could see his hands spinning the wheel this way and that, his head bobbing as he wrestled with the gear. His sure touch had gone. The car bucked forward, cannoning into the car in front; then back, mounting the pavement.

"What shall we do?" Jane said.

Meh-li said nothing.

At last the Captain had the angle wide enough to pull forward and away. Waving the crowd aside with one hand, he pressed his foot on the accelerator. But the car did not move. The engine raced to screaming pitch, and still it stayed where it was. Six big men had grasped the bumper and lifted the back wheels off the ground; now they were standing in that position, holding the car with ease, and the Captain was helpless.

Then, as if responding to a signal, about a dozen other men, carrying steel hooks, lined up on either side of the car. First they smashed the windows, then began to beat their hooks in unison against the doors. The hollow metal boomed like a drum, fragments of paint flew off like sparks at every impact. As the windscreen disintegrated in front of him the Captain saw Jane and Meh-li; for a second he looked at them, undecided, then turned to the right and pushed open the door. But the rhythm of the hooks never wavered. They pounded on the half-open door and slammed it back in his face. Jane saw the boyish features, till now held rigidly in control, dissolve into fear.

"He's not going to make it!" she screamed. "Look, they won't let him out. We must get the police!"

Together they ran from the doorway, but were almost rammed back into it by a man who sprinted around the corner carrying four beer bottles. Brandishing them over his head, yelling like a demon, he ran to the center of the crowd. A small group gathered around him, heads bent, and began to do something to the bottles. The crowd fell silent; the men stopped swinging their hooks and stood still, except for two who pushed the Captain back as he tried to climb through a window. Jane and Meh-li stood riveted to the spot.

At a shouted command the group in the center split, and flung the four bottles into the car. The Cortina was instantly engulfed in an explosion of roaring red flame. The crowd recoiled, and the men on the back bumper ran for their lives. In the same second a door of the car shot open, and a separate bundle of fire rolled into the road, writhing, kicking, but silent. The little boys watched it, grave-faced. The street filled with the smell of burning plastic and paint. Inside its cocoon of flame the car seemed to blister and melt, turning from red to black; and the shape beside it, now finally still, began to blacken too, curling in the heat.

Meh-li, drawing on some atavistic resource, kept her head. She dragged Jane to Nathan Road and thrust her into a taxi, shouting to the driver in Cantonese to take her to Government House. As the car pulled into the traffic, she saw that Jane was crouched on the back seat, beating the leather with her fists, her mouth opening and shutting in soundless screams. Trembling lightly, but still in control, she waited on the pavement for the police. She found she was holding the parcel of silk. Jane would not want it now.

"Here, try this."

Pershing stood by Jane's bed, a
Nembutal in one hand, a glass of
neat Johnnie Walker in the other,
his heart full of pity. Downstairs
people were still rushing about;
there was nothing they could do,
but to go to bed at the normal time
seemed like an insult to the dead
young officer. For an hour Pershing
had lain awake, listened to the
spasmodic creaking of Jane's bed,
heard her be sick in the lavatory twice. Finally arming
himself with the appropriate cures, he had knocked and
gone into her room.

"Go on, take it, you'll feel better."

She lay on her back in a no-nonsense nightie. Her face
looked bruised and the tear channels showed clearly on
her freckled cheeks. She did not bother to sit up or
make any gesture of respect, and Pershing was pleased.
When she spoke it sounded as if she had a cold.

"The doctor's already given me something. If I take
that as well, I'll never wake."

"Nonsense, I'm an expert on these things. It'll just increase the dose to what you need."

"Oh, all right. What the hell. . . ."

She balanced the pill on her tongue, took a gulp of the
whisky, said "Weuaggh," screwed up her eyes and gasped
as it went down. Pershing found this schoolgirlish sequence
painfully adorable; tousled and without makeup, she
looked younger than usual.

Finally she opened her eyes, blinked and said: "Better.
Much better. Thank you."

"We see so much of each other, Jane, there are times

when you could call me by my Christian name. This is one of them."

"All right, I will. Laurence."

"I detest 'Laurence.' Soft name. I used to be Larry, which isn't quite so bad. My best friends call me that."

"Larry, then."

Jane laughed. She felt slightly mad. "What a daft conversation," Pershing said, and laughed too. Like ships at sea in a fog, he thought, invisible to each other, hooting to give their position.

They laughed again, together, then retreated into silence. Toads belched in the garden. A moth kept diving at the bedside light. After a time Pershing said, as if it was the final word on an unhappy subject: "My wife calls me Laurence."

But Jane was watching the moth, which suddenly stuck on the hot bulb, then fell, body contracting, wings whirring uselessly, to the tabletop. She covered her face with her hands. "Kill it, for heaven's sake!"

Pershing crushed it with a book, then swept it onto the carpet.

"Thank you." Jane let her hands fall back on the sheet and stared dully at the ceiling. "I hate this place. If we weren't going back tomorrow I think I'd disintegrate."

Pershing nodded. "I know. I should never have let you go with him. It must have been unspeakable."

"Just now I was trying to close my eyes and imagine I'd never left home."

Pershing's next remark was almost an outburst. "I expect it will surprise you, but I'd rather go anywhere tomorrow than London."

"The Chinese have put us in a horrible situation; it's hard to know what to do."

"It's more personal than that."

"I thought perhaps it was. Do you want to tell me?"

Pershing did not reply, but sat looking at her veined

hands on the sheet, her bare forearms covered with soft, dark hair like a man's. Ships approaching through the fog . . . He knew that if he raised his eyes he would tell her. "Not now," he said, "it's too late."

Their hands joined: impossible to tell who moved first. "I'm glad you're here," Jane said.

Pershing raised his eyes. Looking at each other without embarrassment, they came easily to the point.

"You know what I would like," Pershing said.

"Yes," said Jane, "I've thought of it myself."

"But it's no good."

"No."

"Someone else?"

"Yes."

"And he's that important?"

"Important, yes. . . . I'm not sure. . . . But if I have an affair with you, he'll be less important. And that scares me."

"Well, I thought as much. I'm sorry."

"Don't be. I'm glad you said it. Really. I feel a lot better. . . ." Her eyes were closing. Exhaustion and drugs were taking their course.

Pershing leaned forward and slowly pressed the side of his face to hers. Her cheek was hot, and the skin slightly rough.

"Good night, dear Jane."

Her head stayed motionless on the pillow, then tilted fractionally in answering pressure. Pershing was not sure that making love to her would have given him more pleasure. He sat up. When he looked down, he saw that she was smiling. One eye was half open, and through the haze of sleep came the tiniest glimmer of devilry.

"Good night, *sir*," she whispered.

Pershing laughed, and put out the light. He sat where he was a moment longer, then walked quietly into the corridor and closed the door. Ships sail on out of sight, unable to alter course.

*Part Six*

# LONDON, PEKING AND THE PACIFIC OCEAN

## MONDAY 13 DECEMBER

# 1

*Extract from the* Globe, *Monday 13th December.*

## HONG KONG IN DANGER?
## MINISTER'S MYSTERY FLIGHT

BY JACK KEMBLE

There was sudden speculation in London last night that a storm had blown up between Britain and Communist China over the future of Hong Kong. The chief pointer to a growing crisis was the arrival in Britain's Far East colony on Saturday of Laurence Pershing, Minister of State at the Foreign Office and a noted expert on Asian affairs. Questioned about his trip at Hong Kong airport, Pershing said it was just routine, and Whitehall last night was sticking to that line. But in fact Pershing cut short his visit to a constituency function at Cleethorpes on Friday night to catch a plane to Hong Kong. This bore all the marks of a sudden change of plan, and at her Chelsea home yesterday Mrs. Pershing said, "I don't know why he's gone or when he'll be back. . . ."

Earlier the same evening there had been another top-level change of plan. Ryder Bennett drove down to Chequers where Ministers were meeting to discuss the estimates for 1977–78. This too was an improvised visit, which some political observers at first connected with rumors that Bennett was soon to move from the Foreign Office to the Treasury.

Then a third piece of evidence came to light. It became known that an hour or so before he left for Chequers the Foreign Secretary had had a talk with Hsu Teh, China's Chargé d'Affaires in London. Neither the Foreign Office nor the Chinese Legation in Portland Place would comment over the weekend on a story that this meeting had been stormy, and that the two men had virtually come to blows.

The question being asked last night was: What did the Chinese diplomat say to Ryder Bennett on Friday afternoon? Was it serious enough to send the Foreign Secretary scurrying down to Chequers, and Laurence Pershing on his hurried mission to Hong Kong, or are all three events unconnected? MPs hope to find an opportunity to probe these stories when the House of Commons meets today.

"Yes, I have read Chiang's telegram from London," said the Prime Minister. "What is your conclusion from it?"

Wang Yao-pang, Head of the West European Department of the Foreign Ministry, shifted his feet on the carpet. This was the trouble when the Prime Minister took personal charge; alone of the Politburo he had the habit of asking for opinions before giving his orders.

"In my opinion the British are a paper tiger," he replied. "Ryder Bennett's intransigent talk to the Chargé d'Affaires was bluster. The British masses will not allow the bourgeoisie to drag them into an imperialist war for Hong Kong."

"How do you know?"

The Prime Minister was sitting in an upright chair by the window, savoring the bright winter sunlight. He was not looking at Wang, but out of the window across the lake to the big white pagoda of the Pei Hai and the confusion of golden rooftops which was the Forbidden City. There were skaters on the lake, and their cheerful shouts and the noise of the inevitable loudspeaker came indistinctly into the Prime Minister's room.

Wang, despite his natural deference, was irritated. His superior was wasting time. Marx had clearly said that discussion which did not lead to action was futile. "It is the only scientific explanation," he replied. "In the present phase of the class struggle in Britain the bourgeoisie still hold the machinery of government, but they are not strong enough to impose a war against the wishes of the

proletariat. However, it is essential that the British proletariat should know the true facts. I therefore support
Comrade Chiang's recommendation that our ultimatum
should be published without delay."

The Prime Minister was still looking out of the window. A small boy in clothes so thickly padded that he was
almost circular came skating on the near side of the lake,
well beyond the staked-out limits of the rink. The loud-
speaker shouted and two burly figures with red armbands
swept down on the boy and hustled him away across the
ice.

The Prime Minister chuckled. "See how efficient is the
Peking Municipal Police."

"The notice boards point out that the ice is danger-
ously thin on this side of the lake," hazarded Wang, who
did not understand the Prime Minister's ironic tone.

"Now it is you who are being unscientific, Comrade
Wang. The ice has the same thickness everywhere. The
danger is that we who work in these offices would come
within range of any reactionary-minded skater who ven-
tured beyond the limits in this direction. But since that
would be difficult to explain on the notice boards it has
been discovered with the authority of the Peking Municipal People's Government that the ice is too thin on this
side of the lake. . . ."

Wang's impatience began to show. "Do you agree about
publishing the ultimatum, Comrade Prime Minister?"

"Ah, you don't see the connection with the skating. You
come here, Comrade Wang, and tell me you have analyzed
the situation as a good scientific Marxist and deduced that
the British will not fight for Hong Kong. That is, you have
read the notice board, and it says the ice is too thin for
the British to skate. But you produce no evidence, you
have not tested the ice yourself. And what happens if the
British, like that small boy, cannot read your notice board?

After all, I believe they have not always been slow to fight, nor have they always lost."

"But that was at a different stage of the ideological struggle; then they had a technological superiority—"

"Quite so, Comrade Wang, quite so. I am not saying you are wrong, I am just saying you have not proved you are right."

The Prime Minister, having amused himself, settled down to serious business. He turned away from the window and his thick black eyebrows drew together. "And if you are wrong, if there are warmongering elements in British public opinion which would want to reject the ultimatum, then we might do better to keep it quiet, and play behind the scenes on the fear of the British Ministers. That, you remember, is how Hitler won at Munich."

Wang began to expostulate, but pulled up short when the door opened and the plump girl with spectacles and black pigtails brought in a single envelope. The Prime Minister showed his annoyance but the girl spoke quickly.

"You asked me to bring the daily report from the Bank of China in Hong Kong as soon as it arrived."

While the old man read the report, Wang studied the photograph on the wall of the Communist leaders at Yenan. He felt a pang of fear to see that two of those men who had joked and chatted on that morning thirty-five years ago were now expunged from history, Communists famous in the China of Wang's youth, of whom Wang's children would neither hear nor read a single word.

The Prime Minister looked up from the report and said suddenly: "What do you know of this Lord Maltby?"

"He is the Governor of Hong Kong."

"That I know." The tone was again ironic. "But how important is he, how well-informed?"

"He was a friend of Wilson, and the Tories kept him on. He is influential."

"Then here is your scientific evidence, Comrade Wang. You were right. Please arrange for the ultimatum to be made known in Britain without delay."

He passed Wang the piece of paper. It was headed in Chinese: "Extract from notebook of His Excellency. Date: 11 December. Source: the usual." The text below, laboriously copied by a hand which was not at ease with English characters, read: "One of the most significant days in my political career. I am in truth the only real democrat in Hong Kong. Fane and the General think only in military and police terms. Pershing is superficially intelligent but too much of a Tory to grasp the essential political fact: that once the British people know about the ultimatum, they will force the Government to surrender the colony. All my experience in the Labour movement makes this clear. What then should be my role in these next few vital days? . . ."

Wang handed back the report and the Prime Minister showed him to the door. "I tell you what I told Chiang," he said as they parted. "The Chairman is particularly anxious that this matter should be handled well. He is following it with close attention."

Wang shivered. "That is good news for us all," he said.

It was nine in the morning, and
the wood above Chequers was still
dripping from the rain of the night
before. The Foreign Secretary
stood in the ride with his gun over
his arm listening to the discreet
sounds of the beaters getting into
position a quarter of a mile in
front of him. By his side was a stick
in the ground with the number 6
marked on the white piece of paper in its cleft. Twenty yards up
the ride was a similar stick, as yet untenanted. Ryder
Bennett had made sure the American Ambassador was
drawn 5, and waited impatiently for him to take his place.

The scene tickled Ryder Bennett's sense of the dramatic. It was he who had persuaded Harvey that after an
interval of some years pheasants should again be reared at
Chequers. It was he who had arranged a diplomatic shoot
for the second Monday of December, and solved the tricky
problem of deciding between sporting and unsporting
Ambassadors. The gossip columns had been delighted, particularly when he had said he would take part in the first
two drives himself before leaving for the Foreign Office.
Ryder Bennett had few chances to shoot nowadays and he
had been looking forward to that hour stolen from a Monday morning. But on Friday the Chinese ultimatum
had thrown out all plans, and the keeper had been told
that after all the Foreign Secretary would not be there.

At the far end of the wood the beaters were still quiet,
but something had frightened a woodcock and sent him
flickering through the misty trees toward the guns. Ryder
Bennett raised his barrel, but the bird's jagged flight took

it to his left, over the Romanian Ambassador, who succeeded with his second shot. Ryder Bennett automatically
marked the thicket where the woodcock fell, and tried not
to think of the frustrations of the weekend.

Harvey and he had spent Sunday at Chequers talking
and waiting. Waiting for the President to make up his
mind, waiting for him to have the courtesy to speak on the
direct line from Washington. The British Ambassador
had got nowhere with Secretary Percy at the State Department; all rested with the President. And the President
was at church, then at lunch with the Korean Prime Minister, then asleep, then on a drive to Mount Vernon, everywhere except where he could be asked if the Seventh Fleet
could be used to save Hong Kong. At midday on Sunday
the party at Chequers had been joined by the Chief of
Defense Staff, but there was nothing new to talk about.
The rain had lashed the windows and meal had followed
stodgy meal. Ryder Bennett had not even dared to go for
a walk in case the President came through. This inertia in
the middle of a crisis drove him into one of his famous
tempers; he stormed at the Private Secretary who fed him
through the day with red boxes. The day petered out,
and even the operators on the White House switchboard
became embarrassed. At 11 P.M., after his second whisky,
Ryder Bennett told the Ambassador to go around to the
White House himself and not to leave until he had an
answer, but at that moment the President came through
on the direct line and spoke to Harvey.

The professional charm had gushed across the Atlantic.
The President had been thinking about his British friends
all day. Whatever happened, there must be no damage
to the Anglo-American alliance, which he had always
looked on as the foundation of American policy. He, of
course, had his difficulties, with Congress, with President-
elect Lindsay, with his own party. But he was sure something could be worked out. He had sent his ideas half an

hour before to Louis Kertzenburg, his Ambassador in London, and told him to discuss them with the British first thing on Monday morning. No, he didn't think it would be right to discuss the matter any further on the telephone. There were too many complications. Louis Kertzenburg was fully in his confidence and would explain everything. . . . Louis Kertzenburg was a true friend of Britain, the British could rely on him. . . . "And whatever happens, Prime Minister, you can rest assured that my thoughts and prayers are with you."

Harvey had been depressed by this conversation, but Ryder Bennett, listening on the extension, had let his natural optimism take charge. It wasn't the President's fault that his manner was phony; it was a good sign that he was going to act through Kertzenburg, the best Ambassador the Americans had sent to Grosvenor Square for decades. Able to act at last, Ryder Bennett had thrown his pent-up energy into rearranging the pattern of the next few days. He telephoned Kertzenburg and asked him to come to the diplomatic shoot as planned; it would be good camouflage for their talk. He got the Secretary of the Cabinet out of bed to tell him that the special Cabinet meeting would have to be postponed till Tuesday morning. He left a message for Pershing with the duty officer at Foulness. He even managed to cheer up Harvey over a final whisky; then, as was his habit, he fell asleep within five minutes of turning out the light. His last thought was of the next morning's pheasants.

Now, waiting in the ride for Kertzenburg, he was still cheerful. He had never believed for a moment that the President, with the President-elect breathing down his neck, would authorize the use of American forces against a Chinese attack. All he hoped for was some threatening maneuvers from the Seventh Fleet and a White House statement ambiguous enough to scare the Chinese off.

Of course, putting back the Cabinet meeting another

twenty-four hours was dangerous. The risk of a leak was growing fast. Kemble's piece in the *Globe*, which he had read with his morning tea, was sailing very close. But it looked as if he was still groping, and the rest of the press had nothing. With luck there would be no leak before Harvey got to his feet in the Commons after question time on Tuesday afternoon. And the delay would give time for a proper talk with Pershing before Cabinet. He would have to rely a lot on Pershing this week.

A portly figure was making its way up the line of guns. It wore rust-colored plus fours and a green Tyrolean hat with a cheerful blue feather. Louis Kertzenburg was so rich he did not mind how he looked. He was not Anglo-Saxon, did not read Jane Austen or dress in Savile Row, but for knowledge of Eurodollars, containerization, critical path analysis and other facts of modern Britain he could beat any British politician. He was also a wise man.

He came up to the Foreign Secretary wiping the mist off his black-rimmed spectacles. Behind him lolloped a Labrador as fat as his master.

"The son-of-a-bitch won't do a damn thing," he said.

"What do you mean?" For a moment Ryder Bennett thought he was talking about the dog.

"You name it, the President won't do it," said the Ambassador, cuffing the Labrador. "No Poseidons, no Phantoms, no Marines. Even the State Department has been told to keep its mouth shut. You'll lose Hong Kong, and the great United States won't raise a bleat."

"Then what the hell did he mean on the telephone to Harvey last night? He said he was sending you some good ideas."

"Sure, sure, he's got ideas. He means to go on the box before the week is out and announce a big security conference in Tokyo, all Asian heads of state, himself in the chair, Hong Kong top of the bill."

"But that'll be too late, for God's sake."

"Of course it'll be too late. His idea is that losing Hong Kong will scare the neutral Asians into some new security setup grinning with teeth. Then he can bow out gracefully next month, and the papers will yak about a blaze of glory."

At the far end of the wood the beaters had begun to advance. In the mist their shouts and the crash of sticks on the undergrowth sounded closer than they were. The Labrador was quivering with excitement.

Ryder Bennett swallowed his anger; it was no good ranting at Kertzenburg. "Can you get this changed?" he said.

"Not a chance. The polls say the people are still sick with the post-Vietnam bug, and strong against any kind of U.S. risk-taking in Asia. The President reckons that the slightest move in support of Britain would bring Lindsay and Congress down on his neck."

"Is that right about Lindsay, do you think?"

"Look, you're forgetting I'm just an Ambassador. Any thinking I do is strictly a leisure activity." Then, dropping the jaunty tone: "My law firm has done a lot of work for Lindsay in New York these last years. I tried to get on to J.L. yesterday. He was fishing upstate, and I could only speak to one of his tame professors, so I left a message. I got this back early this morning." Kertzenburg fished a telegram from one of the innumerable pockets of the rust-colored plus fours, and handed it over.

Ryder Bennett read it in silence. "So that's final, then?" he said.

Somewhere in front of them a beater shouted "Forward!" A cock pheasant flew fast and high across the clearing where Kertzenburg should have been, and settled in the safe half of the wood, clucking with satisfaction.

Kertzenburg loaded his gun from the cartridge belt around his waist. "I'm still trying, but you'd better take it as final."

"Then go and shoot your pheasants while I pick up the bits." Ryder Bennett tried to find a light tone.

"We know each other pretty well," Kertzenburg replied, "so I can chance saying this. You British have got into the habit of finding other people to solve your problems, pay your soldiers, blockade your rebels, sell you planes on the cheap. You're smart at it, but it's a bad habit. Don't you think this might be a chance to break the habit before it sets too hard?"

As the Ambassador ambled off toward the stick with his number in it, Ryder Bennett faced the wood and took his gun off his arm. Kertzenburg's question found no response in his mind. He felt tired and detached. What did it matter, after all? Even without Hong Kong, there would still be pheasants in the woods and a Secretary of State for Foreign Affairs.

In front of him the shouting and noise of sticks increased as the beaters came nearer. A cock pheasant ran across the glade, too experienced to get up. Then two hens in quick succession rose from the bushes in front of him. He took one in front and the other behind as she dodged among the birches. The guns were in action all along the line now, and some pellets from a dubious shot by the Romanian Ambassador spattered among the leaves at Ryder Bennett's feet. The shapes of the beaters began to appear in front as they worked this way and that, forcing the birds out of the undergrowth. Suddenly half a dozen pheasants were in the air within his range, and in the familiar excitement he forgot his troubles completely.

As he turned to mark a fallen bird he noticed Harvey standing nearby. His jacket and trousers had a suburban look about them, and he was staring in distaste at the mud on his highly polished brown shoes. The Prime Minister had never quite got the hang of country life.

The beaters emerged into the clearing, faces scarlet with exertion; a fifteen-year-old boy had already picked two birds from the bushes in front. Ryder Bennett unloaded, and told Harvey the bad news.

The night before it had been Ryder Bennett who had been cheerful and Harvey depressed. Now it was the other way around; the two men were used to supporting each other in this way.

"Well, we shall be on our own, then," Harvey said.

"According to Kertzenburg, yes. But what's the use of being left on our own with only pawns our side of the board?"

Harvey laughed. "That's when you change the game from chess to poker."

The two men turned to walk toward the car which would take them back to Chequers and then to London.

His verbal report to Morgan and
the Brigadier finished, Langton
reached for his tea. Hot, strong,
Indian, with milk, in the blue-
striped cup with his initial on the
side; after two days of supersonic
teabags and Chinese rubbish, it
was nice to be back.

4

"Thank you, Langton," said the
Brigadier. "Who's with Pershing
now?"

"Miller, sir. He took over at the
airport."

"Good. Well, I'd hoped we could give you the morning off, but the Cabinet's been postponed to tomorrow,
which doesn't help. Targets scattered all over the
place. . . ." The Brigadier turned to Morgan. "Can Langton do relief shifts today?"

Morgan glanced at a chart on the wall. "Yes, I've got
him down for that. He can take over the Financial Secretary at one; two directors of Jardine Matheson are giving
him lunch, and we've booked the next-door table." Morgan paused while Langton pulled a pad from his pocket.
"That's one o'clock at the Ecu de France, Jermyn Street.
Report back here afterward."

As Langton left the room the Brigadier said: "Try the
steak au poivre. It's two bob over your limit, but I don't
think you'll regret it."

"Right, sir. Will do." Langton's pencil hovered over
the pad. "That was steak oh . . ."

"Poivre. French for pepper."

The door closed, and the Brigadier turned back to Morgan. "Good man, that. Think he missed anything in Hong Kong?"

"I doubt it."

"So Pershing's clean?"

"So far, yes. Mind you, there isn't much to leak yet; it's after the Cabinet we'll have to watch him."

"You still think he's our man?"

"He was in Cambodia."

"But you've seen the file—there's no suggestion that he was responsible for that. I must say, he seems perfectly sound to me."

"Seems so, yes."

"Then what are you going on?"

"A feeling, just a feeling. I know the man well, our paths have crossed several times since Malaya, and I've never been sure of him. He has a soft core. As you say, his exterior's perfectly sound, but under that he's a mess— about as stable as a yo-yo."

"He caught Chiang in Sungei Siput, he can't be that wet."

"He was lucky."

"I recommended his MC myself; I thought he deserved it."

"And you picked a bar to your DSO. The soldiers got the credit, and who, I ask you, did the work?"

The Brigadier seemed about to answer the question, then thought better of it. Instead he conceded the point with a nod and gave Morgan the look which he reserved for examples of poor form. "All right, Gareth, that was a long time ago. So Pershing's a mess—what's the cause?"

"A combination of factors. He was an only child, for a start. He's a solitary bastard—you can tell most men by their friends, but not this one." Anticipating the Brigadier's protest, Morgan's face folded into a broad smile. "That's the first thing to do, you know, rid the Cabinet of only children. While the rest of us drink and play football, they sit around growing weeds in their heads. Security risks, the lot."

Morgan's paunch heaved in a wheezy chuckle and after a quick double take the Brigadier laughed with him. "I'll see to it," he said. "What else—"

But Morgan was already serious—he had the interrogator's trick of changing moods faster than his victim. "When you get close, you sense there's a sort of vacuum in him. He fills it with romantic notions of himself as this or that —but he can only sustain the act as long as the audience are clapping. Shift the scenery, change the audience, and as likely as not he'll take a different part. Tory patriot becomes savior of the proletariat."

"I find that hard to believe."

"Of course, he'd be no more reliable as the second than he is as the first—still, if they caught him at the right time. . . ."

"What about women?"

"Basically they scare him, the only ones who appeal are mothering types or waifs. His wife's not much good in either department—carries on behind his back, and he probably knows it."

"Is she a risk?"

"Depends how much he tells her. But I doubt it—all her boyfriends come out of the top drawer."

"No peccadilloes on his side?"

"He's ambidextrous, I'm sure of it, but too timid to put it to the test. And we've never found a girl friend. There's a female Private Secretary, but she's a pillar of virtue."

"In other words, no evidence at all. We're back to your hunch." The Brigadier looked unhappily at Morgan: untidy body completely at ease in the undersized Ministry of Works chair, no trace of irresolution in the eyes. In some odd way he felt dwarfed, almost suffocated by the man's presence. "However," he said, "I'd be the last man to discount your instinct. What do you want to do?"

"If you don't mind, I'd like to take on Pershing myself now and stay with him right through. Things are running quite smoothly here."

"Won't he recognize you?"

"I'll keep my distance. If I need another man I'll buzz you."

"All right." The Brigadier picked uneasily at his mustache. "Do you think I should say anything to the PM at this stage? There's a rumor Pershing may be made Foreign Secretary—that'd be awkward."

"They won't swap horses in the middle of this stream. I'd be inclined to keep quiet till there's more to go on."

"You're probably right. One more thing—what about Hong Kong? The Cabinet will need to keep the Governor and Commander British Forces in the picture. We mustn't forget them."

"I've telegraphed the colony's security people."

"Well done. That's it then?"

"Yes."

Morgan shuffled his papers together and slipped them into a folder, then tapped his pipe into the coke fire. The Brigadier swiveled his chair to face the window and stared pensively at the jumbled architecture of Victoria. "Uncanny, isn't it," he said without turning around, "that you and I should be lined up against Chiang again? Makes you believe in destiny. When I saw that face in the papers, you could have knocked me down with a feather. Thought we'd seen the last of that little blighter."

"We stopped him in Malaya, we must stop him again."

"We should have strung him up while we had the chance. If you ask me, we were too damn lenient."

"I bet Pershing wishes he'd put a bullet in him."

"Yes. By the way, what's Pershing's zodiac?"

"Let's see, he was born in March. . . ." Morgan looked in his diary. "Pisces."

"Ah."

The black Foreign Office car drove off, leaving Jane on the pavement outside her flat. As she rummaged in her bag for the front door key she found that she was whistling. This was a bad sign of light-headedness, in particularly poor taste just now. She had seen a man burned to death, the world was seething, there might be a war by Wednesday—these were the things Jane Richardson should be thinking about. But they all seemed utterly remote. This was Tedworth Square, on a raw December morning; same peeling cream porticoes, same skinny trees; garbage men clattering among the dustbins, and a female traffic warden poised in doubt over a Bentley. The apprentice accountants two doors down, late for work as usual, spilled down the steps and, shouting something to her about a dirty weekend, piled into their souped-up Volkswagen. Jane waved happily. She was back.

She turned the key and gave the front door the necessary bang with her suitcase. Everyone else in the building had already collected their letters, and Jane's sat in a little pile on the mottled marble slab over the radiator in the hall. She remembered with a slight prick of shame that she would not recognize Jack Kemble's handwriting. Probably by the age of thirty he had forgotten how to hold a pen. Anyway, it didn't arise; just a bill or two, a cocktail party in St. John's Wood, a sale at Fenwicks. She shoved them into her bag and maneuvered the heavy suitcase upstairs, trying not to feel disappointed. He would have telephoned, of course, but getting no answer, what would he have done?

5

More rummaging for the flat key, and then she was really at home, back with the phonograph, the black hearth-rug, the rugged bookcase which her brother had made for her, the magpie on the wall pecking at a scarlet blossom. The picture reminded her of the man who had given it to her. Five minutes before the same black car had dropped Pershing at Cheyne Row, and he had stood at the door face turned not toward his house but outward to watch her drive away. Was it better to come back from a foreign journey as he had and find warm rooms, the coffee on the stove and someone who no longer loved you—or to return as she did to nothing but a few familiar objects?

Then Jane noticed an unfamiliar object. A bunch of daffodils, rubber band still around their stalks, standing on the coffee table in a red jug which normally lived in the kitchen. Large drops of spilled water marked the dusty surface of the table. As she wondered Jane heard a well-known hum rising to a shrill wail as the kettle boiled in the kitchen. Hope got the better of fear and she hurried to the kitchen door. There, eyes fixed complacently on the kettle, stood Jack Kemble. His jacket had been thrown onto the kitchen chair; three days of wear had not improved the bright blue shirt and its top button was undone under the string tie.

Jane stopped, feeling like a schoolgirl. "Hello," she said. "How did you get in?"

"I seduced the landlady and stole the key from under her pillow."

"No, seriously."

"I turned up two hours ago, lurked outside till she collected her milk. I said I was your brother back from six years in Canada and wanted to give you a surprise."

"So she let you in?"

"She let me in and lent me this." Kemble pointed to the jar of Nescafé by the kettle.

Jane still felt awkward—as if anything she said would

make him go away. "There was Blue Danube in the cup-
board if you'd looked."

"If you're going to live with Kemble, my love, Nescafé will be your upper limit."

"Who said anything . . . ?" she began, but her eyes let
her down, and then her face was held in firm hands, and
she was kissed by the lips which she had once thought too
thick.

"I'm tired," she said, to explain the tears, and then
feared he would take it differently. But he didn't.

"You're tired, Jane, and we'll alter the script."

Kemble marched into the bathroom and turned on the
taps. He found a bottle of pine essence and poured in most
of it; the tiny room filled rapidly with strong green fumes.
Then he shouted to her over the noise of the water. "Get
your clothes off. With this smoke screen you'll be invisible
till I actually scrub your back."

A few minutes later the coffee was balanced on the soap
rack and Jane lay in the jungle-green water counting her
blessings. The most immediate of them stood leaning
against the toothbrush rack, cup in hand, asking about
Hong Kong. She told him about the dockers with cargo
hooks, the ADC, the fool of a Governor, and then, throwing fairness to the winds, about Pershing's pass. She
yearned to tell him about the ultimatum and the fearful,
exciting game in which she had a bit part, but held back.
A woman in the Foreign Office had gone to prison for
showing a singularly boring dispatch to her Balkan lover.
Jane's love was strong, but not yet ready to brave the
official Secrets Act.

Kemble rubbed her back with his hands, then kissed
her down the spine; and still the questions came. At first
she thought it was loving interest, then wondered if he
was just putting off the moment when he would have to
talk about their future. So far he had not even asked her
out to dinner that evening.

The bath grew tepid, but she did not want to get out in case he went away. Drops of condensation glistened on the ceiling.

"But honey, what was it all about? Why did you and that lecherous Tory rush out there in the first place?"

Through the clearing steam she saw him glance quickly at his watch. She lay still in the bath. A slow, complete anger began to invade her.

"When's your deadline?" she asked quietly.

"What?"

"When do you have to file your copy, if that's the right phrase?" Then her anger overcame her. "Get out!" she shouted. "What the hell do you mean coming in here at all? I don't owe you a living, you mean bastard, so go and ask your questions somewhere else!" She began to rise from the water.

Kemble made for the bath. "What the hell's the matter, love?"

He tried to clutch at Jane's dripping body, but a wet forearm lashed out, and for a moment Kemble thought she had broken his nose. He backed away, elbow up, soapy water spreading across his blue shirt. He paused at the door, then went out.

She heard him put on his jacket in the kitchen. A final spasm of anger made her shout: "Don't forget to put the coffee on your expenses!"

She heard the door of the flat slam. There was no towel in the bathroom and she had to cross the cold corridor to the bedroom to find one. On the way she stumbled against her suitcase. She had never hit a man before, never thought it possible that she would swear at one like that. She forgot about the towel and lay on her bed, tears and bath water soaking through the coverlet. What in the world had become of Jane Richardson?

Pershing too had felt the need to start the day with a bath. But washing seemed too great an effort, so he lay still in the hot water and listened to the sounds of home. The girls on the top floor, crying in rotation (all three had whooping cough, bad enough to keep them out of school but not to keep them in bed); the voice of the Swedish au pair, pleading for peace; at intervals a savage bark

# 6

from Moira, followed by a short-lived hush; feet pounding on the stairs; the "Jimmy Young Show" on the kitchen radio; the plumber, hammering a frozen pipe on the wall outside.

He lowered his head until his ears were underwater. The extra displacement raised the water level slightly so that a plastic whale floated off the soap rack and bobbed down to his nose. Poor whale, Pershing thought, pushed about by the currents, no control over your life at all, eyes permanently popping, a fixed smile for the crowd . . . inside you, nothing. Join the party.

Morgan parked his car in Oakley Street and took a microphone from the glove compartment.

Miller, huddled for shelter in the door of the Catholic church in Cheyne Row, heard a buzz under his coat and pulled a gadget from his pocket.

"Anything doing?" Morgan said into the microphone.

"No, sir, pretty quiet. There's a plumber in there, and an FO messenger's just pulled up."

Miller watched as a black van with a crown on the side

parked opposite the house and a tired-looking man in blue uniform carried an envelope up to the front door.

"All right," Morgan said, "I'll be with you in a moment."

Pershing lifted his ears above the surface as a noise, louder than the others, penetrated the water.

"Laur-e-nce!" Moira's voice would split concrete.

"Yes, what is it?"

"There's a message from the Office; you've got to come and sign for it."

"All right." Lifting himself with a sigh, Pershing put on a bathrobe and went down to the front door. A man in the familiar blue uniform was waiting with a stiff white envelope inscribed "Personal for Minister of State—By Hand."

"Do you need a reply?" Pershing said.

"No, sir, If you'd just sign here . . ."

Pershing signed to acknowledge receipt, closed the door and opened the envelope. Inside was a smaller envelope, of flimsy paper, with the words "Please read in private" written across the front. He examined it with a puzzled frown, then smiled: odd procedure, but typical of Ryder Bennett—the man could never resist a touch of drama. In no mood to question instructions, he returned to the bathroom and locked hmiself in. Sitting on the bidet he opened the second envelope and read the letter inside.

DEAR PERSHING,

You will not, I am sure, be surprised at my contacting you. Indeed, you may have wondered why my Government allowed so many years to pass without using your services again. The answer is simple. We have never deceived ourselves that the considerations which swayed you in Cambodia were of a permanent character. We knew that if we needed your help again we would be obliged to threaten you, and therefore preferred to wait until an issue of sufficient importance arose.

That time has now come. We require your cooperation, and unless we receive it, we shall allow certain evidence of your previous indiscretion to fall into the hands of the British Security Service, which will end your career and send you to prison.

Your first instruction is as follows: you will go this evening, at any time after 8 P.M. to room 501 in the Rundall Hotel, where you will receive further orders. To signal your consent, kindly draw the curtains on the top floor of your house within five minutes, then destroy this letter.

Do not imagine that you can alert Security Service without my knowledge.

> Yours sincerely,
> CHIANG LI-SHIH

Pershing sat staring at the letter for a full two minutes, waiting passively for some reaction in himself. But he felt nothing, no shock of surprise or fear to stir his thought processes. He had prepared for this moment by not anticipating it, believing a decision would materialize automatically; but now that it had come, his mind refused to move, aware of a choice but incapable of making it. After four minutes he left the bathroom and started to mount the stairs, but still could find no reason for doing so. On the top step he paused to give his brain a last chance, and it responded with a tactical point: the choice could be deferred, nothing would be lost by going to the hotel to find out what was required of him.

"Daddy, why are you drawing the curtains?"

"It's a game."

"Oooh, ghosts! Can we play it?"

"Yes, if you like."

With banshee howls the girls attacked the nursery curtains, then ran down from floor to floor, drawing all the curtains in the house. Pershing stood in the darkened nursery, and through a gap in the curtain saw a black van pull away down the street. "Ready!" squealed the girls from below, and he moved obediently toward the door.

Suddenly he had a vivid memory of last year's Christmas Eve—Moira standing by the door while he crept about the room with rustling Rugby socks, then fell with a crash over the rocking horse, Father Christmas revealed, tears, candies, everyone laughing, stockings opened at midnight. . . .

And this year how would it be? "Sorry, darlings, Daddy's gone away for a while. . . ." Father Christmas in jail.

That was why the curtains had to be drawn.

By the time Morgan arrived at the church the van had gone. Miller made a negative report and walked up to the King's Road. Since taking over from Langton at the airport he had stuck to Pershing like a leech, and was sure he had missed nothing. But in the last minutes of his watch there were two small things he might have noticed.

Government vehicles do not carry Glasgow registration letters, and at the last count the FO messenger corps did not include Mr. Frank Barker, ex-official of the Amalgamated Engineering Union and now Secretary of SACU, the Society for Anglo-Chinese Understanding.

Kemble thrust a note and a fistful of change at the taxidriver, then stood swaying in the center of Portland Place, flakes of sausage-roll still on his trousers. He had spent the morning in a Fleet Street pub, trying unsuccessfully to push behind him the disaster at Jane's flat. Story lost, girl lost and pride lost; it was a sign of middle age that the last hurt most. The message that he was wanted urgently at the Chinese Legation had barely lifted the pall of alcoholic self-pity. Another sign of middle age.

# 7

He turned up his collar against the wind and crossed the street toward the Legation building. A frayed red flag flapped above the roof and every window was shuttered. Sure that behind at least one of the shutters a pair of eyes was watching, Kemble tried to steady his steps. As he reached the pavement a policeman barred his path.

"Excuse me, sir."

"What's this—a breath test for pedestrians?"

"Routine matter, sir." The policeman nodded at the building behind him. "We like to keep a check on everyone going in and out of there. Would you mind giving me your name? You're not obliged to do so."

"It's a pleasure." Kemble held out his card. "Send a posse if I'm not back before sundown."

The policeman smiled tolerantly. "I'm afraid we couldn't do that, sir." He held a walkie-talkie to his mouth. "Embassy One to Embassy Two. Mr. Jack Kemble of the *Globe* moving in. Will clear when he comes out. Over."

Kemble walked up the short flight of steps and pressed his thumb on the bell at the second attempt. The door was opened immediately by a young Chinese in baggy blue uniform.

"What do you want?"

Kemble showed his card again. The Chinese looked at it as if the very act would contaminate him. "Come in, please."

"Thank you, Confucius."

Kemble lurched in. A bare, shabby hall; dark brown paneled walls hung with framed Chinese writings; above the stairs a portrait of Big Brother himself, seven foot square.

"This way, please."

The Chinese ushered Kemble into an almost unfurnished waiting room. It must have been the dining room of the original house and the garlands of white plaster trailing across the ceiling made a pathetic contrast with the colored portrait of the Chairman and the propaganda sheets on the central table. Above the marble fireplace hung a massive photograph of Young Pioneers planting trees on a bare mountainside. Kemble shivered. Suddenly he regretted the morning's drinking; he felt vulnerable, and slightly sick.

For five minutes he stood by the table thumbing idly through the pamphlets. The house was silent as a morgue. Then he heard a door open, and steps in the hall; a booming, vaguely familiar English voice, cut off as the front door closed; a muttered conversation in Chinese, followed by the same total silence.

Kemble sat on a chair and held his head in his hands. That voice—gravelly, aggressive—it was definitely familiar. He groped through his mental fog for the memory, but it didn't come.

A slight noise made him turn nervously.

The Legation Counselor, in the same light gray uniform he had worn at the Albanian party, stood by the door. Without speaking he advanced into the room and handed Kemble a sheet of paper. Kemble focused with difficulty, then more easily as professional excitement pulled his faculties together. Slowly he read the Chinese ultimatum.

It was always a golden moment when the event exceeded the guesswork—particularly for political commentators, forced to alleviate the dullness of parliamentary business with riotous speculation. But this beat anything in Kemble's career. Whatever happened, he knew already that his column that morning would go down as a historic piece of prescience. His gloom evaporated; Miss Richardson could go and stuff herself. . . . But it would not do to let the Counselor in on his pleasure. "What am I meant to do with this?" he asked.

"I understood that you were a journalist, Mr. Kemble." The Counselor's small upturned nose twitched with amusement, but his mouth did not smile.

Kemble remembered the familiar voice in the hall. "Have you given it to anyone else?"

"To no other journalist."

"Well, who then? Come on, I need to know."

But the Counselor was already out of the room.

One minute later Kemble stood on the Legation steps, stone sober, calculating his next move. Could he be sure it was a scoop? If the Counselor had told the truth, he was safe from the evenings. But who was the man with the loud voice? Robin Day? Peter Snow? John Morgan? Must be one of those telly boys. . . . On a sudden inspiration he ran toward the policeman on the pavement.

"Officer—"

"It's all right, sir, they can't touch you now."

"Yes, I know, thank you." Bloody fuzz. "Tell me, who

came out of there just before me? English, with a loud voice."

"Now, sir, you know very well—"

"Look, I'm not pulling a fast one, it won't bounce back."

"I'm sorry, sir, we have to go by the book. No names."

"A clue then."

Something in Kemble's face made the policeman weaken. Looking first to right and left, he leaned forward and whispered: "MP, Conservative, I think. Fat fellow, red face . . ."

"Enough! Bless you."

Kemble ran all the way to Oxford Circus before he found a taxi. For half a minute he flopped exhausted on the back seat, unable to speak, then pulled down the inner window and said weakly—"Carlton Club, please, as quick as you can."

Though he now sat in Parliament as an Independent, Barnett Coper was still sufficiently recognizable as a Tory to keep his membership at the Carlton Club. When the porter brought him Kemble's card he was preparing for his lunch with a gin and tonic. His mind was already drifting toward a vision of smoked salmon and beef Stroganoff; he liked his food strong and spicy. But he had never in his life refused to see a journalist.

As Jack Kemble approached the deep armchair Coper pocketed the sheet of club notepaper on which he had been scribbling and the paper which the Chinese had given him at the Embassy. He made no effort to haul his bulk out of the chair. For such a flabby man his handshake was surprisingly firm.

"Well, young man, what's this urgent business? It'll have to be good to keep me from my lunch."

Purple neo-Fascist slob, thought Kemble, any more of that patronizing talk and I'll kick you in the crutch. But he told his story with the right mixture of modesty and pleading.

Coper always enjoyed turning down a request. He even summoned the waiter to give Kemble a drink.

"I'm a slow chap from the provinces," he said, chewing the lemon slice from his gin and tonic. "Let me make sure I've got it straight. You're offering me a thousand quid to write an article on Hong Kong in the *Globe* tomorrow?"

"That's right, provided you don't use in the House today the information you and I both got from the Chinese this morning."

"What d'you think my marginal rate of tax is, young man?"

Kemble had authority from his editor on the phone to go up to twelve hundred pounds, but saw this would not be enough. "You can have it in cash," he said.

Coper had an upward-slanting smile, like a shark, "None of your London tricks. I go to chapel and declare my income like a Christian. What d'you think I'm in politics for, anyway?"

Kemble didn't like to say.

"Not the money, boy, I can tell you. I could make five times as much sitting on my arse in Wolverhampton. Not the power either. No one's going to put someone like me in the Cabinet. No, it's the thrill of the game—and of course," he added, shark-like again, "I want to serve my country. And those are two good reasons for raising merry hell in the House this afternoon."

Coper heaved himself to his feet and began to lumber toward the dining room door. Kemble had failed, and his exasperation showed.

"I'd just like to ask why the hell the Chinese gave you this information? You're further to the right than anyone else in the House."

"Precisely." Coper did not slow down. "I'm an Independent now, so no bloody whip holds a padlock to my tongue. And the Chinese like to keep me sweet—my firm sells precision gauges to their car factory in Tientsin. But the third reason is the best: they know I hate Harvey's guts."

Freed at last by Ryder Bennett, Pershing slipped out of the Foreign Office and walked to Prunier's, where Moira had been promised a make-it-up lunch. The restaurant was an old haunt, relied on to mend quarrels, but today the magic was missing. Moira went through a dozen oysters and a cold lobster, but Pershing could see she meant to finish with a pound of flesh.

His own mind was not on the job either. The discussion of his Hong Kong report at the Office had occupied his mind completely; he had been concise, logical, constructive, and knew that Ryder Bennett had been impressed. But now the horror of his situation kept coming back to him, destroying his appetite, obliterating Moira's words. It's the usual story, he thought; as long as I'm on-stage I can turn in a brilliant performance, it's when the lights go off I'm done for. Moira was waving her fork at him.

"Laurence! You're not listening to me."

"Yes I am."

"What did I just say?"

"You had a good weekend."

"I said, friend, did *you* have a good weekend?"

"Pretty exhausting—the usual official round."

"Well, mine was perfectly ghastly. Slow fox-trots with that sweaty brute Bamberg till three on Saturday morning, then back on a cold train to a houseful of screaming kids. Really, Inga is useless; she'll have to go."

"Yes, I'm sorry, it must have been grim."

"Why did you have to go to Hong Kong anyway? I

read Jack Kemble in the *Globe* this morning, and he's right—something funny is going on."

She was on a collision course, and knew it. Pershing considered evasive action, but decided he couldn't be bothered; the way to make her really mad was to be inaccessible. "I can't tell you," he said.

"I bet the Chinese want it back. That's it, isn't it?"

"Don't talk rubbish."

"Quite right, too. It was theirs in the first place. You don't stand a chance against them, do you? Not a chance."

"Let's talk about something else."

"You used to tell me everything."

"Well, I can't discuss this."

"But you can with that Richardson girl, I suppose? Because she's British, and looks like an athletic nun, and went to Oxford. Oh, very cozy. I can just imagine, serious faces all round and footy-footy under the table. . . ."

"You're being childishly jealous."

"Jealous? That's good! You wouldn't have the guts to sleep with the girl if you wanted to."

"She happens to be my Private Secretary."

"And I happen to be your wife, friend. I have a mind too—or have you forgotten?"

Your mind, Pershing thought, it always comes back to that maltreated, overlooked, strangely reticent object. "I think we'd better go," he said.

"Yes, I'm going, you stay if you like."

"We're both going. Strangely enough I have one or two things to do."

"Just be back by eight. The Drummonds are coming to dinner."

Pershing looked up from counting fivers into a saucer, and the color left his cheeks. "I can't," he said.

"What do you mean, you can't? We agreed last week to ask them tonight."

"Something's cropped up; I'll be late."

"You and your stupid politics. You think you're so important, don't you?"

"The Drummonds won't mind."

"You bet they won't. I'll get Willy Mumford-Pyke instead, he'll take us to Annabel's. We'll have a lovely time. No boring bloody politicians looking at their watches under the table and wondering when they're going to get to bed—lovely!"

Pershing let it go at that. Oddly enough he felt better. Walking back across the park he wondered why he had never accused her of being unfaithful. He knew about it, she knew he knew; but the subject was never mentioned. Why, for that matter, didn't she confront him with it? How often she must have longed to! The answer, he thought, is the same for both of us. It's more important to stay married than face the truth, because staying married is a precondition of success. The woman can't bear to give me credit for anything, she sleeps around, but she knows that without me she'd never do as well; and I know divorce loses votes. United we climb, divided we are stuck halfway. Success, that's it—important to me for lack of anything better, but for Moira the Holy Grail.

Out of curiosity, he tried to remember the wide-eyed sylph from Sweden he had found paying double for an ice-cream soda in the Champs Elysées. But it was too long ago. All he could see now was this expensive, dirty-minded London hostess, age honing her ambition to a razor-edge.

As if by thought-association, Chiang's words came back. "Unless you cooperate . . . we shall allow certain evidence of previous indiscretion to fall into the hands of the Security Service, ending your career and sending you to prison. . . ."

That would ditch her.

Prime Minister's Questions had gone well and at 3:30, as the House began to empty, Harvey slipped out behind the Speaker's chair. He had called a meeting in his room in the Commons to decide how Hong Kong should be put to the Cabinet next morning. Ryder Bennett hated being messed about by colleagues and wanted to ask for a free hand for Harvey and himself to manage the crisis. But Harvey knew that was out of the question; the colleagues would be in a high state of nerves.

Joynson, his Press Secretary, stood in the anteroom of his office among a cluster of pretty typists, flicking through the second edition of the evening papers. He looked up as Harvey came in. "So far so good," he said.

"What about the *Globe*?" asked Harvey.

"Kemble was drinking hard all morning. He didn't look like a man with a scoop."

"Never mind, have him in, give him patriotism, the official Secrets Act or plain denials, I don't care which. Tell him his piece this morning was dangerous rubbish. He can print what he likes on Wednesday, but tomorrow I want the press quiet till they get the news from me in the afternoon."

"OK, OK, but I bet Kemble's lost the trail already."

Joynson scuffled with one of the pretty secretaries for a telephone. As Harvey headed for the door to his own office the gray figure of the Chief Whip handed him a folded sheet of paper.

"Damn," said Harvey, reading it. He never used a stronger word. "Any chance of getting him off it?"

"None at all," said the Chief Whip. "Coper is carnivorous and today he smells blood."

Wearily Harvey walked down the long, book-lined corridor and back into the Chamber.

*Extract from* Hansard, *Monday, 13th December, 1976*

> **The Leader of the Opposition (Mr. J. Wellbeloved):** May I ask the Leader of the House to state the business of the House for the next week?
>
> **Mr. Barnett Coper** (Wolverhampton East): On a point of

order, Mr. Speaker, I see the Prime Minister has returned
to his place. May I ask him if he will make a statement
about the Chinese ultimatum demanding an immediate
British withdrawal from Hong Kong?

**Several hon. Members:** Order, order.

**Mr. Speaker:** The hon. Member for Wolverhampton East
(Mr. Coper) knows that the time for Ministerial statements today is past and that the House has moved on to
discuss its business for next week. Neither the hon.
Member nor I can compel Ministers to make statements
if they prefer to remain silent. Nevertheless, should the
Prime Minister now wish to make a statement on the
important matter raised by the hon. Member, the House
would, I believe, be disposed to give him a hearing.

**The Prime Minister (Mr. Patrick Harvey):** I would only say,
Mr. Speaker, that I am satisfied that it would be unwise
and very damaging to the national interest if I were to
comment in any way on the question put by the hon.
Member for Wolverhampton East (Mr. Coper).

**Lt.-Col. Thistletone-Thwaite** (Shropshire South-West): On
a further point of order, Mr. Speaker, is it in order for
an hon. Member to make nonsensical allegations of this
kind (Interruption) based on rumors in the gutter press,
simply in order to gain cheap personal publicity?

**Several hon. Members:** Withdraw.

**Mr. Speaker:** Order, order. I would not have shown the
hon. Member for Wolverhampton East (Mr. Coper) the
indulgence which I have if I had believed that he was
simply embroidering on a story in a newspaper.

**Mr. Edward Hobart** (Bolton): Would the Prime Minister
give an undertaking that if he receives such a request
from the Chinese Government he will immediately enter
into friendly talks with them so that this shabby chapter
in the history of British imperialism can be brought to
an early end?

**Hon. Members:** Answer.

**The Leader of the Opposition (Mr. J. Wellbeloved):** Surely
the Prime Minister does not propose to leave the matter
there? He must realize that the hon. Member for Wolver-

hampton East (Mr. Coper) has made a most serious
statement, going far beyond the speculation which appeared in the *Globe* newspaper this morning. The House
and the country are entitled to know at once whether
this statement is true, and if it is, what the Government
mean to do about it.

**The Prime Minister (Mr. Patrick Harvey):** I really must
ask right hon. and hon. Members not to press me on this.
It is true that we have received a communication from
the Chinese Government. (An hon. Member: What did it
say?) I am not at liberty to disclose its contents.

**Mr. Coper** (Wolverhampton East): I know what it said. I
have got it here. (Interruption.)

**Mr. Speaker:** Order.

**The Prime Minister (Mr. Patrick Harvey):** I am perfectly
ready to discuss the matter with the right hon. Gentleman
the Leader of the Opposition through the usual channels.
I hope to be in a position to make a further statement
to the House tomorrow. Today we are just not ready to
go into this in any detail. (Interruption.)

**Mr. Coper** (Wolverhampton East): How can the right hon.
Gentleman say that, when he has had the Chinese Note
in his pocket since Friday afternoon? Is this not proof of
even more than the usual incompetence?

**Mr. Speaker:** Order, order. We must go back to discuss the
arrangements for the Christmas recess. Mr. Jeremy.

**The Lord President of the Council and Leader of the
House (Mr. Jeremy):** It is proposed that the House
should rise . . .

The clock bolted to the bulkhead
of the control room had two sets of
hands: one showed that it was
Monday 4 P.M. in London, the
other that it was midnight in the
Pacific. Below the clock two huge
consoles of dials and screens,
banked in a semicircle around the
periscopes, twitched and flickered
under the eyes of alert, immobile
young men. For ten minutes now,
or perhaps twenty—it was hard to

**9**

keep a sense of time on these long runs—the only sound in
the room had been the whirr of the air-conditioning. The
engines were going flat out but they could not be heard
from here.

Commander Harry O'Brien surveyed the scene with
satisfaction. The course chart showed they were past the
reefs of Bikini and on schedule. Twelve of the missiles
were armed and ready to fire. Everything was as it should
be. It was time to catch up on his sleep. But before he
could move a message from the wireless room was thrust
into his hands.

Wearily he skimmed through the transcript of the news
bulletin. One of the disappointments of being appointed
to command His Majesty's Polaris Submarine *Revenge*
had been the discovery that however far from home they
sailed—under the polar ice cap or, as now, through the islands of the North Pacific—the flow of paper never
stopped. But suddenly his eye was caught by an item halfway down the page, and he began to read more closely.
Someone had had the sense to record in full the BBC's ac-

count of Question Time in the House of Commons and Mr. Barnett Coper's subsequent statement to the press.

O'Brien's lips pursed in a silent whistle. "So that's it. As usual, we're the last to know." He passed the transcript to his First Lieutenant.

The younger officer's eyes flashed with excitement as he read the news. "We're in business then," he said.

"Could be."

"The Chinese have hardly started on their ABM's—we should get something through."

"I doubt if it'll come to that. Let's hope not, anyway."

"You're probably right."

O'Brien smiled at the First Lieutenant's efforts to recover a peace-loving expression. The First Lieutenant smiled back. He was no novice. "You look bushed, sir," he said.

"Yes, I'm turning in now. Hackett's taking over. Wake me half an hour before crew change."

Catching sight of himself in the mirror above the basin in his cabin, O'Brien was shocked by his face; the tan picked up in Hawaii that turned to a sickly yellow and his eyelids were raw red. They had been hard at it since Saturday morning when the first terse message from London had sent them veering away from the Phoenix Islands, with hurried apologies to the Seventh Fleet, on a course northwest. A second message, bearing the Prime Minister's code-sign, had instructed them to proceed at full speed to a point a hundred miles south of Okinawa. In twenty-four hours they would be there.

Lying on his bunk in the half-darkened cabin, O'Brien visualized the map. Okinawa was a good choice. From that position they could hit most of the big cities: Shanghai, Hankow, Canton. . . . Or perhaps the north was more likely: Tsingtao, Tientsin, Peking. . . . What did it matter. They would never know what the targets were.

The computer, fed by its coded tapes, radio-controlled from London, would do the aiming. At the first salvo the Chinese radar would plot their position; and the British Polaris Fleet would be down to three.

Reverting to a well-tried drill, he steered his mind toward home and the cottage in the Orkneys he had bought for his retirement.

The lobby of the Rundall Hotel had just had its decennial going-over and the new motifs were transparent plastic and foliage—convenient for Morgan, who was able to observe Pershing from behind what appeared to be a balloon full of rubber plants.

# 10

Pershing was on a stool at the cocktail bar, where he had been for half an hour. No one had recognized him and the barman had abandoned the effort to make conversation. With his first drink he had bought an *Evening Standard*, glanced at the banner headlines about Hong Kong and read through a half page of instant tub-thumping by Barnett Coper; now the paper had fallen in an untidy heap below the stool and he was staring abstractedly into the mirror behind the bottles. Morgan wondered what he was waiting for.

At 8:15 Pershing glanced at his watch and paid for his drinks, then walked quickly across the lobby. Morgan made as if to follow, then saw that Pershing was heading for the lift, and stepped back behind his cover. The lift doors closed and the numbers above them began to flash. One, two, three, four, five. Ping. Without haste Morgan crossed the lobby to an alcove in the corner, and picked up the house telephone.

"Surely this is unnecessarily dangerous," Pershing said.

"Dangerous perhaps, but necessary," Chiang replied. The Chinese who had let Pershing in disappeared into the next room and closed the connecting door. Without mov-

ing from the armchair Chiang pointed to the end of the
bed. "Sit down, Pershing, you look frightened."

Pershing was in fact shaking all over. "You could have
sent someone else," he said.

"But I wanted to see you myself. There are some things
which cannot be left to subordinates."

"That Legation is watched. You were probably followed."

Chiang smiled—that same all-purpose movement of the
mouth, but this time the eyes showed that he was gen-
uinely amused. "Fortunately this hotel uses the same ex-
cellent Chinese laundry as our Legation. I was brought
here in a basket of sheets. An undignified means of trans-
port, but not uncomfortable."

"And supposing I was followed? It's not impossible."

"As you see, we reserved two rooms. If we are disturbed,
I shall go into the next room and down the fire escape to
my laundry van. You will be found alone in the bedroom
of a London hotel. Surely a British politician could think
of some explanation for that."

"Very thorough. You must have been sure I would
come."

"Yes."

Chiang was sitting with his hands linked in his lap. The
harsh ceiling light showed that he had hardly aged at
all: no surplus flesh, no gray hairs, the lines in the sallow
face only fractionally deeper. Pershing found himself
once again admiring, envying, maddened by the man's
composure. "What made you so sure?" he said.

"You have much to lose—your home, your family, your
career, the respect of the British public. When we
met before you were a young man, frustrated because your
society would not allow you to be a hero. Now, like all
bourgeois, you rely on your possessions and your position;
without them you are nothing."

"What do you want to know?"

"That is obvious. I wish to know what your Government will do about Hong Kong."

"There's been no decision yet. I thought your friend Coper had made that clear to everyone."

"Harvey was unwilling to make a public statement— that proves nothing. He and Bennett have talked together for many hours, they must have decided privately what to do, and you must know their thoughts."

"I've no idea what they're thinking," Pershing lied. "They don't confide in me." He had a grip on himself now: shaky, but a grip.

Chiang was looking hard into his eyes. "I see you are telling the truth," he said after a while. "So the decision will be taken by the Cabinet tomorrow morning. What will happen then?"

"I expect Ryder Bennett will call you to the Foreign Office to tell you what that decision is."

"And he will probably lie."

"I don't see why he should."

"Do not play games, Pershing. You are not as stupid as that. Bennett will probably lie, but you will know the truth. Will you be with him?"

"Perhaps."

"Then this is what you will do. Before we meet, you will write the Cabinet's true decision on a piece of paper, which you will carry in your hand—like this." Chiang opened the palm of one hand to reveal a small ball of paper. "When I leave the room I shall shake your hand and take it from you."

"But Ryder Bennett may prefer to see you alone."

"Of course. Or you may not have time to write the message, or it may not be appropriate for me to shake your hand. In that case we shall use another method of communication."

"I'll be at the Foreign Office all day."

"But you will go home in the evening."

"Late, probably."

"It does not matter. Put your message to me in a match-box, and when you go home take a walk along the river —the Embankment, you call it?"

"The Embankment, yes."

"—toward Chelsea Bridge. A man in a black van will stop and ask you the way to Fulham Road. You lean on the door to tell him, like this"—Chiang got to his feet and went through a poker-faced mime—"and drop the matchbox into the van. Do you understand?"

"Yes."

Chiang sat down again. "There is one other thing I want to say to you. You may think you can lie to me your-self about the Cabinet decision. That would be a false hope. If we learned that you had deceived us, we would destroy you immediately."

"All right, all right, now for God's sake let's break this up."

Chiang rose to his feet and called in Chinese toward the connecting door. "I shall go first. You will wait here for five minutes, then leave by the way you came in."

Pershing stayed sitting on the bed after Chiang had gone, his elbows on his knees, his hands covering his face. So this was where the escalator had brought him. Balls of paper, matchboxes, laundry baskets; blackmail in a hotel bedroom.

*Part Seven*

# LONDON, HONG KONG, PEKING AND THE PACIFIC OCEAN

TUESDAY 14 DECEMBER

Moira came in just before six. The clatter of Willy Mumford-Pyke's Aston Martin, silencer broken, merged with the throbbing in Pershing's head and finally woke him. In thirty seconds he was undressed and between the sheets, vomit-splashed shirt thrust under the bed.

1

Feigning sleep, he watched her creep about the overheated room. One by one the clothes came off that slim white body. Slip, bra, garter belt, stockings. Now she was standing in front of the wardrobe mirror, stretching, naked, and enjoying it. Her lipstick was smeared, her dark hair falling loose; the tautness had gone from her face, and she had that dazed expression she always had after making love.

Pershing watched her without a twinge of desire or jealousy. In the old days the early mornings had always been the best time; but now she was irrelevant. When she was asleep, he swallowed a handful of pills and lay on his back waiting for the pain in his head to ease. Wide awake now, he thought of the day to come. Last night's collapse had purged him of self-pity, left the instinct to survive intact. The Cabinet had been fixed for 10:30. He would need all his wits for that.

*Extract from report of Working Party of the Official Defense Committee, circulated to the Cabinet on the morning of Tuesday 14 December as document CD(WP)(76)1*

# 2

In the time available the Working Party was not in a position to finalize an agreed recommendation to Ministers. Although various modifications would be possible, there appear to be four main courses of action open to His Majesty's Government:

(i) to announce at once their acceptance of the Chinese ultimatum and to enter into talks with the Chinese Government aimed at achieving the orderly evacuation of British troops and adequate safeguards for British commercial interests in Hong Kong.

The remaining courses of action all presuppose an intense effort during the next two days to convince the Chinese Government that His Majesty's Government intend to reject the ultimatum and are ready if necessary to go to war. This effort would consist of diplomatic approaches, public statements and obvious military preparations. Should this effort fail to secure the withdrawal of the ultimatum, His Majesty's Government could then:

(ii) accept the Chinese ultimatum a very short time before its expiry;

(iii) reject the Chinese ultimatum and conduct a conventional defense of Hong Kong without engaging in wider hostilities;

(iv) reject the Chinese ultimatum and employ all means, including nuclear weapons, against the People's Republic of China.

As already stated, the Departments represented on the

Working Party have not succeeded in arriving at an agreed recommendation at official level. They concur, however, in advising against the adoption of course (iii) above, which would in their view result in heavy casualties and the partial destruction of Hong Kong without any commensurate gain.

As a Minister of State at the Foreign Office Pershing had attended Cabinet once or twice before, usually on unimportant occasions representing Ryder Bennett. This was the first time he had been asked in his own right because of his special knowledge of Far Eastern affairs. When the summons came he had thought for a moment that the Cabinet would actually ask his advice, and his indecision in face of Chiang's request grew even more agonizing.

But in the event he was not asked his opinion. The Cabinet had listened quietly to his account of his trip to Hong Kong and then passed on to the argument which was still raging. Seeing a chance to escape his dilemma, Pershing had made a move to go. He could then tell Chiang that he had been kicked out of the Cabinet before there were any decisions. But Harvey waved him back into his seat at the end of the table, and there he sat silent for the next hour, half his mind fascinated by the argument going on around him, the other half obsessed with his own problem.

He watched Broom, now bucketing through the argument like a bulldozer through thick clay. Broom, his rival for the Foreign Office, was tough and relentless, black hair brushed straight back from the pale, heavy forehead, a powerful frame, large hands. His talk was always full of "I's." Pershing had once seen him in the swimming pool at the Hurlingham Club; his body was startlingly white and somehow at forty-five its bulk was not fat but still muscle. Broom had a two-star brain, and had never known a moral doubt in his life.

"I can't understand what all the fuss is about," Broom said, not trying to be polite. "Of course the Americans don't want to come in. I never thought they would. But I've always said the whole point of having Polaris is that we can trigger the Americans off, pull them into our quarrels whether they like it or not. I'm quite clear that if the Chinese attack Hong Kong we should go for them hammer and tongs, Polaris, the lot. I reckon the Americans would be in the war in three days, and Hong Kong can easily hold out that long. The only thing that should stop us would be a Chinese capability to attack Britain—and all the joint intelligence reports show that they have no nuclear submarines completed and that the missiles in Sinkiang can't get farther than Warsaw. We, on the other hand, hold their cities in pawn. In such a favorable strategic position I'm amazed there should be any doubt about what we should do."

He glared across the table at Ryder Bennett, who cut in at once: "Quite apart from the assertion that Hong Kong could hold out for three days, an illusion which I thought Pershing here had dispelled in all of us, I'm not prepared to be responsible . . ." But Harvey lowered the temperatures by calling on the Chancellor of the Exchequer. Sir Richard Wroughton had aged fast in the last twelve months, and in Cabinet nowadays he was inaudible except when announcing bad news or criticizing his colleagues.

"Two twenty-four and three quarters," said the Chancellor, clear as a bell, "that's where sterling stood half an hour ago, a full cent down on yesterday, and the Governor reckons we'll be bumping along the bottom by tonight. The Bank is supporting the rate already and we can't keep that up for more than a few days." He started to mumble about IMF standbys and the Group of Ten, then ended at full volume: "I must add, Prime Minister, that if the matter could have been presented differently in the House last night, the effect on the markets might not have been nearly so serious."

Pershing saw Harvey flush. Odd that after twenty years of politics the Prime Minister should have kept so thin a skin. Then Harvey began to speak. He had held himself in reserve for this moment; most of the colleagues were beginning to feel weary and impatient for a decision. His words carried much more weight than they would have an hour earlier. In fact, they were irresistible.

*Extract from Cabinet conclusions of Tuesday 14 December*

The Cabinet
  (a)  approved course (ii) in document CD (WP)(76)1;
  (b)  in consequence authorized the Prime Minister, the Minister of Defense and the Secretary of State for Foreign Affairs to take all possible measures to convince the Chinese that an attack on Hong Kong would provoke the maximum retaliation by this country, including the use of nuclear weapons;
  (c)  decided that if these measures did not induce the Chinese to withdraw their ultimatum, *it should be accepted two hours before its time of expiry—i.e. at 10* A.M. BST, *Wednesday 15 December.*

The room in Security Department was just like any other in the Foreign Office, too tall for its furniture, underpainted and overheated; coffee and chocolate digestives were on the table; but Jane Richardson still felt ill at ease. In her career she had had several contacts with the intelligence services, and they always made her nervous. She felt as if she had been summoned to a police station. And there was something rather frightening about this colossal pear-shaped man with his studiously polite manner and bad breath; you felt he might be capable of some sudden violence.

$3$

"Can we go over one or two points again?" said Morgan.

"Yes, of course. Mr. Pershing won't be back from Cabinet yet." The man's breath really was appalling. Jane was convinced that once or twice her nose must have wrinkled.

"This Chinese woman who alleged she was the sister of Chiang Li-shih—she came with you in the ADC's car when you left Government House?"

"That's right."

"And you're sure it was the Bowring Hotel she was staying at?"

"Yes."

"What sort of person was she?"

"Oh, a homely sort of body, with a lot on her mind."

"You're obviously a shrewd observer. Did you get any idea what was on her mind? She was worried about her brother, perhaps."

"No, it was her parents, I think. She seemed to think

Mr. Pershing could help them—with money, I suppose."

"That's interesting." Morgan scribbled on the pad in front of him. "So she came to Government House to get help for her parents."

"That was the impression she gave me when I brought her up from the gate."

"Are you sure Pershing didn't invite her there?"

"Oh, quite sure. He was as surprised as I was."

"Why did he agree to see her? It was rather an unusual thing to do."

"He hoped to get some useful background on her brother."

"I see." Morgan paused to light his pipe, and Jane inhaled the aroma of Balkan Sobranie with relief. "Were you there when Pershing saw the woman?"

"No. They walked in the garden of Government House alone for about half an hour."

"And where was Langton at the time?"

"Asleep, in his room."

"Now, afterward, did Pershing tell you what had happened?"

"He said—"

"I want you to think carefully about this."

"Yes, I remember quite well. He simply said that as a fact-finding exercise on the brother it was a waste of time. Chiang Meh-li hadn't seen her brother for years, and she hoped that we would have news of him."

"He said that, did he?" Morgan looked at Jane for a moment, then scribbled again in the pad. "Nothing about the parents?"

"No."

"Isn't there a slight discrepancy here? Your impression was that she had come to get something for her parents, but Pershing said that she came for news of her brother."

"I'm sure there's no discrepancy really. I was probably wrong about her—or there could have been things in their conversation Mr. Pershing didn't bother to tell me. He seemed rather bored by the whole thing."

"Yes. Well, I think that's all. Now I must let your people have this room back." Morgan smiled and got up. "Thank you very much, Miss Richardson. We're most grateful for your help."

Jane paused in the doorway, not quite easy in her mind. "Can I ask you why you are asking me all these questions? Wouldn't it be simpler to ask Mr. Pershing direct?"

Morgan took a biscuit from the plate by the telephone and began to nibble it. "No need to bother him; we know he's very busy. It was just an odd little unexplained incident during his visit, just the kind of thing which can come up and hit you later if you ignore it. So we felt we ought to clear it up. And I think that's just what we've done, thanks to you."

Pershing, standing by the window, watched the two men confront each other. The winter sunlight from St. James's Park caught the two faces—Chiang's smooth and pale under sleek black hair, Ryder Bennett's rough fair skin beginning to line, with touches of color on cheeks and forehead. The Foreign Secretary had decided on Pershing's advice to play it stiff and formal. Chiang in the presence of foreigners was never anything else.

4

"I'm grateful to you for coming at such short notice," said Ryder Bennett, motioning Chiang to sit. "You know Mr. Pershing, I think?"

Chiang half-turned to Pershing and gave a little bow. "Yes indeed." No irony in the voice, no gleam in the dark eyes. Chiang did not enjoy the act of blackmail, thought Pershing, nor did he dislike it; it was simply something he did for the Party, automatically and without feeling. In his waistcoat pocket Pershing fingered a sheet of paper torn from his memo pad, now folded four times into a neat and tiny square.

"Mr. Pershing and I have just left a Cabinet meeting which discussed Hong Kong," continued Ryder Bennett. Sitting now behind Lord Curzon's desk the Foreign Secretary looked older and more authoritative than in Cabinet. His tone was harsh. "I was asked by my colleagues to express our very strong resentment at the Note Verbale which your Chargé d'Affaires handed to me four days ago. Both the tone and the contents of the Note are unacceptable.

We do not doubt either our legal and moral right to remain in Hong Kong, or our ability to do so."

Ryder Bennett stopped, and there was a pause. Chiang's
expression did not change, but Pershing had the impression from a slight movement of his hands that he was dis-
concerted. He had expected more.

"Am I to take this as a final rejection of our just demands?" Chiang asked.

"You will receive tomorrow a formal reply to the Note
Verbale," Ryder Bennett said. "But I thought it right
to let you know at once our strong reaction to your demand."

Chiang rose from the chair in front of the desk. Halfway down his mind Pershing admired Chiang's crisp ele-
gance, the way he moved his body in one piece, not awk-
wardly limb by limb like a European.

"Then there is no point in discussing the matter further," said Chiang in his perfect English. "The Government of the People's Republic of China is not interested
in the emotions of Mr. Pershing or yourself or your colleagues, since these cannot affect the outcome. We simply
wish to know whether the British Government intend to
leave Hong Kong peacefully or whether they prefer to be
evicted by force."

"You will have our reply in writing tomorrow," said
Ryder Bennett. "But I can tell you now two things which
it will contain. We offer to open negotiations at once on
all matters now at issue between your Government and
the Government of Hong Kong. Pershing here can tell us
the details."

Pershing was prepared. "There is the water supply
agreement to be renegotiated, the tax position of the Bank
of China, police jurisdiction in the walled city of Kowloon
and fishing rights at the mouth of the Shumchün river.
The Chinese side may have other points to suggest."

If only I could take the big decisions as competently as

I can deal with these trivia, Pershing thought. He felt sick with doubt.

Chiang twisted the knife for the first time. "We know already of Mr. Pershing's expert knowledge of Chinese affairs. But all these matters are totally irrelevant to our demand for the liberation of Hong Kong."

"Then I will say just one thing more." Ryder Bennett rose from behind the desk. "Do not underestimate us. Do not be misled by what you read this morning in those"— he pointed to the newspapers stacked tidily on the lectern by the window. "Our editors and journalists are telling us to turn tail and run. They're a nervous lot and think the British public are as timid as themselves. But it isn't true, as every politician worth his salt discovered long ago. And don't suppose that you could confine fighting to Hong Kong. Remember, we have powerful allies, and powerful weapons of our own. Do not doubt that if necessary we are ready to defend ourselves by attacking you."

As Ryder Bennett spoke, Pershing had made up his mind. Other people could talk about abstractions like Britain or Hong Kong, and perhaps mean what they said. But he was not made like that; he must think first of himself. The chatter in the smoking room, the hush in the village hall as he rose to speak, the neat bundles piling up as the votes were counted, loudspeakers, blue rosettes, red boxes, the reporters scrambling for a word, the policeman saluting him in New Palace Yard—Chiang was right, these were the things which sustained him now. If the price of self-respect was a prison cell, it was too high. He took the folded piece of paper out of his waistcoat and held it ready in his palm.

Chiang had shaken hands with Ryder Bennett and was turning toward the door. Pershing moved to open it for him, and for the first time that morning their eyes met.

And a peculiar thing happened. Pershing was overwhelmingly reminded of Meh-li. The set of the eyes, the curve of the chin, even the slight angle at which Chiang held his head was the same. . . . A plump little woman sitting in the Governor's gazebo, tears rolling down her cheeks; losing her home once again, perhaps her life this time, before the march of politics. . . . Was it only two days ago? He had promised to put the parents on the evacuation list, but afterward had decided it would look too suspicious—and done nothing.

For a second after opening the door he put both hands behind his back.

"Thank you," said Chiang, and held out his hand, Pershing shook it and showed Chiang out into the corridor, where an aged messenger was waiting to take him to the lift. Pershing went back to the Foreign Secretary's room.

"Well, what d'you make of that?" asked Ryder Bennett.

"Impossible to say. He certainly listened." Pershing was surprised to find himself speaking crisply.

"I suppose that's something. And he didn't shake his fist at me, like that damned poet on Friday." Ryder Bennett looked out of the window at the plane trees and the chilly waters of the lake. "By this time tomorrow we shall know," he said.

The folded piece of paper in Pershing's left hand was soggy with sweat. Carefully he put it back in his waistcoat pocket.

The three men talked among themselves, so softly that Meh-li could not hear. The Eurasian called Robert Foo seemed to be in charge; it was he who had asked her all the questions. A tall man in a shiny blue Western suit, his head smelling of sweet oil.

**5**

The room was hot and airless. It had no windows, and the strong naked bulb hanging immediately in front of Meh-li's face was making her head ache. The leather thongs which tied her arms and legs to the chair sent stabs of pain backward and forward across her body. It was several hours since these men had flung her into a car outside the Bowring Hotel, bound her eyes and driven off into the unknown. It must be late afternoon now. She wished that it was over.

She heard the Eurasian say, "Tell London we're doing our best; we should have something soon," and then he came back to her, walking lightly on the balls of his feet. He spoke in English, the words dropping softly from between his even white teeth.

"Why did you go to see Pershing?" he said.

Meh-li repeated what Pershing had told her to say. "I hoped he would bring news of my brother in London."

"That is a ridiculous lie," the Eurasian said casually. "You were with your brother in Peking last week, you have lived with him for years." Meh-li's heart sank: so they knew that too. Suddenly the Eurasian leaned close to her face and spat out the question again. "Why did you go to see him?"

The steady drip of repetitive questions had worn away her resistance. She no longer even looked for the traps. "He is an important man; he could help my parents, he could help them escape if there was trouble."

"Why should he help two old Chinese to whom he owed nothing?"

Weariness closed in on Meh-li. "Because I gave him information." This was the fourth time through this round of questions, and each time she told a little more. She closed her eyes and the man in the blue suit kicked her on the shin with his narrow pointed shoe.

"What information did you give him?"

Among all the unintelligible confusion in Meh-li's mind one thing was clear: Pershing, who was a good man, had told her not to answer that question. She said nothing.

"What information did you give him?"

Again no answer. Without waiting to be told the two assistants brought two metal pincers and clamped them on Meh-li's wrists. Red and green leads ran from them to a black cable plugged into the wall.

"What information did you give him?"

Meh-li did not fear pain, but the electricity might kill her, and then what would happen to her father and mother? She had to get back to them, she had to get out of this horrible little room and back to the hotel before it was too late. Pershing would understand. "I told him there was an agent of the Communists in the British Government."

The interrogator bent over her, and the smell of sweet oil was sickening. "How did you know that? Did your brother tell you?"

"No. I read some papers from his briefcase."

"What was the name of the agent in the British Government?"

"I cannot remember."

"Of course you can remember." At a sign from the Eurasian one of the assistants moved to the point where the black cable reached the wall. "Just tell me the name, or I shall have to hurt you."

"There was no real name; I think it was a code."

"All right, what was the code name?"

Meh-li did not reply. But the assistant did not touch the switch, and the Eurasian seemed to think of something else. "What did Pershing do when you told him?" he asked. "Was he surprised?"

"He laughed. So he knew already about the agent?"

"No, he laughed."

"No—that is what I thought at first, but then he told me the information would be a great help. He laughed because he was pleased I had come to him." Meh-li saw that the second assistant was writing her answers in a book. It must be nearly over now. When they had finished would they let her go or would they kill her?

The interrogator seemed about to walk away, then suddenly he whipped around and slapped her across the face. He was shouting at the top of his voice directly into her ear. "The code name! What was it?"

Meh-li kept her eyes and lips tight shut, feeling her cheek turn hot from the blow. I must hold back something, she told herself. The Englishman promised to get us out of Hong Kong; for his sake I will try a little longer.

"I cannot remember," she whispered.

In the corner of the room the first assistant made a movement. The flood of pain from her wrists seemed to last forever. She tried to force herself into unconsciousness, she groped for comfort, but it would not come. Another movement in the corner, the pain stopped and the names of the saints tumbled desperately out: "Peter, Paul, Thomas, Jude . . ." But then another blow struck her, this time from inside, spreading outward, a warm, almost kindly pain which brought the unconsciousness she was seeking. She slumped forward in the chair; only the thongs kept her from falling. The three men tried hard, but they could not revive her.

Carried by the gale from the south, the rain was coming across the river in horizontal gusts. The lower half of Pershing's body was protected by the Embankment wall, but his head and shoulders were exposed to the blast. Shivering with cold, he paused to check that the pavement behind him was empty, then turned up his collar and, right hand clutching the matchbox, walked on toward the bridge.

# 6

It had been a grueling day: protest and counterprotest at the UN, the Americans panicky as hell, Moscow on the hot line, wild scenes in the Commons—Tories yelling support and Labour split as usual, right-wingers nervously carping, left-wingers loud with rage. The only short lull had been early in the afternoon. Jane had produced sandwiches and beer, and they had lunched together in his office. Poor girl, she was longing to hear about the Cabinet; but only the Permanent Under-Secretary was in on the secret. Extraordinary how comforting it was to talk to her. Afterward, sitting quietly alone at his desk, he had seen what to do at last. If the British bluff worked, Harvey would have to keep the Cabinet decision a secret—otherwise the Chinese would simply renew the ultimatum. Chiang had said he would get to know the truth eventually, and he might. But there was just a chance . . .

"Excuse me, can you tell me the way to Fulham Road?"

Scottish; Glasgow, probably. Burly type, getting on. Ah yes, the messenger of Monday morning. No crest on the van this time.

"Yes, certainly." Right hand on the door; release match-box. Scotsman smiles. Wonder who he is. "Turn right at the lights, keep going and you'll cross it."

"Thanks. Good night."

"Good night."

Car across the road. Pulling out behind the van. Coincidence, must be. Keep it natural; walk as far as the bridge, then back for a hot bath.

All over now.

Kemble switched off the television.

"So Harvey's taking us to the brink," he said.

7

The wind rattled against the windows of Tedworth Square, followed by a violent hiss of rain. Jane sat on the sofa, the Prime Minister's words echoing in her head. She shivered. "It's fantastic," she said. "All that stuff about resisting the Chinese demands by every means at our disposal . . . a time of grave danger for the nation. . . . He must mean the bomb. What else could he mean?"

"Whoa there, whoa. I said *to* the brink, not over."

"Is there a distinction?"

"There'd bloody well better be. I reckon that speech was very carefully drafted, ditto his statement to the House this afternoon. If you look at them closely you'll see he hasn't committed himself entirely. Harvey's no warmonger."

"You mean it's a bluff?" Jane thought of that feverish day in the Foreign Office. "No, that's impossible."

Kemble looked at her out of the corner of his eye. Did she know more than she was pretending? No; discreet as a Trappist monk she might be, but she couldn't lie to save her life. So even Ministers' Private Secretaries were in the dark. His faith in his theory took a knock, but he went on: "Impossible—why? Take a lesson in political realities from the mastermind at the *Globe*. The bomb has always been a bluff, except perhaps in the case of an attack on the sovereign territory of a nuclear power—a point which de Gaulle and I realized years ago. Now, imagine you're trying to maintain that bluff in the final hours of some confrontation. You can hardly expect the other side to believe it unless you tell your own side that war is on the way."

"Preposterous," Jane said, but clever, she thought— and just possibly right. Yes, Jack Kemble, you're the most astute political observer in the land. Bravo. Just don't imagine that's enough to keep me at your feet. All right, I slept with you—and that went to my head. But I'm over it now. You're sitting there pleased as Punch because you think you're forgiven. Wrong, my clever friend. I called you here tonight for a purpose; but first I shall feed you up on pasta and cut-price Chianti. . . ."

"A Conservative Government is an organized hypocrisy," said Kemble. "Know who said that?"

"Disraeli. Let's eat."

The table was set in the corner of the room; Finnish tableware, black candles in painted wooden holders, cloth from the Ghana Gift Shop. After she had brought the coffee, Jane said: "Anyway, now that it's all come out, you know why I couldn't tell you about my weekend."

Kemble wiped the traces of meat sauce from his mouth and shifted uneasily on his chair. He had wondered when it would come. "Of course you were right, my darling; I should never have asked you. If it's any consolation, this has become an office joke." He pointed to the bruise on his nose where she had hit him.

They moved back to the sofa. She stroked his wrist. "Yes, I'm sorry, it does look rather awful. It was good of you to come."

"Then I'm forgiven." He nuzzled her cheek.

"Actually I was lucky to get away on time; most of the Office will be at it all night. But for some reason Pershing suddenly decided to go home, and he packed me off too. He looked white as a sheet. I do hope he doesn't crack up."

"If he's lived with that whoring bitch of a wife for years, he can live with a crisis for a day or two."

Jane added lack of taste to a growing list of points against Kemble, and steered the conversation back to its starting point. "Of course, there's lots more I can tell you now. Did I say anything about the Chinese woman, the one who came to Government House to see Pershing? She's the sister of the grim-faced man they've sent over from Peking to handle the ultimatum."

"Chiang's sister?" Kemble swung his legs off the sofa. "I've been chasing that bastard all day. What's his sister got to do with Pershing?"

"I'm not sure. It's all rather a puzzle."

Jane recounted the events of Sunday evening. She knew she was being naughty. Even if he hadn't said so, the fat security man had implied she was to keep it to herself. But the thing had been on her mind all day; there was something odd somewhere. Why *had* Meh-li come to see Pershing? Why, if she had lived there all her life, did she seem to know so little about Hong Kong? Had Pershing compromised himself unwittingly? In the middle of the afternoon Jane had seen a way to solve the mystery and, pretending love, had telephoned Kemble. The *Globe* would be able to find out the truth. Now, as he listened to her story, that look she knew well came over his face— like a fish, stupid with greed, rising to the bait.

"Can I use your phone to ring Hong Kong?"

"What on earth for?"

"This Chinese bird of yours has a story in her. I want to get our stringer onto her before anyone else tumbles to it. Bowring Hotel, was that it?"

Without waiting for an answer Kemble reached for the phone, asked the *Globe* switchboard for a number, then called the international exchange. The exchange said there was no hope of a line to Hong Kong that night, then, in-explicably, called back in a few minutes.

Listening hard, Jane cleared the table and began to wash the dishes.

"Hello. Hello? Hell-O!"

Saucepans first. Nothing worse than congealed spaghetti. Keep your cool, mastermind.

"Hello? I'd like to speak to Joe Allott please. . . . That's right, Joe Allott of the *Morning Post*. . . . Well, wake him up. It's urgent."

Kemble lit a cigarette, pulled at it rapidly, fingers drumming on the coffee table.

"Joe? Kemble here. . . . Yes, I know what time it is. Now get hold of this. . . ."

Kemble gave his instructions, Jane giggled. Her tame newshound.

". . . Yes, I'm sure it's getting tough your end. . . . But one riot's much the same as another, you've seen one, you've seen them all. . . . Bullets, eh? Well, wear your tin hat and wave your press card. . . . Yes, the usual fee—no, tell you what, we'll double it. Danger money. Can't be fairer than that. . . . Bank it in Geneva? All right, leave it to me. . . . Attaboy. . . . Ask her about her brother, and ask about Pershing. And ring me back as soon as you can . . . 842-7182 . . . Yes, I'll be here all night."

"That's what you think," said a small voice in the kitchen.

Thirteen Ming Emperors lay buried in the valley, each tomb with
its pine-clad mound, its courtyard,
memorial tablet and gray encir-
cling wall. No one was sure
whether this had anything to do
with the choice of the valley as the
secret seat of government in an
emergency. It might have been
simply that the twenty-mile road
from the capital was good, and the
main effects of blast and radiation
would not reach so far.

8

Wang looked at his watch: it would be late Tuesday
evening in London now. But here in Peking it was already
dawn on the final day, and he still had no idea what the
Prime Minister was up to, or why he had been summoned
at this early hour. The car stopped while a heavily padded
guard peered through the window, then drove on.

The yellow alert had been in operation for two days
now, and the evacuation of the Politburo to the Valley of
the Ming Tombs was complete. The Prime Minister's
offices were established in a vast bunker scooped out of the
ground fifty yards from the tomb of Yung Lo, the greatest
of the dynasty. Scarlet persimmons hung from the leafless
trees around the entrance. Northward, toward the Great
Wall, the rims of the hills were sharp in the cold light.

Wang's driver drove the little Skoda into a nearby clearing, two days ago a threshing floor, now the car park for
senior officials. There was one other car there, a big black
Russian Zim. Wang waited to be sure that his driver remembered to put on the camouflage netting. Then he was
led through the main gateway of the tomb into a little

courtyard with carefully stunted trees. In the center a dusty bronze griffin bared his teeth.

"You have seen the message from Chiang." The Prime Minister's opening remark was half question, half statement. The underground room was small and bare; a desk, two chairs. The butt of the last visitor's cigarette smoldered on the floor. There was no ashtray.

"Yes. Pershing says that the British threats are genuine." Wang was uneasy; he saw slippery uncertainties opening before him.

"What then is your assessment?"

Again, the disconcerting habit of asking for advice instead of giving instructions. None of the other leaders was so unreasonable. Wang decided to be bold and voluble.

"We have three pieces of evidence, Comrade Prime Minister, that the British mean what they say. First, there is the copy of the British Cabinet minutes photographed by our agent in the Home Office. You have seen a summary; it states that the Cabinet decided to resist by all possible means the Chinese attack on Hong Kong, including the use of nuclear weapons."

"It was a very definite document."

"Yes, but there are three puzzling factors. Our agent works at a low level in the Ministry and normally only sees Cabinet papers when they deal with home affairs in her sector; it is extraordinary that the girl should have been allowed to see a paper of such importance. Secondly, this was the first classified document which has passed through her hands for several months. She had begun to think she was under suspicion. Thirdly, these minutes arrived in the Home Office office earlier than usual by several hours."

"The intercepted orders to the supply ship of the Polaris submarine are more important. They appear to be genuine." Wang saw that the translation of the intercept was on the Prime Minister's desk.

"In my opinion they may be genuine, but still designed mainly to mislead us. The message included an unnecessary amount of information: for instance, that the submarine *Revenge* had ceased maneuvers with the American fleet and would be within range of the Chinese mainland by this morning; and that the supply ship should be prepared for a scramble."

"I was going to ask about that. What is a 'scramble'?" The Prime Minister faltered over the English word.

"We do not know exactly, except that it is the name the British have given to a procedure for concealing the position of these submarines after they have fired their missiles. This fact was published recently in a British naval magazine, which they must know we read. But that is not the only strange thing."

"No?"

"The message was transmitted in a new code, difficult to break but not impossible like the one before, which was introduced only two days ago. In my opinion the British imperialists are desperately following tactics of disinformation. They intend to yield at the last moment if we persist."

"What is your third piece of evidence?"

"The behavior of the traitor Pershing. In his message to Chiang this evening he wrote that the Cabinet had decided to fight. But, as you see, Chiang says that he thinks the man may be lying. Pershing had a message in his hand during the meeting at the Foreign Office, but at the last moment evidently changed his mind. I have read the file on him carefully: he is a typical adventurer, but I fear we may have underestimated the extent to which he is restrained by his instinctive class loyalties. He could well have decided to take a chance on our not discovering the true proceedings of the Cabinet."

"You are evidently a 'psychologist,' " Again the Prime Minister used the English word. "But you will recall that in the People's Republic there are no longer any psychologists. And how do you assess the attitude of the Soviet Union?"

Wang felt the clouds gathering, but it was too late to look for shelter. He gave the answer from the rule book. "The Soviet Union would not dare to seek to restrain the just demands of the Chinese people."

"So you would attack Hong Kong?"

"Yes."

The storm broke. The Prime Minister normally spoke educated, straightforward Chinese without the usual larding of official jargon. Now he showed that he had the jargon ready for use when necessary.

"It is clear, Comrade Wang, that you failed to apply the technique of socialist analysis to this problem. It is surprising that a cadre of your seniority should be defective in political education. It is a fault which you must openly admit and strenuously work to correct. You have neglected the teaching of our Chairman. Do you not recall his saying: 'Before sowing on the mountainside make sure that the fields in the valley are planted?' The first duty of the revolutionary is to harvest the fruits of the Chinese revolution. Yet the infantile petit bourgeois adventurism which you advocate would put our revolution in great danger. We do not know for certain what the British will do. We do know that they have the power to destroy our biggest cities with rockets from a single submarine. Our defensive system is not ready, nor have our own rockets the range to hit London. The American imperialists may help the British; the Soviet Union will certainly not help us. We must clearly in these circumstances observe the Three Imperatives of revolutionary struggle: Vigorously Consolidate, Vigilantly Prepare, Victoriously Advance."

So he had jumped the wrong way. Counterarguments and counterquotations crowded into Wang's brain, but he held them back. The tiny, bare room reminded him of a prison cell. He merely asked: "Then the original decision of the Politburo to reoccupy Hong Kong—"

"—was based on the assumption that the British imperialists would not fight. That assumption may still prove correct. For your sake, Comrade Wang, I hope that it does."

The feline smile came and went so quickly that Wang was not sure if he had seen it. He was not one of the Prime Minister's protégés, and he would be broken without hesitation. His only hope now was to be humbly efficient.

"I admit that my analysis was superficial and incorrect. I will study to improve my ideological standpoint. What now remains to be done?"

"Here is a telegram for you to send at once to Chiang. He asks for a chance to verify Pershing's statement, and I agree it is worth the risk. He is to use the emergency procedure to arrange a second meeting. But if there is no firm word from Pershing or elsewhere by 11 A.M. London time that the British are bluffing, he is to accept their offer of negotiations over the water supply and the other administrative points at issue between China and Hong Kong. We will then announce that as a great stride forward toward our goal of liberation."

Wang took the piece of paper from the Prime Minister's hand and read the message. His brain worked to find a helpful suggestion.

"Chiang will have heard in London that his sister has been interrogated in Hong Kong."

"That is true, Comrade Wang; this time you are right. Add a sentence that so far as we have been able to discover she gave no information which would compromise the emergency contact procedures."

There was a pause while Wang scribbled, then the Prime Minister asked: "Is the woman dead?"

"I heard there was an accident during the interrogation."

"No need to mention that." Again the quick cat smile.

The road back to Peking is flanked by the Avenue of Beasts, great stone figures standing and kneeling in pairs—elephants, camels, unicorns, warriors, statesmen—guarding the entrance to the valley where the Emperors rest. As Wang's Skoda bumped down the road, a big black car overtook it and fouled it with dust. Through the yellow cloud Wang saw the Zim which had been parked on the threshing floor. Except that now a red flag fluttered on its hood. Seeing the hammer and sickle, Wang cursed himself. If he had been properly observant, and realized that the Russian Ambassador too was visiting the bunker, he would have jumped the other way and landed safely. As it was, his future was obscure, like the swirling dust on the road to Peking.

"We are rather proud of those minutes." The soda siphon gave its death rattle as Ryder Bennett refilled his glass. "And they worked like a dose of salts. The silly girl popped out of the Home Office and they were in her usual letter box within the hour."

9

"Good," Harvey said.

"We've held back the proper minutes, haven't we?"

"Yes, Sir Norman's keeping them close to his bosom till tomorrow noon. How are you managing in the FO?"

"We told the PUS, no one else. They all think they're going to war. Some pale faces, one or two squeals, but they're doing all right."

"They're not going to like it when they know."

"Leave it to me."

"Gladly." Harvey was in his purple silk dressing gown. He had canceled his official dinner and speech at the Farmers' Club and the evening had been full of summoned visitors and telephone calls. Now it was past eleven and everything possible had been done. But he did not feel like bed, and was glad that Ryder Bennett had come across from the Foreign Office for a final summing-up.

"So we planted the phony minutes," he said, "and then there was the radio message to the Polaris supply ship. Anything else in the same line?"

"I saw the Russian Ambassador, as we agreed, after your statement in the House and put on a real jingo act. He muttered something about peace and went away

looking more beetle-browed than ever. I think he might
help. Then I had some fun with the BBC."

Harvey noticed that as usual his Foreign Secretary was
enjoying a crisis. And the Director-General of the BBC
was an old enemy. "What sort of fun?" he asked.

"Well, I reckoned it was as insecure a place as any in
London, so I rang the DG and told him as pompously as
I could that I was giving him an informal warning that
within a day this country might well be at war with China,
and the BBC should behave itself accordingly. He got in
a fearful tizz and began to sound off about traditions of
impartiality and so forth. So I said I'd been looking at
the plan Kilmuir drew up at the time of Suez for the
Government to take over the BBC in an emergency, then
hung up while he was still spluttering. With any luck the
Corporation roof is now crowded with fellow travellers
semaphoring across Portland Place the news of a wicked
Tory war."

This is the difference between a friend and a comrade,
thought Harvey, looking across his study at the flushed
face under the lamp. Friendship meant tastes in common;
he and Ryder Bennett had none. Comradeship meant
days of shared exhaustion; of that they had piled up a
rich store—Rhodesia last year, and now this. Perhaps comradeship forged the stronger link. Men opened up when
they were tired; women, or at least his wife, closed down.

"What drives them on?" he asked suddenly.

"It's nothing but a great garbage bin for misfits."

"I was referring to the Chinese."

"The Chinese? Oh. Laurence Pershing explained it to
me once. They are the one genuine imperial power left
in the world. Even when we were clobbering them a hundred years ago they went on thinking that China was central and unique. We've all thought that about ourselves
at one time or another. But we British stopped long ago,

the Russians stopped after Stalin and the Americans never really started. To the Chinese the foreigner is still someone who owes tribute to the Emperor, and the sooner he pays up the better."

There was a pause. Above them Mrs. Harvey pottered audibly about her bedroom. Ryder Bennett thought of Hong Kong, snipping among the skyscrapers, refugees crowding onto the tarmac after the last planes had gone, the harbor tangled with escaping ships, looting, panic, invaders pouring through the hills and dropping lazily out of the sky. Britain, without a fight, losing her last big possession. After so many editorials, the final performance, the real end of an era.

Harvey thought of the effect on sterling, on the pending by-election, on the Monday Club, the new American President and the King. If the bluff failed, there would be a lot of explaining to do. The party, the House of Commons, the public—in that order they would have to be told the truth: that all today's noble statements of defiance had been an elaborate charade. He began to rehearse the speech in his head. ". . . It was therefore necessary, as part of our policy for attempting to dissuade the Chinese from aggressive action, for me to give the House a false impression on Tuesday. . . ." How odd that in all the millions of words written on the exigencies of the nuclear age, no one had thought of this one.

Aloud he said: "It's going to be damned awkward, Ryder. You'll have to stay on a bit at the FO. I'll try to prop the Chancellor up for a few more weeks. Couldn't move you so soon after an upset like this."

"You assume we're going to lose."

"Our bluff's got only eleven hours' life in it." Harvey emptied his brandy. "The Chinese have given us till noon, but as you said yourself in Cabinet, we must give in by ten at the latest, so as to be sure of forestalling their attack."

"I know. If nothing breaks, I'll have to see Chiang at ten."

There was a pause.

"Pershing's done well," said Harvey.

Ryder Bennett saw the train of thought. Typical of Harvey to talk about Cabinet appointments at a time like this. "Well enough to take my place when the right time comes?"

"I think so, if you stick to your recommendation."

"Of course I do. He's much the best choice."

"You don't think . . ." But Harvey did not complete the sentence. He knew a man under strain when he saw one, and he'd seen Pershing quite often in the last few days. But it might be so many things—excitement, that Swedish woman, or simply lack of sleep. As you grew wiser, you learned that it did no good to hunt about below the surface of complicated men; the truth always escaped. It was usually safer and more just to take them at face value. And Ryder Bennett had evidently noticed nothing.

"All right, he shall have it. Let's aim at March," he said.

The Brigadier rubbed his eyes and poured himself another coffee. He had been in the office in Queen Anne's Mansions for two days now. His shirt was beginning to smell. In the corner a bed had been made up; sheets smooth, hospital corners on the blanket. He looked at it longingly. As soon as Morgan had phoned he would be able to catch a nap.

# 10

The night before they had sat together for an hour, mulling things over. Fatigue seemed to have worn away Morgan's reserve, and for the first time he had opened up about himself; talked of his childhood in the Rhondda valley, his struggle to break away from the poverty and filth, the drab little mining village where his brothers and sisters still lived. And at last the Brigadier had understood him—the driving ambition, the enjoyment of luxury, the caution over money, the jealousy of a man like Pershing.

It must be jealousy. Why else would Morgan insist on pursuing the man when there was nothing against him? The only oddity was Pershing's visit to the Rundall Hotel. Morgan had lost him there, but a check on the register for the fifth floor had produced nothing to go on. Nobody had turned up to claim a telephone reservation on rooms 500 and 501; but that happened all the time.

The telephone rang.

"Ah, Morgan, it's you. Anything to report?"

For about a minute the Brigadier listened. "I see," he said eventually. "And he's gone to bed now. . . . Well, you'd better get over here straightaway. . . . We've got some decisions to make."

The early sun shown down on the
flat, empty sea south of Okinawa.
A hazy, windless day; hot and still.
Not a plane or a ship in sight to
disturb the seven-thousand tons of
British hardware cruising slowly in
a circle below the water.

11

Of the 143 men aboard only four
knew where they were, and of those
four the two most vital, the Captain
and the Polaris Systems Officer,
now stood together on the top
deck of the missile compartment. When the moment came
their every move would be checked by four other officers,
but the ultimate responsibility was theirs. O'Brien would
receive, decode, authenticate the teleprinted instructions;
the Polaris Systems Officer would open the safe to which
only he and one other knew the combination, and extract
the trigger; with the key tied to his waist O'Brien would
unlock the safety catch; and the PSO would press the
button. But that had been rehearsed a hundred times;
they did not need to discuss it now.

"We're out of chipolatas," said O'Brien.

"If we don't reach that supply ship soon they'll have
eaten the lot."

"I think I'l go down to the galley and see if we can't do
better."

Walking forward between the white-enameled tubes
O'Brien watched his crew, padding quietly about their
business in white T-shirts and gym shoes, and thought of
the thousands like them, buried in the silos of Arizona,
flying their bombers above the Arctic, manning the

Early Warning radar from Alaska to Fylingdales; fit, hand-picked men, checked for every psychological defect, perfect extensions of the machines they served.

Still, they had to be fed.

The call came through just before midnight. Jane was half-undressed and half-asleep on the bed. Through the open door she saw Kemble lift the receiver. He turned and nodded to her. She lifted the extension by the bed in time to hear the London operator say: "Hong Kong on the line. Go ahead please."

When the call was over Kemble came into the bedroom and sat heavily on the bed.

"Poor Meh-li," Jane said. "I wonder what they did to her."

"I hate to think," Kemble said.

"Are you sure it's true?"

"Oh, no doubt about that. Allott works for those people, we've known it for a long time. That's why he was so nervous about telling me."

"What will you do now?"

"I could phone it through—it's not too late for the last edition."

Jane's eyes widened with alarm. "But you won't, will you?"

"No. Can't possibly publish a thing like that until we know what effect it'll have. It's no time to be rocking the boat."

"Why don't I talk to Pershing?"

"Do that."

Later they sat together on the bed, clutching mugs of cof-

**12**

fee. "Well," said Kemble, "that's that. You got what you wanted out of me. I'll be off now."

Jane looked at the floor. "Was it that obvious?"

"You're not much of an actress."

"Well, eye for an eye. Now you know how it feels."

"Yes." Kemble pulled himself to his feet and began to fumble with his tie. Brown pouches had formed under his eyes. He wondered how many times he had been through this scene, how many times he would do it again.

"You look tired."

"I am."

She was by his side, smiling gently, her hands unraveling his tie. "Just for tonight then," she said.

*Part Eight*

# HONG KONG, LONDON AND MONGOLIA

## WEDNESDAY AND THURSDAY 15 & 16 DECEMBER

The wireless crackled; General Lamont was being stubborn.

"Don't exaggerate, man. There'll be no danger till this evening. I'll be with you in half an hour. Over."

"OP four. Roger, out."

There was no point in pushing it. Duthie turned away from the set and took up the bionoculars again. Through the glasses, beneath and beyond the Gurkha Observation Post, he gazed at the sight with which his imagination had so often played.

He was now in the main OP, overlooking the central section of the frontier. From Shumchün, about a mile away on the Chinese side, two roads led to the main crossing points below them—the station at Lowu and the road bridge at Man Kam To. Both roads were easy to pick out because of the trees which lined them. And through the trees Duthie could see the tanks and troop carriers, nose to tail, lumbering southward like some slow, inexorable reptile.

They had been on the move since just after dawn. No attempt at concealment, not even at the frontier, where the infantry were deployed, some in trenches, some out in the open among the rice stubble, right up to the fence itself. Duthie was reminded of the diagrams of old battles which had fascinated him as a boy: Blenheim, Oudenarde, Malplaquet, black and white arrows showing the regiments and squadrons as they neatly maneuvered and died. Tomorrow would be like that; or would it be tonight, or even today?

Not a plane in sight. Some MIGS had come over soon

after first light to have a look, but nothing since. The British had always expected bombing and an artillery barrage before the frontier was crossed. The Chinese gun positions were marked with crosses in red chinograph on the talc pinned to Duthie's map; no sign of life from them so far.

Probably the General was right. The Chinese were a formal, literal-minded people: their ultimatum expired at 12 noon British time, which meant 7 P.M. Hong Kong time, which meant that they would not move a man into British territory till then. Eight hours to go then; they would not be easy to live through.

A series of heavy thuds reverberated through the hills. That would be the engineers, blowing the roads and railway behind them. The Gurkhas muttered softly to each other, but kept their eyes to the north. Colonel Duthie tried to concentrate on the questions he needed to ask the General.

Thirty minutes later the two men were standing together at the embrasure of the pillbox.

"Nice to get some fresh air," said the General, then, more quietly: "Quite a show they're putting on for us down there."

In the sharp light the khaki of the distant Chinese uniforms and vehicles contrasted with the darker brown of the fields. The blotches of khaki were spreading fast across the landscape.

"What's it like in Hong Kong this morning, sir?" asked Duthie.

"Much as you'd expect," the General said. "The civilian evacuation is going quite smoothly. Some demonstrations and a bit of looting last night, and a big crowd not far from Government House this morning, but so far the police seem to be pretty well in control. It'll get worse today, of course. The Governor's quaking like a jelly, but

Fane's managed to get him to agree to a curfew from five
this evening until further notice."

"Any change in our own plans?"

"Not really. The ultimatum expires at seven, so the
odds are on a night attack, and probably some landings
under cover of darkness. I've reinforced the position at
Shatin and sent a company to Junk Bay. That'd be the obvious place for them to go for if they wanted to take the
airport."

Duthie was not sure how to phrase his next question.
He himself was not particularly interested in the answer,
but he was responsible for his men, and it had to be asked.

"About the evacuation, sir," he said.

"Yes?"

"Well, the original plan supposed that there would be
a surprise attack, and that the evacuation of civilians
would start as soon as possible after the Chinese crossed
the frontier."

"Quite right."

"Well now, because of the ultimatum, there's no surprise and we've been able to start the evacuation a day
before the attack starts."

"Well?"

"Well, sir, doesn't that mean a day cut off the time we're
supposed to hang on in the New Territories? Doesn't it
mean that more of the civilians will be got off by air than
in the original plan, so more ships will be available to
take off the army?"

"In theory, perhaps." The General suddenly felt tired.
"In practice, no. I've been specifically told to make no
change in our defense plan."

"I see." Duthie did not see, but it was the answer he had
expected, and he was content with it. But the General,
watching the Gurkhas scurry about the Observation Post,
was not content. Apparently faced with the choice between a prison camp and death by shell, bomb or bullet,

they were smiling and cheerful. The General felt an un-military need to explain himself.

"You see, in London they still think all this may be a bluff."

Duthie watched the reptile of vehicles worming southward. He had just heard on the field telephone that a Chinese troop train had drawn into Shumchün.

"A bluff, sir?"

"Yes. They think if we stand absolutely firm nothing may happen."

"But we're not strong enough to call their bluff. It can't matter much to the Chinese whether we fight here or not —just a few hours and a few thousand lives either way."

"You're forgetting the Polaris submarine." Duthie's face showed his surprise. "If I start pulling you back onto the ships, the Chinese won't believe we mean business with the Polaris."

"And do we?"

"Yes, we do," lied the General. At the Imperial Defence College refresher course they had spent a whole day on Morale. It had boiled down to saying that in modern limited "political" wars officers and men must be taught to have complete confidence in the backing they would get from London. Explanations, if needed, could be given later to those who survived.

Duthie believed the General, and was on the whole glad. He thought the Gurkhas would be glad too. So it would be a straightforward scrap on these hillsides, his men against the khaki horde gathering beyond the fence, their first proper fight since Borneo '66, their last fight.

An orderly carrying two steaming mugs of tea was tacking up the bare slope toward them. Duthie thought of Pershing and his visit three days earlier, of how uncertain and harassed he had seemed in his success.

"Those politicians have more guts than I bargained for," he said.

The bell rang for the third time.

"All right, coming," Pershing shouted. As he fiddled with the latch a blast of freezing air went up his pajama legs. Pulling his dressing gown closer, he opened the door. And suddenly the cold was inside him, running through his body like an electric current.

"You," he said.

"Yes, me," said Morgan. "May I come in?"

"Yes—yes, of course."

Morgan wiped his feet. Pershing took his mackintosh and hung it in the hall; the snowflakes melted almost immediately. They moved to the drawing room and Pershing switched on the lights. The central heating had been on for half an hour, but had hardly made an impression.

Morgan settled into an armchair. The long hairs which he grew to cover his bald patch were standing ridiculously on end. He brushed them flat with his hand. Pershing stood by the fireplace, reached for a silver box, offered it to Morgan.

"No thanks. Mind if I use this?" Morgan held up a pipe.

"Not at all." Pershing lit a cigarette, and his fingers were steady. Now that the end had come he was not afraid. "Rather early for MI5, isn't it?"

Morgan withdrew the pipe from his mouth, but kept his eyes on the match poised above the bowl. "Traitors keep odd hours," he said softly.

"So do Ministers of the Crown, but not this odd. Why have you come to me?"

"Because you're the man I want."

LONDON 7:30 A.M.
*(Hong Kong 2:30 P.M.)*

"That sounds very threatening. Next thing I know you'll be saying you've come to arrest me."

"The police do that. Our job is to collect the evidence." Morgan looked up. "Come on, Pershing, stop mucking about. You're finished, admit it."

Pershing walked to the window, Morgan's eyes on his back. The light was already stronger. A milk van was working down the street. What was the use.

"I admit it." An odd little thrill as he said the words, the bittersweet thrill of self-destruction.

Morgan nodded. "I thought you'd be sensible."

"What put you on to me?"

"That must wait for the moment. First we have things to do."

"Things to do?"

"Yes, we do," lied the General. At the Imperial Defence I've been keeping you company for several days, and when you took your walk on the Embankment, I was with you. It was clear you weren't out there for your health, nor mine for that matter"—Morgan blew his nose—"so I assumed you were there to meet the fellow in the van, and I followed him. To cut a long story short, your message to Chiang Li-shih was passed on by telephone, and we were able to listen in. This information was immediately passed to my superior, who in turn took it to Downing Street." Morgan smiled. "I'm afraid you're not much of a spy, Pershing."

Pershing put out his cigarette and sat down. Now that it was over he felt almost lighthearted. "Lack of training," he said brightly.

Morgan went on. "A meeting was then held at Downing Street to decide what to do with you. The first question to be asked was why you were working for the Chinese. I had raised the suggestion that you were the source of their information in Cambodia, and that you were now being blackmailed. I also thought it likely that this was the first

time you had been approached since then. I was instructed
to verify this."

"Correct on every count. You should be promoted."

"The second fact to be noted was that in your message
to Chiang you maintained the same line as the Foreign
Secretary. And that, it was felt, was evidence of patriotism
on your part."

Something in this remark of Morgan's—the rather careful phrasing, as if he were repeating something he had
been told—struck Pershing as odd, and then he realized
that Morgan himself did not know the truth about the
Cabinet decision. Surprising. No, not surprising. Since the
Rhodesian affair Harvey had distrusted MI5, and in any
case security men were rarely told about the secrets they
were protecting. Pershing enjoyed a moment of superiority over the man sitting beside him. "Patriotic?" he said.
"It was no more than the truth."

"Quite so. But it seems our friend Chiang does not believe you. Early this morning he decided to contact you
again, and this time he was less than cautious. We intercepted the message before it reached you."

"What did it say?"

"He wants to meet you again."

"Oh no."

"Oh yes, and it is of course imperative, if the Chinese
are to be dissuaded from aggression, that you maintain
your earlier line. I have therefore been instructed to ac-
company you to the rendezvous."

"But he knows who you are, he'll see you."

"No he won't. I'll come to that in a minute."

"And when I've done my bit, I'll be arrested."

"Perhaps."

"Perhaps? What is that supposed to mean?"

"If you cooperate, there's a chance that your earlier
misdemeanors will be overlooked."

Pershing could hardly believe his ears.

"I see you're surprised," Morgan said. "Yes; well, I don't mind telling you I was surprised too. However, mine not to reason why. Here's what I'm instructed to tell you. The head of MI6 was also at the meeting, and he pointed out the advantages of recruiting you as a double agent. The Prime Minister, it seems, was sympathetic to your case and gave the proposal a fair wind. The idea is that I will run you—a prospect which I need hardly say I find extremely distasteful."

"Run me?"

"If the Chinese contact you again, you will come to me to learn what your reply should be."

"Harvey agreed to this?"

"Nothing has been decided. You will be put under surveillance, and I am to interrogate you. The decision will be taken after I have submitted my report. Meanwhile, I repeat, your best chance is to do exactly as you're told."

"Yes, of course."

"Good. Now, the meeting with Chiang is at nine. That gives us just over an hour. You'd better get dressed."

As Pershing left the room Morgan sat staring straight ahead. "You're a lucky bastard, Pershing," he said, and his voice was dull with resentment.

Four hours to go, thought Fane. This was the day of crisis, his day, and he was ready for it as a police officer should be: no spare flesh on his body, no spare emotion on his mind.

*3*

Even through the closed windows and the wooden shutters the two men heard the shot. Someone had fired again into the garden of Government House.

"I must insist on having authority to raid the Bank of China," said Fane. "The Communists are issuing machine guns and ammunition from the vaults. The place is simply an arsenal."

"Then why not get your men to guard the exits?"

"I am." Fane no longer said "sir." "But they're under fire from inside the bank."

On the advice of his detective Lord Maltby had had his desk moved away from the window. He sat fiddling with a piece of paper with the red royal crest on top. Now that the shutters were closed the room was in green semidarkness. "Out of the question," he said. "It's too provocative. Peking is bound to take grave offense. None of you seems to realize this isn't a police problem or military problem, it's political. I've tried to get Pershing on the phone—"

There was a rap on the door and a police inspector came in without waiting for an answer. The white-coated Chinese butler hovered protesting in the doorway. The inspector gave an envelope to Fane.

"The latest sitrep," Fane said. "Evacuation of listed British and Chinese proceeding according to plan. Over-

253

all deterioration in security position. Looting and arson widespread in Kowloon and Victoria, appears to be well co-ordinated. Crowd of fifteen hundred with grenades and LMGs forming in vicinity Connaught Road praya, ignored order to disperse. Seventeen members Kowloon City Station arrested for desertion by army personnel. . . ." Fane broke off and looked up. "If you don't authorize me to take control of the Bank of China, I shall act on my own."

Lord Maltby got up from behind the desk. An explosion somewhere in the city below rattled the windows. Fane looked at his superior in the dim green light and knew that he had won. Authority had fallen away from the Governor like a suit of armor, leaving him flabby, fat, uncertain.

"You must do as you think best," Lord Maltby said. And then: "Tell me, do you think I could cut out the FO and send a telegram direct to the Security Council?"

But Fane had already left the room.

"Two tea and toast."

"On me," Morgan said and walked to the counter. Pershing cleared the dirty cups to one end of the table and swept the cigarette ash to the floor. The air was thick with smoke and the smell of frying. Three lorry drivers sat at a table in the center, barracking the woman at the cash desk.

# 4

LONDON 8:50 A.M.
*(Hong Kong 3:50 P.M.)*

Morgan came back to the table in the corner. "Don't stir unless you like it sweet," he said.

"No, that's fine." Pershing sipped his tea, and Morgan took a bite from the toast. The windows of the café were opaque with heat on the inside, streaming with sleet on the outside. Beyond the petrol pumps the motorway was just visible; heavy traffic heading into London, a trail of spray behind every vehicle. Margarine was running down Morgan's chin.

"Ten to nine," Pershing said.

"Yes; now listen carefully. Here's what will happen. Chiang will almost certainly arrive in the back of an Embassy car. The Chinese make a regular run up the expressway on Wednesday mornings to pick up a bag at the airport. They'll probably stop here for petrol and Chiang will be out and into the café before the Special Branch car closes up. Don't look around or anything; let him find you. I'll be sitting over there, in the far corner. And please don't forget I've got this." Morgan held up a gadget looking like the flash attachment to a small camera. Pershing recognized a directional microphone.

"Don't take any chances, will you?"

"I'll get into position now. Enjoy your breakfast."

Schoolboy games. Whatever made a man like Morgan do a job like this? He was clever enough to make money, live twice as well as he did. The protection of the system, the knowledge that the highest in the land were in his power? Pershing was still wondering when a neat black-suited figure slid onto the bench opposite him.

"Good morning," said Chiang.

Ten minutes after they broke into the Bank of China the police found the tunnel they had been expecting. They had spent three hours under fire in Des Voeux Road, waiting for orders. And now the defenders had gone, taking their arsenal with them.

# 5

The police were angry, but not so angry as to assault the tunnel at once; there would be booby traps and probably an ambush at the other end. While the Superintendent talked to Fane on the radio his men searched the bank.

By one window they found a dead sniper, twisted on a bed of broken glass. They took his gun, kicked his body and passed on. In the next room on the neat metal desks and filing cabinets was spread a mess of eating bowls, chopsticks and spilled rice. At the farther end was a locked door, and they worked off some of their frustration smashing the lock. Then they were in a room without windows, cut off from the noise of shots and explosions outside. On the floor lay the body of a middle-aged Chinese woman. She looked dead, but when the Sergeant touched her she stirred and muttered. They were looking for guns and Communists, not women, and they let her lie. But the Superintendent was a methodical man, who in times of stress clung to routine like a raft. When he heard about the woman he jotted her down as a suspect for interrogation and had her sent to Queen Mary Hospital in a jeep.

"Then Bennett was telling the truth?" Chiang said.

"Yes," said Pershing.

"Why did you not pass me your message in the Foreign Office?"

"I told you, I thought the Foreign Secretary had seen me put it in my hand."

"So the British really mean to use nuclear weapons?"

"Yes, yes; how many times must I tell you? Now please get out of here before someone sees you."

# 6

LONDON 9:10 A.M
*(Hong Kong 4:10 P.M.*

Chiang stood up. In the mirror behind him Pershing saw Morgan put the microphone in his pocket and blow his nose.

"I have one other question," Chiang said.

"What is that?"

"Where will your Foreign Secretary be at eleven o'clock this morning?"

"Downing Street. The operation is being run from there."

"Thank you."

Pershing watched Chiang stride from the café. None of the drivers looked around. Morgan came back to the table and together they watched in silence as the slight black figure, head down into the sleet, walked down the ramp to the motorway and crossed to the London-bound lane. A minute later a large white van pulled into the emergency lane and the back doors opened. Chiang climbed in, the doors slammed shut and the van pulled away.

"Well," said Morgan, "that's that. Good work. How about another cup?"

"Let me get it this time."

"All right."

When Pershing came back to the table Morgan was still staring out of the window, chin in hand. "Hardly changed at all, has he?" he said.

"No, he's just the same."

"Hard as nails, not soft and fleshy like us. Clever, too."

"Clever, but blinkered."

"They used to call him The Tiger; it was a good name."

"Yes, I remember."

"Remember when I came to get him in the helicopter? The greatest moment of my life, that was. And he just stood there looking at his dead sister; that poor bloody little corpse, for all the expression on his face she might as well have been a dead dog."

"Yes, he was a worthy adversary."

"Hard as nails."

The drivers yelled with applause as the jukebox burst into life. The café became an inferno of electronic sound, and conversation stopped. Morgan grinned at Pershing and turned back to the window; he seemed in no hurry to move. The drivers plied the machine with coins, and disc followed disc.

Pershing thought of that distant day in Malaya, and the three of them standing around the stretcher. Poor Ah Ming. Even her killer could hardly remember her now, no longer held himself responsible. It was just a chain of bad luck. If she'd signed the surrender message she'd have been all right. If the villagers hadn't seen the sandal-maker talking to Morgan she'd have been all right. The villagers warned Chiang, but he still didn't know who had betrayed him, not until the first shot was fired. Then it was Ah Ming who didn't run, Ah Ming who put on a brightly colored scarf. Chiang sees a chance to punish his sister and save his neck; takes the scarf, kicks her into the bushes. She is wounded, panics, runs. If she'd stayed where she was she'd have been all right. We chase her, catch up. Even then, if she'd lain down or called for help, she'd have lived, and none of this would have happened.

The music stopped. Morgan looking out of the window, sleet pattering on the glass.

"Morgan."

"Yes."

"Now that I've done my party piece, tell me: how did you get on to me?"

"Ah, that. Yes." Morgan came out of his reverie. "It was Chiang's sister, Meh-li. That was your big mistake; you should have kept away from her. Our people picked her up and she talked."

"What did she tell you?"

"The same thing she told you—that the Chinese had an agent in the British Government."

"But she didn't know who the agent was."

"No, that's true, but she gave us plenty to go on."

"Did she give you the code name?"

"No, but that didn't matter either. From her description of your behavior it was obvious the agent was you. When she gave you her information, you laughed; you did not report it afterward; and to buy her silence, you promised to get her parents out of Hong Kong. A promise you didn't keep, incidentally."

Pershing said nothing, and Morgan turned back to the window. For a minute they sat in silence, watching the queue of cars at the petrol pumps, then Pershing said quietly: "She fooled you, Morgan."

"I beg your pardon?"

"Poor old Meh-li, she fooled you all."

Morgan shifted quickly on his chair.

"What are you talking about?"

"Shortly after you questioned my Private Secretary—"

"Miss Richardson had no business telling you about that."

"Well, she did, and shortly after, Meh-li was pulled in by your people, right?"

"Yes, that's right."

"What you forgot to mention is that 'your people' are the secret service of the People's Republic of China."

Two tiny bombs exploded in Morgan's eyes; but he did not move or speak.

Pershing went on. "Meh-li was taken from the Bowring Hotel to the Bank of China on the orders of one Robert Foo, ostensibly a director of the bank, in fact the head of Chinese Intelligence in Hong Kong."

"Where did you get this nonsense from?"

"After her chat with you, Jane Richardson had the sense to check up on Meh-li through a journalist friend, and rang me late last night. I thought nothing of it at the time. Meh-li was a defector, the Communists had good reasons to want her; I just assumed the British had been too slow off the mark."

"That is the case. I told you we were holding her, to induce you to—"

"Don't be so bloody ridiculous. It was you who had her interrogated by the Chinese, and I know why. After you'd talked to my PS you knew Meh-li had come to ask me a favor; you guessed that in return she had offered me information, and that she must have pinched this information from her brother, probably read his instructions for London."

Pershing leaned forward, stabbing his finger at Morgan. The jukebox was going again, but he did not hear it. "Now, Morgan, you knew what those instructions were, and what scared you was not that she had discovered my part in this operation, but *yours*. Well, that's exactly what she had done. As soon as I read the paper she'd copied I knew the agent wasn't me. The code name was Polo, and he'd helped them in Cambodia—all right, that could have been me. But this man had also worked for them in Malaya, Paris and London—and that I had not. Now you see why I laughed. There wasn't enough then for me to guess who it was, but I know now. Polo was Gareth Morgan."

"Now just a minute—"

"You see, this document Meh-li copied was a memo from Wang, in the Chinese Foreign Ministry. And it ended with the instructions that if information was unobtainable from the source in the Foreign Office—obviously a reference to myself—then this Polo was to be used in an 'emergency contact procedure.' That, I think, is the little game we have witnessed this morning. All that stuff about intercepting Chiang's messenger. You *were* the messenger, and the only object of this whole exercise was to find out if I'd told Chiang the truth. Blowing your nose, that was the signal, wasn't it? Damned awkward maneuver with a microphone in one hand, and you haven't even got a cold. What were you going to do if I was lying? Pick your teeth?"

The music stopped again, and Pershing realized he had been shouting.

A muscle was twitching in the side of Morgan's face. He was giving off odor, like a wounded animal. He opened his mouth but no sound came out.

Elated with his own cleverness, eager for the kill, Pershing lowered his voice and pushed on. "All that rubbish about me becoming a double agent—I must say, it's a great tribute to your powers of deception that I swallowed that one. Of course, I see the point now. You couldn't carry the charade through as far as having me arrested, could you? If you did that, you'd have too much explaining to do—about Meh-li, and about this morning's episode. No, Morgan, you didn't go to your boss, or if you did you didn't tell him anything. And your boss certainly

didn't go to Downing Street. I thought it was damn peculiar that Harvey hadn't told you—"

Pershing's brain flashed a message to his throat, and the words were cut off. But the damage was done. Morgan was half on his feet, gripping Pershing's lapel. "Yes?" he said. "Go on—Harvey hadn't told me what? Hadn't told me the truth about the Cabinet decision, eh? That was it, wasn't it?"

"No."

"You lied to us, Pershing. No one's going to fight for Hong Kong, are they? The whole thing's a bluff."

"No."

"Come on, man, the truth!"

The whole of Morgan's enormous body was quivering with rage; flecks of foam had appeared at the corners of his mouth. Pershing felt as powerless as an insect under a boot. "No," he said again, "I've told you the truth."

The lorry drivers were watching them. "Knock it off, you two," one of them said. "None of that here."

Without letting go of Pershing, Morgan sank slowly back into his seat. He put his free hand inside his raincoat, and suddenly Pershing felt a hard pressure on his knee. He looked below the table to see a short-barreled revolver aimed at his loins.

"Let's finish this outside," said Morgan quietly.

On the way out Morgan pressed a coin into the jukebox, stabbed the buttons at random.

Behind the café was a patch of wasteland. Most of it was open territory, but Morgan, who seemed to know his way around, headed for a hollow at the back, invisible from the windows of the café. At first Pershing made quite a noise but not enough to drown the Rolling Stones, and by the time Morgan had finished only a person within six inches of Pershing's mouth could have heard him say: "Yes, it's a bluff."

Meh-li had woken to find herself between rough blankets, and all around her the hubbub of a hospital in a city dissolving into war. A piece of paper had been pinned to her dress. It read: "The death or discharge of this detainee to be notified to the police in accordance with para 26 Emergency Regulations. J. E. Brabazon, Superintendent, HK Police." This meant nothing to her, so she had crumpled it up and thrown it under the bed.

# 7

HONG KONG 4:40 P.M. *(London 9:40 A.M.)*

Getting out of the hospital was surprisingly easy. A wave of giddiness swept over as she shifted her weight from the bed to her feet, but it passed. The ward was full of people, nurses, stretcher-bearers, relatives, shoving and shouting; no one had time to spare a glance as, slowly and with several pauses, she made her way into the less crowded passage.

Another stretcher came past. It carried a young man with the left side of his face burned gray-black. His body under the blanket was humped and contorted, but no sound came from his lips. Meh-li found a water fountain in a corner, drank and felt better.

She followed the lights marked Emergency Exit, and came out into the backyard of the hospital. There, suddenly, she gave up, defeated by the glare of the sun, the unfriendly white walls, the tightness around her chest, the faintness in her head. Whimpering softly to herself, she sat down on the pavement.

"Feeling better, love?" A freckled face under red hair leaned sideways out of the window of an army ambulance.

"I'm on civvy work today—just off to Kowloon to pick up another load of misery. Can I take you anywhere?"

Meh-li just had the strength to say: "Thank you. The Bowring Hotel."

Hand on the horn, lights flashing, Morgan took the Hillman up to eighty and held it there. As they mounted Hammersmith fly-over the sleet became heavier, piling into the corners of the windscreen, but he did not slow down. The fast lane emptied in front of them.

# 8

Pershing sat beside him. Both men were soaked to the skin, their clothes smeared with mud. Waves of pain and nausea still coursed through Pershing's body; he was holding his stomach, and every so often his head keeled sideways against the window. But his brain was clear.

His watch showed 9:45. The Cabinet had decided to back down at 10. Chiang had asked where Ryder Bennett would be at 11, and that could mean only one thing. Problem one: get a message to Downing Street in the next fifteen minutes. Problem two: stop Morgan warning Chiang. But can't do the first without disposing of Morgan.

Morgan glanced sideways, seemed to read Pershing's thoughts. Without relaxing the speed of the car he began to speak, rapidly and precisely.

"Sorry about the roughhouse. You'll be all right, just don't let the wife see you in the bath for a week or so. And don't be tempted to pay me back. For one thing, I'm driving. For another, I'm trying to catch Chiang, and it's in your interest that I do so. I shall tell him the truth, of course, and he'll then know that you lied. But he can't touch you. If he had you arrested, you could expose me— and I'm too valuable, I run their whole London net."

"What if you don't catch him?"

266

"I'll get to him sooner or later, it'll come to the same thing. But you'll have spoiled his timing, and that will rile him. When the Chinese get riled, there's no knowing what they'll do. Logic doesn't always come into it."

Pershing said nothing, stared at the half-white rooftops flashing by the window. He must think of something.

"Still have visions of saving the realm, do you?" It was uncanny, this power of Morgan's. "Let me do your thinking for you. There are just two ways you can stop me reaching Chiang: you can kill me, or have me arrested. But I warn you, if you start a fight, you're the one who'll get killed. You forget I'm armed; I could even pass it off as in the line of duty. And if you turn me in, I'll take you with me. I'm sure you're too fond of life for that. We sink or swim together. So shut up and stay still. Ah, there he is."

Morgan braked, pulled into the slow lane behind a white van. Happy Valley Laundry, Pershing read through the sleet. The road dipped. Nothing would happen until they were off the clearway.

He really thinks I'm too fond of life, thought Pershing. Chiang too. That's their big mistake.

Traffic lights ahead, turning yellow. Van goes across. Morgan accelerates after it. To the right a black Ford, waiting at the lights in Earl's Court Road. Police. Now.

As they went into Cromwell Road, Pershing yanked the wheel to the left and a lamppost carved through the hood of the Hillman. Pershing turned just in time; his back thudded into the instrument panel and glass cascaded over his head. Morgan went into the steering wheel. His hands fished for the door handle, then dropped to his side; his head sank slowly forward, lids fluttering over the whites of his eyes.

A red mist was descending through Pershing's head, the world was spinning. He fought it with all the strength he had left; gripped the back of the seat until his knuckles turned white, focused his eyes on the whitening knuckles.

Voices, far away, then nearer.

"He pulled the wheel, officer, I saw him."

A head at the window, blue-peaked cap. A strong hand reaching out to steady him.

"Easy does it now. Think you can make it?"

"Yes, thank you, officer, if you'll just open the door."

Pershing stood on the pavement, breathing the cold air. The mist cleared, buildings stopped lurching about. The laundry van had gone.

Five minutes of hard talking, and he was in the patrol car, connected by radio and telephone to Downing Street.

". . . Yes, this is Laurence Pershing, Minister of State at the Foreign Office. Get me the Foreign Secretary as quick as you can."

The policeman, half-convinced, looked at him nervously. If this was a hoax there'd be hell to pay.

"Ryder? Laurence here. . . . Yes, I'm sorry, I've been delayed, I'll be with you as soon as I can. . . . Look, I've got some important news. They're going to back down at eleven. . . . Yes, quite sure. . . . I can't explain now, you'll just have to take it from me. . . . I know it's risky. . . . Well, look—hold it till I get there. Will you do that? . . . Good, I'll be with you in twenty minutes."

Pershing handed back the microphone. The policeman's face was a picture of relief, bewilderment, curiosity.

"Convinced?" Pershing said.

"Yes, sir, I'm sorry, it was just that with you looking in such a mess . . ."

"I understand. You took a chance, and I'm grateful."

An ambulance, siren blaring, pulled up in front of the Hillman. The other policeman was bending over Morgan.

"How is he?" Pershing said.

"Him? He's out cold."

"Look, there's one other thing I want you to do, and this is just as important. Can I borrow that?" Pershing took the policeman's pad and wrote a number on it. "I'd like one of you to stick with him, go to the hospital, don't let him out of your sight. If he tries to communicate with anyone, ring this number. It's the Prime Minister's office."

"Very well, sir."

"Just for the next two hours, then Special Branch will take over. Now, can you find me a taxi?"

Standing on the pavement again, Pershing watched as Morgan was lifted into the ambulance. It was all explained now—the long chain of coincidence, the odd little un-answered questions which had dogged him for twenty years. Chiang's fantastic success as a terrorist—not luck, but an operation controlled by the head of Ipoh Special Branch. Ah Ming's death—not bad luck, but a carefully planned sacrifice. It was Morgan, not the villagers, who had killed the sandal-maker, because the sandal-maker knew that the surrender message had come from Ah Ming; Morgan who had torn Ah Ming's name from the bottom of the leaflet to make the message anonymous; Morgan, not the villagers, who had sent a courier to warn Chiang. Chiang must have had time to break camp, but he stayed where he was; Morgan could have destroyed the message, but he passed it to the army—why? The two of them had done a deal, that was why. The pace was getting too hot, so they set the whole thing up: Chiang to eliminate Ah Ming and pose as the author of the message, Morgan to get Chiang repatriated to China and see him right with the Party.

And the photographs of Moira in bed with the French-man—Morgan had been in Paris during the Phnom Penh conference. And the fat shape, half-recognized, behind the rubber plants in the Rundall Hotel—Morgan again, supervising the rendezvous with Chiang. . . .

The doors of the ambulance slammed shut, and it pulled out into the traffic. Pershing felt relief as he watched it go, but he knew that the feeling was false. Morgan's career was over; but he was alive, and in his head were the facts which would bring ruin.

Barricades, fallen buildings, overturned vehicles, streets jammed
with frightened people or emptied
by machine-gun fire; all the normal routes were blocked and it had
taken them an hour to reach the
hotel, but the freckled driver
seemed determined to keep his
promise, and in the end they made
it. Meh-li thanked him and
watched the ambulance disappear
down the street, then walked up
the steps to the faded cream portico.

# 9

HONG KONG 5:45 P.M.
(*London 10:45 A.M.*)

She found her mother counting bills. The army families
had left in lorries for the airport early that morning; there
had been some confusion about their accounts, and the
old lady had made them sign every bill. Since many of
them had also left her their remaining Hong Kong money,
there was just a chance that the Bowring Hotel would
show a profit out of the proceedings. Upstairs the beds
were made and the rooms cleaned for whoever might present themselves that evening. On the sofa by the old lady's
side was stretched the red flag of the People's Republic of
China, fresh from a recent scrubbing.

"Where is my father?" said Meh-li.

"He is at the warehouse. He always goes there on
Wednesday."

"The warehouse?"

"In Jordan Road. He had been buying silks with the
money from the hotel. That is where they are stored."
Her mother spoke as if Meh-li should have known all this.

Jordan Road. She had seen the street sign from the ambulance two or three minutes before they arrived at the

hotel. And she had seen something else. Part of the street was on fire.

"But it's dangerous! How could you let him go out at a time like this?"

"You should not shout at me, Meh-li. Your father wanted to count the silks before Chiang Li-shih comes. One day they will be his."

For a moment Meh-li believed it. "You have heard from him?"

"No, he is too busy to write. But if the Communists come, he will come."

Once again her mother was evidently stating the obvious. Meh-li saw there was no point in arguing. She must hurry to Jordan Road.

"You are leaving again?" said her mother. "You come and go, you tell us nothing. I am old, and there is much work for you in the hotel."

As Pershing was shown through the door, both men exploded.

"For God's sake, Pershing, where have you been?" said Harvey. He was the calmer of the two.

Ryder Bennett was pale with fury. "You said twenty minutes," he shouted. "It's bloody nearly eleven now."

# 10

LONDON 10:55 A.M.
*(Hong Kong 5:55 P.M.)*

Pershing stood in the middle of the room, his clothes dripping onto the carpet. "I'm sorry, the traffic was terrible; Whitehall's full of demonstrators."

"Never mind; let's get to the point," Harvey said.

"That *was* you on the phone, I suppose?" Ryder Bennett asked sarcastically.

"Yes, it was me, I'm afraid the line was rather poor. You haven't spoken to the Chinese yet, have you?"

"No," Harvey replied, "but what I need from you quickly is a reason why I should wait a minute longer."

Pershing brought out the answer he had rehearsed in the taxi; the essential fact, stripped of explanatory details, the minimum needed to convince them. "At his request, I had a secret meeting with Chiang Li-shih this morning. In the course of our conversation it became clear that his orders were to climb down if we hadn't accepted the ultimatum by eleven o'clock."

"Jesus Christ." Ryder Bennett was incredulous, affronted. "What an extraordinary thing to do. Why did he do that? And why, for that matter, didn't you tell me?"

"That can wait," Harvey snapped, and to Pershing: "You're quite sure of this?"

"Yes."

"You'd better be, because I've just had the CBF Hong Kong on the line to say that Chinese troops are moving up to the frontier."

"That'll be part of the bluff; they've been bluffing all along."

Harvey looked at Pershing grimly. "I hope for your sake you're right." He pulled a watch from his waistcoat pocket. "We'll know soon enough, anyway. The switchboard has been told to connect me to the Chinese at eleven, so unless that phone rings in the next two minutes, we've lost."

Pershing's legs could hold him up no longer; he dropped into the nearest chair. For the first time both men noticed his condition.

"Are you feeling all right?" Harvey said. "You look as if you'd just crawled out of the river."

Ryder Bennett circled behind Pershing's chair. "What have you done to your head?"

Pershing mopped at his scalp, and the handkerchief came away red. Fragments of glass were still falling from his hair. "It's not serious. I had an accident on the way."

Ryder Bennett was less than sympathetic. "Did the press get a picture of you looking like that?"

"No, I came through the Scottish Office."

Again Harvey pulled the conversation back to essentials. "All right, now as quickly as you can, tell us what Chiang said."

But before Pershing could answer the telephone rang. All three men jumped. Ryder Bennett was first to the receiver.

As he listened the corners of his mouth began to twitch, then settled in a slight upward slant.

"Thank you, I am ready to receive him now."

He lowered the receiver. Pershing and Harvey waited while the Foreign Secretary enjoyed a last brief moment of suspense. Then, imitating the English of Chinese officialdom, he announced: "The office of the Chargé d'Affaires of the People's Republic of China request an immediate interview for Chiang Li-shih, to discuss a peaceful end to the Hong Kong dispute."

Harvey was still cautious. "Well, where is he? Can we be sure it's genuine?"

Another telephone rang. Ryder Bennett snatched it, listened, nodded, put it back. "That was the Foreign Office. Chiang's at the Park Door."

Harvey sank into the chair behind his desk. "Thank God."

Ryder Bennett slapped his thigh. "We've done it, Patrick!" he shouted.

"You'd better get over there straightaway to make sure," Harvey said.

"Yes, I'll ring you as soon as I can." Ryder Bennett moved to the door, then seemed to remember something. He looked back at Pershing, and his face creased in an awkward smile. "Good, Larry," he said. "I shouldn't have doubted you."

After he had gone Pershing and Harvey sat in silence for a moment. A clock was striking the hour. The rain had stopped and they could hear the crowds chanting in Whitehall. Pershing wondered if Meh-li was dead.

"Well, Laurence, the method was a little odd, but it looks as if you were right. I'm grateful to you."

Pershing did not reply, and Harvey pressed a switch on his desk. "I'm expecting a call from the Foreign Secretary in about fifteen minutes, then I shall want to speak to General Lamont again. No other calls till then. If the White House comes through, tell them I'll ring back."

Harvey released the switch and swiveled his chair to face Pershing.

"Now, while we have a few moments, you'd better tell me how you came by this information." Pershing nodded weakly. "But let me get you something first, you really do look frightful. Brandy do?"

"Thank you."

As he watched the Prime Minister busy himself with bottle and glasses, Pershing felt a pang of regret, not for himself, but for the fresh shock he was about to give this kindly, beleaguered man.

As Meh-li turned the corner into Jordan Road groups of Chinese in twos or threes were coming away from the fire. Some were openly carrying armfuls of half-charred silks, others had concealed their takings in baskets and suitcases. No police had been seen in that part of Kowloon since early morning, and the call to the Fire Department had not been answered.

**11**

HONG KONG 6 P.M. *(London 11 A.M.)*

The warehouse was almost gutted. The roof had fallen in and the pavement was deep in smoking rubbish. The watching crowd, looters, and non-looters, had begun to disperse. The moment of drama was past. Flames crackled and billowed through the blackened window frames; they would leave little of value now.

The first group whom Meh-li approached answered her question at once. Yes, there had been an old man in a gray gown. He had shouted from a second-floor window and then thrown himself out. Some people had tried to catch him, but he had fallen on the pavement. They had carried him into a bar in Battery Street, and the barkeeper had given him some water.

The barkeeper was still there, hunched over the till as if protecting his child. It was dark inside and Meh-li did not at first see her father.

"Please take him away," the barkeeper said.

Meh-li could feel that the spine was broken. His face was untroubled, and she thought for a moment of the young man on the stretcher in the hospital. Even if you did not believe in Mary and the saints it was better to die

276

quietly, thinking about your life. Perhaps her father had been able to do this, lying in the corner of the bar. Perhaps with old people the pain was less.

She lifted the thin body, but her weakness came again and she let it drop. Something small and hard fell to the floor from the pocket of the gray gown. It was her father's seal, ivory with a black dragon carved on one side, and at the one end dry red ink clinging to the incised characters of his name. They had often played with it as children, covering sheet after sheet of paper with the red imprint, until their father had come in saying he would go bankrupt unless he had it to sign his business letters. Once it had been lost for a day, and he had been very angry.

"He is too heavy for me," she said to the barkeeper. "I will go and get help."

She put the seal in her pocket. It had been made for her grandfather after he had come second in the imperial examinations at Peking. Somehow she would send it to Chiang Li-shih; but it would mean nothing to him.

As she walked back to the hotel Meh-li tried to mourn for her father. Present or absent, he had been the governor of her life; she had risked much for him; but already he was just a body with a broken back, a huddle in the corner of a dingy bar.

They had left on Wednesday evening, hurrying without a sideways glance through the crowd of reporters and cameramen. Sitting together on the plane, they had picked at their food, slept a little, finished their separate reports. It was Thursday morning before they spoke.

# 12

MONGOLIA 8 A.M.
## Thursday
*(London Wednesday midnight)*

"This has not been a happy week for China," said Hsu Teh, formerly Chinese Chargé d'Affaires in London, his soft, intellectual voice clearly audible through the noise of the engines.

The Ilyushin was climbing out of Ulan Bator on the last leg of the journey to Peking. Below them the town seemed absurdly small, a few modern buildings around the big square, then a conglomeration of shacks and white tents spilling out over the brown frozen plains of Mongolia. Chiang could see a herd of wild horses in a dried-up watercourse. He wondered whether to answer. Hsu Teh was a negligible man with no Party background, a poet left over from the past, a diplomatic figurehead; ordinarily a man to be snubbed without hesitation. But here they were in the same plane, flying back to face their superiors, sharing a common failure.

"The Chinese people will certainly liberate Hong Kong," he replied.

"Of course," said Hsu Teh. "But why was the attempt made now and in this way? The People's Republic gains much profit from Hong Kong as things stand. We receive back most of the Colony in twenty-two years' time when

278

the lease expires. Why not wait till then? Why shake the tree before the fruit is ripe?"

Chiang was surprised. In London Hsu Teh had been a silent, terrified spectator of events; now, when for him the moment of danger was greatest, he seemed calm and talkative. "You do not understand the impatience of the Chinese people. They could no longer stand idly by and watch their brothers suffering under imperialism."

"You talk in slogans." Hsu Teh actually smiled. "For China, what is twenty-two years? There must have been another reason."

Chiang looked around them. The seats in front and behind were empty. The plane was Russian; any microphones would be Russian too, and so not immediately dangerous. He was tempted to hear more. "What do you mean?" he asked.

"I will tell you. I used to know the Prime Minister well in the old days; that is why he sent me to London. He would never have handled the matter so clumsily except on purpose. Today everyone in the world is saying that the Chinese Government has been outmaneuvered, humiliated. That is what he wanted."

"You are talking nonsense," said Chiang. But to his surprise he did not feel indignant.

"The Prime Minister has enemies, men and women who have the Chairman's ear, whispering against him, frustrating his plans, breaking up the machinery of government, enemies of whom he would like to be rid. I believe that he lured them into a trap. Ever since the Cultural Revolution they have been pressing for us to seize Hong Kong. Suddenly, having opposed it for years, he agrees to the plan—and it fails, as he had predicted, so that his enemies are discredited."

Chiang said nothing; he gazed down onto the waste of desert below. His mind was detached and empty. He wondered if Meh-li would know that he was coming back.

"So you see," Hsu Teh continued, and he was smiling enthusiastically now, "For him it was essential that the British should be willing to fight. Whatever Pershing said, whatever you telegraphed, that is the conclusion he would have believed and reported to the Chairman. For if the British had not been willing to fight, the plan of his enemies would have succeeded. And that he could not afford."

"This is mere speculation," said Chiang.

The Great Wall was ahead of them now, crooked along the crests of the mountains like a writhing snake. They were already over China.

"Of course it is speculation. How can we expect to know the truth? And it makes no difference to us, for we are the agents of failure. However pleased the Prime Minister may be at the outcome, he will do nothing to save us."

That was true enough, thought Chiang, and tried to judge what would be in store for him: prison, obscurity, demotion, a posting to the far West—there were many varieties of disgrace.

But as the Illyushin began its descent over the Valley of the Ming Tombs, his mind clicked back into its groove. He was almost home now. Whatever trouble lay ahead he had been mad to listen even for a moment to such treacherous nonsense. "You are insane," he shouted above the din of the jet. And then more quietly: "You are talking the language of counterrevolutionary intrigue. The Chairman and the Prime Minister and the Politburo are united to serve the Chinese people. Their solidarity cannot be broken, and their orders are the expression of the invincible will of the masses. I will report your remarks to the competent authorities at the first opportunity."

Hsu Teh did not seem to hear: he was intent on the view from the window. The plane circled over Peking, and below them spread the golden roofs of the Forbidden City glinting in the winter sun, delicate summerhouses on

Coal Hill, fragments of massive gray wall, the startling blue of the Temple of Heaven; then southward again over the University and the Summer Palace at Wan Shou Shan; willows bending over the ice on the lake, humped marble bridges, pavilions decked in blue and scarlet. As they veered for the last time the Western Hills came into sight again. On the peak of Miao Feng Shan a line of snow shone clearly in the morning light. On the tarmac below them some tiny figures were assembled.

"It is a beautiful city, is it not?" said Hsu Teh.